Just A STILL LIFE

JUST (e)STATE *Mysteries*

J. Ivanel Johnson

Black Rose Writing | Texas

ISBN: 978-1-68513-033-6
PUBLISHED BY BLACK ROSE WRITING
www.blackrosewriting.com

Printed in the United States of America
Suggested Retail Price (SRP) $21.95

Just A STILL LIFE is printed in Sabon

*As a planet-friendly publisher, Black Rose Writing does its best to eliminate unnecessary waste to reduce paper usage and energy costs, while never compromising the reading experience. As a result, the final word count vs. page count may not meet common expectations.

In memory of Victoria Ivanel Johnson,
my paternal grandmother who supported me
in all my aspirations, however impractical—
and inspired me to JUST write.

As she lay dying, I promised her I would update, revise and complete
the manuscript she began in 1947 and not give up until it was
published. In its various incarnations, it has crossed the Atlantic twice
and North America thrice, reaping the spiritual genius loci of the
Brontes' own moors and Sylvia Plath's hillside all the way to the
Glacier Park Gateway, dominion of Dorothy M. Johnson (no relation).
What a journey! It's had far from *"just a still life"*…

"There he stood, the one I trust
The one and only, whose heart is pure,
Whose courage rages, whose gavel **just**…"
– **V. I. J.** in her original title: *Prison Is A Private Place*

•   •   •

With respect to lost Fredericton Police
Constables Sara Burns *and* **Lawrence Robert ("Robb") Costello**
who are secondary characters working with the
otherwise-fictional 1971 capital police force in this novel.
Their lives were taken in the line of duty, at the end of their shift,
on a very dark day indeed for the little city of
Fredericton, New Brunswick, August 10, 2018.

Just A
STILL LIFE

PART ONE

"Lady, it is to be presumed,
though parts and causes are not found,
All is not sweet, all is not sound."
–Ben Jonson

CHAPTER ONE

1971, New Brunswick, Canada

His nightmares were fraught with the bulging eyes of the three near-retirement chambermaids whose lives he could have saved. Or at least, he *felt* he could have. Despite having left Ontario well behind him, Philip Steele still saw their horror-filled orbs, as his own were squeezed tightly shut, praying for a deeper sleep. The more recent Caswell case in Fredericton didn't keep him tossing and sweating at all; the victim had been a male drug-dealer and they'd found his killer quickly. But those innocent older ladies who'd just been trying to earn a decent day's wages? *No!* So now, to forget, Phil took long walks and smelled flowers. That's what the police psychiatrist had advised him to do, with the straightforward simplicity of the Atlantic-bred. And while he loved stooping to sniff the fragrant, fall Black-Eyed Susans, their name and shape did nothing to erase those grisly images.

The overgrown paths he had once frequented matched his current state of disordered perception, he thought. As Hamlet felt that his 'unweeded' world had gone to seed, so too did Phil's brain in this rather rugged garden. And as had the Prince of Denmark's, he also felt his inner Eden had turned 'rank and gross in nature'.

The huge back yard wasn't *literally* rank or gross, of course. Polly Jane would never permit that—especially now. This was the hallowed time of year for her harvest moon ritual. The winding walkways and borders must be trim and tripless.

"*Tripless*?" He'd teased her gently when she'd coined the term.

"Well, I don't want to trip over anything, so it's an obvious—"

"Yet you go 'tripping' and prancing along. Hmm. Funny old language, huh?"

P.J.'s English garden was indeed still a thing of humble beauty, far from unkempt exactly. But these landmarks: that half-dead tree for instance, whose one remaining branch had coiled to form a perfect 'O', or the sagging rear porch, or the now too-tall lilac bush over which he'd once amused himself playing leap-frog, had changed so much in twenty years that he hardly recognized them now. The village of Victoria and its environs had not stood still with time. Nor *yet* had he! However, he decided as he tossed a twig into the trickle which, long ago, had been a burbling stream—that was not to say he couldn't! *Ahhh, yes, to just stand still...*

Betsy Lawford's grandsons, playing catch in her yard, were bantering back and forth, and their voices carried across to him. "I said throw it low, Wally!"

"I did, you fool!"

"Ya call that low?"

"Chuck it back!"

Phil smiled. He'd played so many simple summer childhood activities here in Victoria as well. And of course, he had expected *some* changes in the two decades since his last visit. He'd not thought to meet any of his boyhood friends among the neighbors, for instance. He'd assumed rightly that the quaint old ice-cream parlor would have closed; he knew the cedar-shingled New England-style saltbox owned by his godmother would have also grayed and hunched over time. But ultimately the reason he had yielded to the insistence of Deputy Commissioner Cobalt (who had urged him to retain, at least for a trial period, *some* connection with the force) was because he had not expected so many *other* changes. Dammit, he should have just quit. Not only for the sake of his unsettled soul, but to help Polly Jane with basic maintenance—before it was too late! Yes, had it been anyone but the D.C., Phil would have stood his ground.

Emotionally exhausted from his mother's unexpected death, followed by the sale of their 'JUST(e)STATE' while simultaneously working one of the first serial killings in Canada—the Gerald Thomas Archer case in Chatham—he'd asked for the transfer to New Brunswick. He knew well this province of primarily rivers, hills and trees. He knew it could instill serenity. But then he had immediately been assigned another homicide case in the small capital city the locals called 'Freddy'. Recognizing that his lack of concentration and distaste for his career was a serious detriment to his work—and now the financial necessity to earn a living had been removed, at least for the immediate future—he felt less inclined for the job than ever.

A baseball whizzed past him as the boys let one slip by. Betsy's yard backed on to Polly Jane's neighbor's, so Phil's throw back to them had to be on a diagonal angle and also had to miss the weeping willow's low-hanging branches. But he managed it. Instead of hearing their cries of thanks, though, he heard Archer's angry and psychopathic taunts as he called to the jury: *"That's only the first strike against me! The ball game isn't over yet!"* And a sentence of 'life' wouldn't mean life, Philip knew.

•　　•　　•

"It's wonderful being here again, P. J.," he told the apron-wrapped body that night after apple crisp.

"I'm so glad, dear." Polly Jane beamed at her godson. "I was afraid you'd find it all pretty dull, but it's certainly a treat for me to have someone else to cook for. I wish you could stay forever."

"So do I. Victoria seems far removed from the rest of the world. So refreshing! So right."

There was a pause as the elderly woman debated broaching a subject she had yet to raise. "You've sounded so bitter lately, Phil. Cynical, even. Does police work do that?"

"I suppose it does. The trouble is, I just don't want it anymore." He explained to the spectacle-clad mop of blue-tinted hair in front of him that his resignation had not been accepted. "I'd have been a lot firmer with the D.C. if I had another direction I'd wanted to take. I mean, you know I've always wanted to write. Or get into local politics, maybe. But the only thing I feel like doing is exactly what I'm doing right now—eating and loafing."

Polly Jane rose to pour the tea into waiting Limoges cups. "You're worn out, my boy. Plain and simple. You're long overdue for a break, what with all the tough cases they've thrown at you, the transfers, your mother passing last year."

Philip sighed.

"Plus, I know how hard the sale of the farm was on you."

"Five generations of us there. Dad used to say it had always been 'Just Us Steeley Traditionalists' on that land. Completely ignoring thousands of years of Ojibwe, of course."

Polly Jane chuckled. "He always told me, when you and your sister were young, that the 'JUST' stood for 'Juveniles Under Strict Training'."

"Huh! He would. And we were!"

"You've been through a lot these last few years. And Rainey, of course…"

"*P.J.*," Philip warned.

His godmother knew she'd pushed far enough.

"Well, have an extra sugar lump. You'll work it off on one of your hikes!"

"Maybe you'll let me dance with you in the garden."

"*Hush* now, Phil! Only you and I know about that, even after all these years. Besides, the full moon isn't due for nearly a week yet. You'll have had plenty of exercise by then."

"Stafford warned me I wasn't to get a belly. Said I had to keep in shape in case I had to 'terminate leave' in a hurry. Fredericton is ridiculously understaffed, it seems."

The senior citizen tutted. "Tssk! You all wouldn't know what understaffed *was*! This village may look like it's changed to you but some things are carved in granite."

"Such as?"

"Well, there's still only Mary and me at the post office, even over the Christmas rush. And we still only have the one sheriff—Chet Anderson, it is now. Remember him? He used to come over and play Sherlock with you. So sweet you both went into law enforcement!" Polly Jane said, apparently connecting this bit of destiny for the first time.

"I can't speak for Chet, but I'd hardly call my career 'sweet'."

"And of course poor Doctor Graham is worked off his bunions because this whole neighborhood is just overflowing with oldies like me, gasping out our last breaths."

"Hmph. 'Last breath', indeed! Woman, you've got more life in you than I do at the moment. Now pass me another slice of that apple concoction, will you? Paunch or no paunch, I do not intend to deprive myself of simple pleasures while on vacation."

The telephone shrilled and Polly Jane hurried out to answer it. Alone in the kitchen, Philip wandered aimlessly about for a minute or two, then switched off the combination fan and ceiling light hanging above the stone walls—mortar crumbling, he noted—and poked his way through the hall to the front rooms. These, for the last four decades since he was a mere three years of age, had housed Victoria's post office. Paneled in deep mahogany, with old-fashioned pigeon-holes behind a sturdy counter, this was Polly Jane's place of business, and where he himself had often sat as a child, intrigued by much of the local gossip and the variety of accents with which it was conveyed. Without turning on any lights, Philip stood at the window, surveying the peaceful vista of the tiny town's maple-guarded main street. Absently fiddling with the blind cord, he noticed that more than half the houses were in darkness, but that Brock's Bakery/Convenience Store far down on the corner was still carrying on its daily trade. There were lights on at Dr. Graham's too and he saw a car backing out of the laneway. That poor man probably never got an evening at home with his feet up!

"No tuffet for *that* toughie," muttered Phil to himself.

A large Victorian-style house, red-bricked and somber in the twilight, appeared to have strangely lit shadows dancing in its windows. As P. J. called his name from behind him, he turned, answering her with a blithe "Got any binoculars? I'm just spying on the neighbors."

His godmother entered the post office and smiled. "That was a call from the Newmans. Laurie said Sonja Sorensen's gone into labor. This'll be her fourth child and she insisted on having it at home with just a midwife. But apparently there are complications, so poor Wilf Graham is off to do a Special Delivery—Express Post!"

"I just noticed him leaving. Whose place is that, now?" He thrust his chin toward the big brick house down the street. "I remember it used to belong to the Sandersons, didn't it?"

"That's right. It's still in their family, of course. But just old Esther Grimball and her niece live there, now. Esther's mother was a Sanderson, so they're the last of the founding families to live here in the village."

"What's causing the Northern Lights effect inside? Looks like oil lamps, or something!"

Polly Jane pulled her wire-rimmed glasses from the top of her head, placed them on her nose and then peered over their tops, completely ignoring the lenses. "Of course they're oil lamps— candles too, if I know Esther. That woman, despite all her money, is the greediest tight-wad you've ever seen. Wouldn't want to burn up electricity for no good reason!" She snorted indignantly. "Poor Bethie, her niece, is a schoolteacher over at Victoria Elementary.

Has lived here most of her life with that crotchety old thing. How she grades her papers at night with only a little stub of wax... Well! It's beyond me. Come on, let's go and have a look at the television, shall we? There's supposed to be a good movie on tonight."

" Not another murder-mystery like last night, P.J.?" groaned Philip. A brand new series called Columbo had premiered the night before, but he would rather have spent the hour and a half quietly reading something far-removed from the topic of cops and killers.

"Now, then. We're not all as brilliant as you, Inspector Steele. I don't know how you figure them out before the first commercial. No, this one is an old black and white comedy/romance. Just what you need!"

She led the way to the library where her softly-faded chintz upholstery, over-stuffed gingham cushions, and warm stained-glass lamps beckoned invitingly. She didn't add, as she'd been about to, that it was more the romance than the comedy he needed.

•　　　•　　　•

Polly Jane slept very little that night, although there was nothing in particular to disturb her. After the film, she and Philip had retired to their rooms where she stood by her gabled window, peering through lace curtains at the small town below as it stood surrounded by the dark silhouettes of hills and their thick forests. A slender ¾-moon cast a pinstripe thread of light over the utilitarian storefronts and the more noble dwellings tucked behind them. Phil was right, of course. Everything was always so peaceful here in Victoria. And yet, distracted, she sighed as she moved to pull away her down comforter from the pillow shams at the head of the antique four-poster. *Why were the jagged ends of a life so hard to scoop together and blend?* Dear Phil! He had always been such a practical, scientifically-inclined boy but now as a man these qualities appeared to work almost to his detriment. He seemed so lonely and disillusioned with his inner-city cases from around the country, his dealings with child abusers, prostitutes, rapists, murderers, the homeless. For a while he'd had Lorraine—Rainey—his cheerfully optimistic fiancé. P.J. had flown up to the Yukon several years ago when he'd been consulting on a case there and had met the fun-loving young woman then, happy she seemed able to bring her godson out of his funks. But after Rainey had been shot and killed during that investigation, he'd never dated since. At least to the best of her knowledge. And she noticed he was talking to himself again as well. Oh, he really needed a family to call his own. Something positive to return home to at the end of each shift. Especially now both of his parents were gone, and the remaining twenty-four-acre Steele homestead, the 'JUST(*e*)STATE' north of Toronto, sadly sold on to developers. Money and job titles were not enough to feed a hungry soul!

Poo. How silly she was, to have these trite, romantic notions at such an age! Of *course,* Philip must be practical and sensible to be so renowned in his position, so sought-after as a consulting investigator across the nation. And he was very good, she knew, at being able to strip people bare of all pretensions, to look into their minds for the truths. If only he could do the same for himself!

Polly Jane hooked her hand around an arthritic left knee and pulled it toward her chest as she tried to wiggle into comfort. Ah, well, perhaps that was what he was doing here. Why else would he take so much time off, right after being transferred to a new position? Being unattached, her godson was always sent to the most obscure locations and because of that, added to his aloofness and skepticism toward other people, he seemed to have few close personal friends. His father and mother had always meant a great deal to him and now they were both gone, she knew he would have a difficult time trying to adjust, even as he approached middle age.

She tried hard to make her mind a blank so she could fall asleep. The mail usually arrived by 7:00 a.m., and she would have to be up and finished sorting it by the time Mary arrived at 8:00. Then, she would be free for a short while to make Philip the blueberry waffles he so enjoyed.

Perhaps she should count sheep. One, two, three…forty-seven, forty-eight…*Oh, fiddlesticks! This wasn't working at all!* Polly Jane moved restlessly to her other side and considered potential women in northern York County to whom she might casually introduce Phil. In her mind she went through every house she had just scanned before crawling under the covers, and then conjuring up each of their inhabitants and their relatives. *Hmm…* Grace LeBlanc was too old, probably, and Stella Cormier a little too young and immature. Helen Richards was a sweet and intelligent computer analyst—someone scientific would do very well for Phil, she supposed—although there was the matter of that unfortunate scarring over poor Helen's right cheek from the fire which had taken her husband's life. But looks were superficial. Would Phil want to adopt her three children, however? Oh, and Daphne Hawkins was recently divorced, of course, and had moved back to the village with her aging father. But she was terribly volatile and had a nasty temper—no wonder her ex-spouse had announced he was gay! Beth Grimball was a possibility. Yet, with an aunt like Esther, Polly Jane was certain no neighborly invitations to dinner would be proffered! What about Genevieve Stroud? Too independent and career-oriented, perhaps…But was that necessarily a negative quality these days? Instead of sheep, Polly Jane Whistler ultimately fell asleep counting eligible bachelorettes under forty years of age.

•   •   •

At the same time that Victoria's post-mistress was finally drifting off, Genevieve Stroud was just climbing into bed. At thirty-four, her energy level was higher than it had been in her early twenties and, capable of managing her *own* affairs to her extreme satisfaction, she was often induced to manage those of others as well. She opened her copy of the latest P.D. James novel with a sigh of enjoyment but found her brain was not yet ready to settle. Padding over to the bureau, she set her radio-alarm clock, which now read twelve minutes after two. She still appreciated living alone. At eighteen she had been married to her social worker, not long after ditching her last bartending job. But it had been a troubled match from the start—too much nit-picking on each other's bad habits, mostly—and they had parted within a couple of years. Since then, she felt free! No noise, no hollering, no one demanding she get into bed at a specified hour. No one insisting the lights were out by eleven. No one telling her when she could and could not leave the house. Her businesses were successful, she was well known all over the county and she was convinced that, despite the overdose of poverty and discipline she'd experienced as a child, she was heading toward financial freedom in her immediate future. Yes, luck harnessed to intelligence and 'street sense' had produced some satisfactory results. Now that she had devised the new plans, her wagon load was much lighter.

Back in bed, she fell into an untroubled sleep as the remnants of a complacent smile still lingered upon her cheeks.

• • •

But while Genevieve and Polly Jane slept, another woman down the street twisted and sprawled like an untethered vine, stretching aching muscles in an effort to attain relief. Finally giving up in vain, she lay still and listened intently to the welcome silence. Flat on her back, her legs thrust long and taut with toes pointed up, her whole being concentrated on the simple act of listening. She breathed so softly her nostrils barely fluttered. From years of practice, she could control her breathing, control her whole body in an unnatural immobility. The violent thudding of her heart, however, was impossible to still. Like piano hammers without their felt padding, each striking pulse pounded a reverberating chord through her chest.

Slowly, cautiously, she sat up and leaned against one flattened foam pillow. Aunt Esther would not allow the luxury of feathered head-rests. Nor would she hear of more than one per bed. Elizabeth knew this, because she had once smuggled in a beautiful cushion which she'd ordered from the Sears catalogue, only to find upon her return home from school the next day, that it had disappeared. Her aunt had not admitted to taking it, but Mrs. Whistler at the post office had mentioned Esther had been in that morning to return the large brown-wrapped parcel. With less courage than a timid church mouse, Elizabeth Grimball now kicked back the covers and was about to climb out of her bed when she thought she heard a noise in the bathroom. Good *Lord*! Twenty-eight-years-old and not an ounce of independent fortitude to muster! She'd better wait a little longer… There—was that a familiar snore? Just another minute or two to be safe.

The shade was down. Yes, that was one thing of which she could be certain. For if ever she was to forget, Aunt Esther would have promptly called her attention to it. The window faced the ravine behind the house. It was extremely unlikely that anyone had ever peered (or ever would) into the room, but her aunt's powerful modesty was not to be taken lightly. She stripped off her ancient patchwork quilt now and shimmied to the edge of the mattress. Damn! If only those springs wouldn't squeak so! She tip-toed to the door, shut it quietly and stuffed her quilt under the crack at its base. As a whimsical teenager, she had called this quilt '*Threads*' because it was on only the strength of these from which she felt both their existences clung. Age had certainly not added to either of their complexions or comforting propensities; nonetheless, she was more grateful for its purpose now than ever. Feeling at last that she was secretly ensconced in her aloneness and, with an inaudible sigh of relief, she lit her candle. She'd gotten a tall, new one from the kitchen pantry tonight.

The room, as revealed by the dismally inadequate yellow glow, was no more cheerful or attractive than it had been in the dark. Of moderate size, it held the iron bed, a chipped Depression-era bureau over which was a blurred, oval mirror and a diminutive, scarred wooden table which served as her desk. The vinyl roller shade covering the only window was shabbily criss-crossed with the cracks of sunlight and age, and her clothes were hung in a corner, covered with a faded rust-colored drape.

Seated at her desk, she soundlessly leafed through her pages until she came upon her most recent watercolor, partially sketched at school. It was of a basket full of fruit which the children had given her, collected from their parents' respective orchard harvests. She was pleased with the dull waxiness she'd given to the apples, and she'd achieved a texture to the dimpled pears of which she was most self-impressed. Of course the actual fruit had never come home; Aunt Esther could not abide fruit-flies in her kitchen. However, the painting added a bright spot to her modest desk while she worked. Putting it aside, she picked up a brown-paper-covered exercise book, innocuously designed with the simple heading: 'Social Studies—Miss Grimball's Copy'. As she opened it to the middle and scanned her latest entries, she decided 'Anti-Social', or even 'Auntie Anti-Social', would be more accurate descriptions of the writings within. For the next forty minutes, she wrote steadily, her pen making a grooved indentation in her thumb and forefinger. Then, the candle fading, she sat a moment longer as if the effort to move called for more energy than she could muster. Finally, the flame flickered out and in the darkness, only a small rustling could be heard as she tucked the book and her artwork away, rose from her chair and gently plopped the quilt back on the foot of her bed. Next, the door opened soundlessly, the mattress groaned protestingly and all was silent again save for the occasional gulping snores from the room across the hall.

CHAPTER TWO

"Oh, Inspector Steele, what a shame you got to be gettin' your own breakfast! Can't I help?" The morning voice of Mary Henry grated like a snow-plow bouncing along a gravel road and Philip winced as his ears were jolted by the sound. She had come in through the kitchen door for some reason, instead of going straight into the post office at the front, where P.J. was still busy sorting mail. "Here! Brought you some cinnamon buns, jes' warm from the oven. 'Course, they almost didn't get here, mind. Some crazy kid jes' bout took my head off with a baseball!"

Philip knew that P.J. had planned to make a special breakfast for him as soon as Mary arrived at work and she could leave the counter for an hour or so. He had simply been adding coffee beans to get the percolator going, but Mary started clattering about, fussing with dishes and mugs, helping herself to the butter jar in the fridge. Polly Jane Whistler was a patient saint, her godson thought, to put up with this creature on a daily basis. He knew she despised Mary more than consistent with her usual accepting equability. Why she'd never hired a different assistant was beyond him. Coolly, he responded to the repeated entreaty to sample a bun.

"Thank you, Mrs. Henry. But I believe P. J. already has something planned." Philip gestured toward the front room, hoping she'd take the hint. "Perhaps for a snack, later."

But Mary was not to be deterred. She fondled his V-necked sweater, marveling at the quality of factory designs 'in these here days', and then proceeded to pour coffee from the pot. For herself!

"Goodness, how strong you like it!" she grinned, slurping at the black liquid. "Really, most big men seem t' need a good jolt of caffeine ta get their engines started! Ain't that the truth, now!" She batted her mascara-thick eyelashes at him. "I can't hardly see how you manage it."

"Actually, the double negative suggests one of us doesn't, dear Mrs. Henry," Philip said with the formality he tended to inject when wishing to disguise scorn. He was only rescued from continuing on into more blatant rudeness when there was a slight 'tssk', and Polly Jane marched in and firmly asked her assistant to take up her position in the post office.

Half an hour later, feeling like he might explode from the weight of eight blueberry waffles with locally tapped maple syrup and a whipped cream topping, Philip escaped outside leaving the two women to continue serving customers and sorting envelopes in the front of the house. It was a beautiful morning. An indolent autumn breeze stirred the gold leaves on the trees; the yellow and orange chrysanthemums fanned languidly toward him in a rhapsody of sun-worship. It was nearly as warm as mid-summer. The village was astir with human activity more vigorous than that encouraged by the nature of the drowsy day. Dust mops reluctantly releasing their burdens of fuzzy gray swirls danced madly up and down as they were energetically shaken from front verandas. Out of houses, children scampered on their way to school, dogs obstructing their progress by running circles around sneaker-shod feet. A mailman with wetly plastered hair tucked behind his ears pushed determinedly down the street with his heavily laden knapsack, away from the cedar-shingled post office.

The bustling reminded him too much of the city life he was trying to escape and, feeling inclined to work off the weighty waffles, Philip decided to explore his boyhood haunts in the gully.

But when he turned through the Town Hall yard to head for the once-familiar path, he discovered a tall boarded fence in his way. There were only four buildings which backed onto the ravine. He walked past three of them in search of an opening: the hall, a white stucco cottage with ivy clinging to its sides, and a faded margarine-tinted clapboard, badly in need of some cosmetic attention.

The fourth house was the enormous red-bricked Victorian he had studied last night—the old Sanderson place. It looked more solid and imposing today in the brilliant sunlight than it had with its windows full of dark, flickering images. It was also barred from the ravine with a fence—but just a simple post-and-rail, easy enough for a fit inspector of police to pop over. However, he had turned into the side-yard and taken only a few strides when the front door opened. Her arms laden with books, a woman hurried down the porch steps but paused uncertainly when she saw Philip.

"I'm afraid I'm trespassing," he said. "But I want to get into the ravine and it seems to be barricaded all the way along. Any objection if I just climb over your fence?"

She hesitated for an embarrassingly long minute. The face she turned to him was pale and blank. Philip had the uncomfortable sensation she was looking right through him. Clearing her throat she said, "I think that's all right", while glancing anxiously toward a second-story window. Then, without another word, she spun about and trudged off in the same direction as the children.

What an odd woman! Phil stared after her retreating back for a moment before continuing to the fence. She had looked almost frightened, barely conscious of his presence. And although she'd been dressed in a navy-blue tailored suit on this warm morning, she had looked cold. Cold and ill. Her haunted eyes had had deep curves cupped under them. Perhaps she was simply shy—and he'd startled her?

Once over the fence, Philip found a steep path heading straight down. The ravine was much more thickly wooded than he remembered it. Another change, naturally. It sloped precipitously down to the stream at the bottom, where he discovered the going was less treacherous. He pulled a few burrs from his sweater and socks, then straightened to gaze about. Philip remembered many rousing hours with the neighborhood boys on this very spot. Two of his friends, the McKinley brothers, had lived in the house on the other side of the gully. It had been possible then to see the top of their place with its high cupola tower. Now, there was nothing to be viewed but brambles and forest. The McKinleys had moved away years ago, he knew, but was there still a path which could reach their farm? He tried to find one by following the course of the stream southward. He trudged along for some time, keeping his eyes up along the ridge for any sign of the place, and going much farther than he'd intended until he realized it must be time for 'elevenses'. Waffles forgotten, he was ready now for at least one cinnamon bun. Why hadn't he thought to bring one along?

He turned back. Presently, he discovered a stony trail leading in the general direction of the village. He followed it, ducking under low-lying branches, and *thinking*, rather than scanning upward this time. Most fitting, he decided. For here he was, hunched over physically, just as life seemed intent on making him symbolically. And following a rough path the end of which was unclear.

"Stoney End," Phil muttered, with Nyro's song, just released yet again, fresh in his mind from the kitchen transistor. "*I never wanted to go down the stoney end...*"

For twenty-one years, he had performed every duty from traffic cop to undercover detective, from as far away as Yellowknife in his R.C.M.P. days, to his more recent work as an expert investigator and consultant on homicide cases throughout the country. Deputy Commissioner 'Blue' had been a close friend of Philip's father and since Supervisor Steele's death many years ago, was the one man in the force for whom Philip could never feel anything but the deepest respect. He was also the only man about whom Phil was never tempted to yield to his growing habit of making derogatory observations. And the main reason he'd sought a vacation in Victoria was that Polly Jane was the only *woman* exempt from these comments. Those two good folk were, he told himself, now his greatest vulnerabilities. The Commissioner wouldn't be happy unless he could keep him on the force; P.J. wouldn't be content until she could engineer his marriage.

At this moment, both prospects were equally distasteful.

After having been reluctantly persuaded to tear up his resignation, Philip had been sent to the headquarters in Fredericton, the one condition upon which he'd insisted. Although only established there for three weeks, and with one murder already successfully solved under this new jurisdiction, he had found his supervisor entirely amenable when he told him he needed this holiday. With no family left except an uncle in England, (his sister had died of an overdose when she was still in her teens) and with his beloved godmother only a few villages beyond Fredericton's city limits, Victoria had seemed a perfect recuperation destination. Hadn't he always felt relaxed here? Hadn't it been his second home throughout his childhood? Although the nightmares of Archer's victims in Ontario still haunted him, by the end of this first week at P.J.'s, he was beginning to feel more restored. Certainly he had not eaten so heartily nor lounged so lazily in years. But where was he to go from here?

Still deep in thought, Phil emerged twenty minutes later, on what he recognized as the old fairgrounds surrounding the Town Hall, only a few blocks from where he had descended. He might have saved himself a nettlesome scramble if he had remembered this section earlier, for it was the same path he, the McKinley boys and Chet Anderson had most often used on their many pilgrimages around the village's perimeter.

He strolled across the grounds, opened the gate, and stepped into the street. From there he could see directly to the main corner of the village and he was immediately aware that something of an exciting nature had occurred. The street was filled with fervently gesticulating people. His instincts caused him to hasten his step before he realized that what he really wanted to do was flee back down into the peaceful gully.

Agitated voices raised in high-pitched titillation greeted him as he arrived on the outskirts of the crowd. "What's going on?" he asked of a woman with a kerchief thrown over damp hair. But it was another figure that turned enthusiastically to answer him.

"Oh, ain't you heard?" In her eagerness to be the first to break the news, the words literally sprayed from Mary Henry's lips with so much force that Philip found himself leaning away. "The bank's been robbed! An honest-to-God holdup! Four men with stockings and caps! And they got over fifty thousand dollars, someone said! Shot Mr. Ouellette in the shoulder. Doc's in there now and Chet Anderson went after 'em—the robbers mind, not the Doc."

An older man grabbed his arm and spun him around. Obligingly, and to avoid a repeated succession of spittle, Phil turned and was again accosted by yet another resident of the once quiet village. "Say! Ain't you Polly Whistler's nephew, or whathaveya? The police feller? They been looking all over for ya!"

A teenager ran up crying "Dad! Here he is! Mr. Steele, I mean."

Another man appeared behind the boy. "Hey, we sure have been looking for you! Come with me, please!" He was grabbed by the sleeve of his sweater where some burrs still remained and where a loose knit was perhaps not as strong as Mary Henry had earlier admired.

In fact, it was at this point that *every*thing began to unravel for Philip Steele.

"I am a Maintenance Engineer here," he was told. Philip could easily visualize the capital letters of the title. The word 'janitor', it seemed, was not a word by which one built pride. "They told me to try 'n' find you. Doc Graham, he said you'd know what's what."

Maybe so, thought Phil rebelliously as he was led through the bank, but who says I want anything to do with this? As soon as the squad cars arrive, I'll be able to fade. *I'm on holiday, dammit!* Once confronted with the group of tense people in front of him however, he professionally concealed his distaste for the job and his authoritative manner had a quelling effect on the hysterical excitement. Calmly, he started questioning the staff. The one customer in the bank at the time of the robbery was introduced to Philip as Mrs. Stroud and she seemed by far the most level-headed of the group. "Fortunately, I had just deposited my money, so they didn't manhandle me looking for more," she said, with a sparkling show of teeth. "I showed one of them my deposit slip and told him to just carry on and get out! My visit, if I may say, has been thrilling entertainment. Providing, of course, you can retrieve our funds."

Mr. Ouellette, the bank manager, favored her with a glare when he heard her flippant remarks. To him there had been nothing amusing about the proceedings. Dr. Graham assured him that his wound was slight, but it was the personal indignity he had suffered—and in front of his employees. And now the whole town—*his* town—was outside waiting, watching!

As Philip delved into the finer details, coaxed forth by deft questions, it came to light that at exactly ten minutes to eleven, three masked men had entered the bank while another had remained behind the wheel of the running car outside. The staff of three tellers, Ouellette, and Nora Knowles, his 'administrative assistant' (it seemed it was also incorrect to use the term 'secretary' around here, Philip thought sardonically) were ordered to line up facing the wall with their hands on their heads. The fact that each of the men was brandishing a revolver ensured immediate compliance. Two of the robbers then scooped up all the cash in the tills, while one covered the group with his gun. Next, Ouellette was yanked out of the line, ordered to open the vault. He refused, with what was described by his staff as "profane objections"—which he vehemently denied—and it was at this point that he was shot, luckily with only enough damage to convince him these men meant business. The safe was opened, two of the men followed him in, the money was speedily removed and the criminals fled.

Coincidentally timed with their departure, Chet Anderson, the local constable, was coming out of the post office having just been handed by Polly Jane Whistler, his most recent issue of "Reel Life". Chet loved fly-fishing on the Wolastoq River and was an avid competitor in local outdoor contests with some of his buddies from the nearby First Nations reservations, so he could perhaps be forgiven for taking several minutes to notice anything out of the ordinary going on down the street. "Reel Life" had beautiful photography in it and he was just admiring the russet colors of a leaf floating down a glistening brook on page four when the rapid slamming of car doors caused him to raise his head. Startled comprehension flooded his boyish features as he ran toward the speeding Plymouth. Apparently, he had only time to leap on his motorcycle, call a hurried explanation to Ouellette, who had come running into the street holding his arm, and Anderson was away, single-handedly in chase mode and without a thought for his own safety. Or the glossy magazine left behind on the gritty sidewalk.

Dr. Graham then explained that he had arrived on the scene and, as he was doctoring Ouellette, had remembered the presence of Inspector Steele in their village.

"But at this stage, you had already notified the district headquarters?" Philip interrupted.

Ouellette, whose patience appeared to be wearing away as much as the color in his face, said, "Yes, but they haven't had time to get here yet. Damn! That fool Anderson won't catch them! Wouldn't do any good, anyway…"

Philip cut him off and directed his next query toward Nora Knowles. "What time exactly did you get through to the police?"

"It was three minutes after eleven," she said. "I–I looked up at the clock, because it seemed we'd been held-up for hours, not minutes! I didn't know exactly who—or where—I should call, since we'd all seen Chet take off. So I just dialed the operator; she put me through to the Fredericton department. Mrs. Stroud got part of their license number from the window and I passed that on to them."

"Well, that's very efficient of you both!" Philip congratulated her, then looked admiringly in the direction of the Stroud woman. "Is this the first bank robbery you've ever had here?"

"Yes," put in Ouellette mournfully. "And it couldn't have come at a worse time! Forty-six thousand dollars in that safe, and over sixteen hundred in the tills! Normally we wouldn't have anything like that sum on hand, but of course during harvest it's necessary. So many immigrant farm workers and also a lot of tourists going through to see the colors in the Appalachians."

"Isn't it odd there weren't more customers in the bank?"

"No, not really. Just before lunch is usually our slackest time of day on Fridays. Because all afternoon, the orchard and potato farmers will be in to get their pay packets."

"Hmm," Philip pondered. "And it does seem rather as if someone knew all that. I don't suppose you've noticed anyone suspicious-looking hanging about lately? Across the street or anywhere?"

"Ya mean—casing the joint?" put in a young teller with the sunlight glimmering above her dimpled cheeks.

A few too many episodes of The Mod Squad? Phil almost asked, but mumbled instead, "Ah, er–yes. I suppose, if you like."

Ouellette silenced her with a glare of pained disapproval, then turned his back to his employees. "No," he said shortly. "Of course we haven't, or we'd have reported it immediately."

"How about the rest of you?" Philip asked, refusing to let Ouellette speak for everyone as he was obviously in the habit of doing.

The shy teller spoke up again. "One of those men today. His mouth…"

"Yes?" prodded Philip. "You noticed something unusual?"

"Well, I don't know. Of course, they all wore gloves and those stockings on their heads. But one of them, I'm sure, had a mustache—dark blond or brown. And, well—" She broke off, looking around the room uncomfortably.

"Do you think you could recognize him again?"

"I don't know. It's not that. It's just—well, my dad has a man like that, about that height with a mousy sort of mustache. Working through harvest for him, you know? He's from the North Shore. Of course, he lives in the bunkhouse, so I don't see him often. But I suppose it could have been."

"Has this man worked for your father before?"

"No. He just came into town a few weeks ago. We were still awfully short of help and Daddy hired him on the spot. Said he had a good strong back and didn't seem to swear much, so why not?"

Smiling with what he hoped was an encouraging presentation, Philip asked, "And he's still there working at the farm?"

"He was when I was home for supper on Sunday night, and Daddy was in to the bank yesterday and didn't say anything about him leaving, so I *guess* he's still there."

Philip asked several more questions of her, jotted down a few notes with her address to hand over to the Fredericton contingent which he saw pulling up outside and announced with relief, "Here are the reinforcements. I'm afraid you're all going to have to put lunch off for a bit. I'll give them the details but no doubt you'll be questioned more extensively."

Genevieve Stroud piped up again. "Who cares about lunch? Do you think Victoria has ever seen such excitement?", and with that she bustled out to meet the newcomers as if she owned the bank herself.

• • •

It was 3:30 before Philip was finally free. Although he had made it clear that he intended to have nothing to do with the investigation, the intention was easier to state than the physical withdrawal. Turner, a fellow inspector at Fredericton, was a red-faced, barrel-shaped man who, while eager to take charge, seemed resentful of Philip's lack of interest and managed to keep him on the job all the early afternoon on various pretexts.

When he finally arrived at the salt-box, Polly Jane welcomed him with mixed exclamations of excitement and dismay: "What a day you must've had!", "Did you get a speck of food for lunch?", "Was it true that over 50,000 dollars was stolen?", "Why would thieves choose quiet old Victoria?"

Philip laughed at his godmother as she handed him three of Mary's re-warmed cinnamon buns from that morning. "It's amusing, you know. Most people, except for Mr. Ouellette, seem to feel rather flattered about the holdup. They're all eagerly awaiting the morning papers. It's too bad you had to be in the post office all day. I'm sure it's been one of this village's most historically momentous events!"

"Well, believe me—I heard most of it, several times over, even if I'm sure half is hugely embellished. Of course, Mary had a two hour lunch in order to be at the scene. Oh, by the way, there's a message for you from the Fredericton station. You're to call a man named Stafford."

Later, while P.J. bustled about the kitchen preparing supper, Philip made several calls to his department supervisors then sat down to a loaded plate of potatoes, tenderloin and coleslaw. "P.J.,

I haven't eaten meals like this for decades. Not since I stayed with you in the old days. I don't know what it is you do to food, but no gourmet restaurant could equal it! What's for dessert?"

Polly Jane laughed, but pretended to be disapproving. "Tssk! Now then, our biggest day of the century and all you can think about is your digestive system? What makes you think I've had time to bake anything, for goodness sakes?"

"Don't tease, you old rascal. Is it cobbler? Pie? Some whipped cream concoction?"

"Peach shortcake."

When supper was over Philip, well fed and slightly somnolent, helped with the dishes and the clearing up before retiring at about 9:00 to the library to read. His godmother raised an eyebrow in bewilderment as he settled down with his book. He knew what she was thinking: How could he concentrate at a time like this? Shouldn't he be working? Making more calls? Out chasing the thieves himself?

Philip ignored her persistent stare. Finally she spoke: "I was just–er–rather wondering if you didn't have to go out again?"

"No. I've done my little bit. A better man than I am has his nose to the scent now." He laughed. "It's all right, P.J. I've been officially excused from participation in the case. I'm to be allowed my uninterrupted holiday, for which I'm duly grateful." He went back to his book, Pierre Berton's newest called The Last Spike. He was able to lose himself in the wilderness for some time until Polly Jane put down the needlepoint at which she'd been squinting in vain over the tops of her glasses, and hurried off to the persistent clanging of the phone. Philip glanced at the clock over the bookshelves. 10:40. Late for phone gossip. But then not many minutes passed before P.J. scuttled back into the room.

"Phil! Phil, for goodness sakes! Something awful…"

Philip leaped to his feet and helped the older woman to her chintz armchair. "What is it? What's happened now?"

"There's been—an accident. Jake Brock's son, Oliver. He—he's dead! Trudy Quigley said Chet Anderson wants you to come right away."

"Where? What kind of accident?"

"He was shot. Chet's sending someone over for you. Oh, my gracious! What's going on in this little place?" She patted her chest as though burping a baby, catching her breath and then hurrying on. "Oh, goodness, I must put some casseroles in the oven for the Brocks. I'd better call Tessa over in Moncton, too! I think she's a second cousin or something! Oh dear, maybe I'd better wait…"

"Yes, please, P.J. Just wait on doing anything."

Philip sighed as he went to answer the door. Obviously some people still reveled in these kinds of situations, found a natural high from a pumping rush of adrenaline. But he was so tired of it all. So very tired.

CHAPTER THREE

An agitated man stood on one foot on the doorstep, wringing his hands nervously. "You Mr. Steele? I'm here to take you to Mr. Anderson. We gotta go quick!"

"Should I get my car out of the garage?"

"No sir. It's quicker to walk."

"What sort of accident has happened?" Phil asked as they half ran along the sidewalk.

"Weren't no accident, sir! That there boy's been shot, sure and certain."

"Fill me in a little, please."

"Wal, sir—don't know how it happened, but we found him just a bitty ways from our place—mine and Mary's, that is. My name's Mort Henry. I didn't hear nothin', personal-like, mind, 'cause I had the TV on. The local news was talkin' 'bout the bank robbery here and then I was watching an Eastwood movie. My wife don't like violence on the telly, but she weren't home—was next door with the old—er, with Miss Esther. They don't have a TV over there, and I guess they heard what sounded like a car back-firing at about 10:15. You din't hear it? 'Course my old lady, she got all excited on account of the robbery, and thought maybe it was a gunshot and maybe them robbers was down in the ravine or somethin'."

"I'm sure those thieves are long gone by now."

"Wal, anyhow them ladies was scared, I guess, and a bit later Elizabeth—that's the old—that's Esther Grimball's niece what teaches school—she come in a few minutes later. Claims she din't hear nothin'. Mary, she wanted her to go out with her to look around, but Elizabeth wouldn't, so my old lady come home and asked me to check it out. I figured it was her 'magination, so I didn't really look too good, you know? I just took a stroll down to the main corner and back. I seen Chet Anderson and before I has a chance to tell him anythin', he asks me have I seen young Oliver Brock? He han't come home from school, never showed up for supper and his mother was fit-to-be-tied, like. I says 'no'. Then I tells him about the shots my old woman thinks she heard, and he says for us to go back and have a look around and we did and... And we—um, we found him."

"You say it was close to where you live?"

"Yeah, we're nearly there."

"Oh I see. You're right next to the old Sanderson house, then? And that's Miss Grimball who lives there?"

"Yes sir. Always been some Sanderson or t'other in that there house. When Esther's mother married John Grimball, they just moved right on in with the old folks. Here's Chet. The body's right down there. Back of the ravine a bit."

A figure approached from out of the shadows. Anderson emerged and as he came to meet them, Philip noticed a gray pallor showing plainly on his face, even in the dim glow of Mort Henry's flashlight. "Phil! Great to see you again! Too bad it's under such dramatic circumstances!" The two shook hands warmly and Philip felt the weight of twenty years nearly doubling as he looked in the eyes of his boyhood playmate. How old they'd both become.

"Yes! You've had a helluva day!"

"Damned right! Spend most of my career chewin' the fat at the tea-room and then wham! All in under twelve hours! Look."

Chet Anderson directed the beam of his flashlight downwards. "Shot in the heart, be my guess."

The body, that of a large fifteen-year-old, looked young and immature in his white death. He was lying on his back, his right arm twisted under him. The light the constable played over him revealed a wet darkness on his chest, as the three men descended to investigate.

"Have you moved him at all?" Philip asked.

"Not really. Just felt for a pulse. Did you call Dr. Graham, Mort?"

"He weren't there. Marcia said she'd tell him as soon as he come in."

"Did you find the weapon?" Anderson asked Henry.

"No, sir. Not me."

"Better call Fredericton in again," Philip recommended.

"Yeah, but you work for them now, don't you? So isn't this in your jurisdiction?"

Philip sighed. "That may well be. But at the risk of sounding facetious, I'm not on duty."

Chet looked at him strangely for a moment. "But, what should I do about searching for the gun? What about the coroner? How about calling—"

"Relax, Chet. Fredericton will want to take over. They'll keep you involved, naturally. But look, it's obviously not an accident or a suicide. You'll need more manpower."

"And you're not the man?"

"It's a long story."

Anderson's face, which since Philip's arrival had regained its normal expression and color, creased now in furrowed lines of doubt. Wonderingly, he commented, "You know, he was always crazy about guns, this kid. He's been a regular visitor to my office, and I don't mean in a good way. So I just assumed... But you're right! There's no gun here, and I've been looking! Hey, Phil? Do you suppose those bank thieves never went away at all? That they led me on a merry chase out of the village, and then came back to some hide-out 'round here? I mean, it would be the last thing anyone would ever think of."

"At this point, your guess is probably better than mine. Have his parents been told?"

"No, I was waiting till after you and Doc had looked him over. Gosh, I don't want to be the one to break it to them! Oh! Who's there? That you, Doc?"

"It's me," said a tired-sounding voice even less enthused than Philip's. "What's happened now?"

"Looks bad. Oliver Brock's been shot—and it's not a suicide. There's no gun here!"

"Good Lord! Is he dead? I'll have to have more light. Uh, Mort, my car's just over there. Turn the headlights on, will you? Hello, Philip! On the job again are you?"

"Not exactly."

"Damn! There is nothing I can do. Jake and Rose don't know about it yet?"

"No. Wilf, what should we do with him? I mean, do we call in the county coroner or what? We'll have to have that bullet if it's still in there."

"All right if I turn him over?" Dr. Graham looked questioningly at Philip who nodded. Gently, Dr. Graham rolled the body and peered for an exit wound "It's still in there, all right. Better call the C.C., Chet, yeah. Right away."

"Philip, would you? I've got to stay with the body. And Wilf— Rosie and Jake..."

"Yes, I suppose I'll have to go."

"I'll call the coroner and then come with you, if you like," Philip offered, feeling it was the least he could do. Both the local constable and the doctor sighed with relief.

•   •   •

There should be something other than adrenaline, Philip thought, which could kick in when boredom and disillusionment take over one's life. For adrenaline was only a temporary stimulant and Philip was going to need a lot more than that, he figured grimly, in the days to come.

"*Bloody busman's hol,*" he said aloud.

Stafford, at Fredericton, had gone against everything he'd said only hours before. Deciding his new Inspector Steele—already at the scene and somewhat familiar with the community—would be an asset, the supervisor had assigned him officially to the case. Vacation be damned. This, along with the wails of a grieving mother and the anger of a confused father, did nothing to change Philip's attitude toward the despicable work of all murder investigations.

A dim glow shone in the little entrance hall of Polly Jane's house when he finally arrived back, well after midnight. The lights were on in the sitting room too, and a wood fire crackled in the grate. The air was permeated with the overwhelming aroma of freshly brewed coffee. His godmother greeted him, pot in hand.

"Oh, Phil, dear! It's just dreadful! And you and Wilf have had to tell the Brocks all about it? That must have been an ordeal for you!" P.J. had always had an awe-inspiring approach to digging up desired information while appearing discreet. Philip assumed that most of tonight's had been exchanged over telephone lines about the urgent need for offerings of banana loaves and hamburger casseroles.

He sank into a chair clutching the steaming mug between his fingers. "It was that, and now Fredericton says I have to head up the case, for the love of God! The boy was shot outright. Nobody had seen him since 5:00 p.m., or at any rate no one's admitted to it. The Brocks are inconsolable: the mother screaming, the father hollering about revenge."

"Yes, I can imagine that. They doted on the boy—an only child, of course."

"Well, it all has a sense of the surreal to me. The kid had failed Grade Eight last year; was repeating it with little hope, apparently, of passing yet again. He skipped out of school early this afternoon and didn't attend a soccer match he'd been expected to play in. But a buddy of his did talk to him at about 5:00 after the game. It was still light then and his friend claims he was leaving after the soccer at the fairgrounds when Oliver called out and asked him who had won."

Polly Jane jumped in. "Perhaps he and some of the others have been playing at cops and robbers, trying to catch the real ones from today?"

"We asked about that," Phil said. "But he didn't have a gun! Chet says he got in trouble with it last month—shot some farmer's cow. Anyway, Jake Brock rather belatedly, in my estimation, took the damn thing away from him and locked it up. He wasn't supposed to have it in the first place, couldn't get a license for one until he was sixteen. Lord, I'm tired. How about we turn in? I've got to be off and running by 8:00 a.m., thanks to Stafford. Mary comes in at 8:00, doesn't she? Right. Perhaps I'll be out of here by *quarter to*, then!" He rolled his eyes in exaggerated aggravation and Polly Jane smiled.

In bed, however, she found once more that she couldn't rest. Such an exciting yet tragic day! True, the national newspapers were always full of break-ins and robberies, murders and slayings but they were so distant, so detached from her village of Victoria—and really very rare in this mostly wilderness-dressed province. Some stranger or strangers must be responsible! Although there had lately been a lot of unhappy, displaced people in the recently-formed Nackawic over the building of the dam, that had settled down some now, with jobs offered at the new mill. There *were* a lot of strangers who'd been moving here from other provinces for the mill-work too, of course. But Nackawic was miles away and all that could have nothing to do with occurrences here in quiet Victoria, surely? Crabbe Mountain had its fairly new ski resort, P.J. pondered, biting a fingernail—but that wouldn't be attracting tourists for months yet. At least the end of November, depending on snow. And while farm workers came into the area each year during harvest, they usually toiled on the land all day and fell into their bunks at night, exhausted. They rarely came into the village unless it was to make a quick purchase at Brocks' store.

Oh, and poor Rose Brock! What a life she has had, thought P.J. with her usual empathy. Such a belligerent, bitter man for a husband, such a foolish and bull-headed son. Sometimes she was grateful for never having had a marriage or children to tie her down, or to which she could become unbearably attached. Besides, Philip was as much a son as she could ever have hoped for. Though he hadn't stayed with her in Victoria in nearly two decades, they often spoke on the phone, especially about some of his cases far and wide. After his detective father had died, she liked to think she'd been the one who was at the other end of the line for him, with whom he could bounce theories or make literary or historical comparisons. There'd been several Christmases and other visits in the many interesting places across Canada where he'd been posted, as well. She was grateful to his parents, her dear friends, for inviting her to take such a special part in his upbringing. She thought about how she'd react if he was killed, a real possibility in his line of work. Yes, it would be like losing a son, and she arrived again at—*what an unthinkable thing to lose one's only child.* What could she do for Rose Brock, she wondered. What to say, what to offer?

Sighing deeply, she realized she was tired after all. Really, it was almost too much for an old biddy to take, all in one day. Laughing at herself, she allowed a yawn to force her eyes closed, and she kept them so.

•   •   •

Coughing harshly, Genevieve Stroud sat curled in her armchair, reading. It was late but she would not be ready for bed for hours yet. She had far too much to think about, to plan.

Tomorrow she must remember despite all the hysterical excitement, that she had an appointment with Ed Wynne about his new insurance policy, and at 4:30 p.m. she had to show a house outside Nackawic to a couple moving there from Charlottetown. The husband would be starting work at the new mill and she hoped they would be the first of many more families moving there to be thus employed. Then, she would have to get on the road to make it to Moncton in time to fly out for the conference in Halifax. And perhaps to a fresh lobster dinner beforehand? She must not let herself become distracted. She coughed again. She was sincerely glad she'd given up smoking. The only trace remaining was this damn lingering chest cough and it only came about if the night air was damp.

•   •   •

"Elizabeth! How many times must I remind you to shut those blinds! Really, you'd think you wanted some crazed murderer in the gully to watch you undressing." Esther Grimball habitually started in on her niece before she remembered Elizabeth was not in that room tonight. Honestly, what was the girl thinking? She'd been acting so strangely lately.

And Esther was frightened. Very frightened. What with the robbery and then the shooting. She supposed it was just as well there was one less Brock in the world. But that kid had wicked friends; Elizabeth had said so herself last year, hadn't she? Perhaps there's even a gang of them out there spying *now*…Oh, for heaven's sakes, that wretched Elizabeth had left the second-floor hall light burning. She'd have to hurry right up and switch it off.

· · ·

Jake Brock fled to his work-shed. He couldn't bear to hear his damn wife bawling another minute longer. He needed time to get himself together. Time to think. Reaching behind the little pot-bellied stove he used to heat the space in the winter, he grasped his rifle, pulling it toward him. He shook his head in disbelief. How could any kid of his not have fought back? How could he just let himself get shot? Jake thought he'd taught him everything he'd need to know in these situations, but perhaps he never should have taken his gun away from him. Who cared about some old Holstein, anyway? If Oliver had still been armed, maybe he wouldn't be lying in a mortuary right now.

CHAPTER FOUR

Polly Jane felt she'd been asleep only a matter of minutes when the clanging phone brought her hastily struggling into her fuzzy pink robe.

"Hello?"

Breathless, a shrill squeak broke into a torrent of incoherent speech. "'spector Steele! Oh, *God*! Get him right away! I can't— Jesus! Is he there? Tell him to come right away. She's dead! I–I *found* her, P.J.! Mort's there all alone. Quick!"

"Who's dead? Come where?"

"Esther Grimball! She's dead—killed herself, maybe. There's a gun right beside her. I don't know!" Mary Henry was hysterically out of control.

"I'll tell him. He'll be right there!" P.J. hung up and using muscles she hadn't remembered she possessed, nimbly thrust herself up the stairs. "Phil! Philip! Wake up, Philip!" She was trembling violently, her heart thudding so sporadically from both the excitement and the exertion that she wondered what it felt like to go into cardiac arrest.

"What the devil! P.J.? What now?"

"Oh, Phil! There's something awfully the matter. I don't know what's happening to this place! I–I'm frightened!"

"Sit down, P.J. Breathe."

"I'm all right. But there's been another death. Esther Grimball. Shot!"

As Polly Jane sat staring through unseeing eyes, her godson bounded to the bureau, pulled off his boxer shorts, and dressed as he dashed to the closet for his shoes. Many hours later, Polly Jane Whistler was to remember that moment and blush modestly at her shamelessness.

"Call Wilf Graham, will you?" Phil was saying as he scrambled to tie his laces. "It's a shame because he's half dead himself with fatigue, but it can't be helped. I'm off. Don't worry, P.J. "

It was shortly after 6:30 a.m., and dawn had not yet completed her full ritualistic ceremony. He ran down and across the street, thinking it was less than twenty-four hours since he had taken his first steps onto the lawn of the old Sanderson house. That first time had been for pleasure, the next two anything but. Mary and Mort Henry were again the not-unwilling heralds of the news. Vainly, Philip wished it could have been anyone else to whom he was obliged to listen. Mary's marble-mouthed voice, her protuberant eyes and her clutching gestures toward both Mort and himself practically nauseated him. And that was without the rain of spittle, which naturally made it doubly worse. He had never had much patience with women, except for his mother and P. J., but this creature was particularly unbearable. She droned on and on. Although he had thought Morton Henry overly garrulous before, Philip would have heartily welcomed even a few words from his clamped lips now. However, his wife had the stage.

"It was just about 6:00 when I come over. See, I know'd Esther'd been worried sick about the Brock boy bein' shot pract'ly in their backyard. Oh, Inspector Steele! We really need someone like you in this town! Huh, Mort? Chet Anderson just don't have the brains. I was just sayin' last week—"

"I think," Philip interrupted rudely, not bothering for once with his formal feigned tone, "we'd better leave all that for now. I'd like to see the body. You haven't disturbed anything?"

"No. Now, mind—I was just comin' to that. See, I always come here and keep Esther company in the mornings before I go to the post office. She always gets up at 5:30, rain or shine, summer or winter. And she's mighty appreciative of my storytelling. That niece of hers is a real loner. Mighty strange girl. Never hardly opens her mouth, and after all Esther's done for her too! You'd think she could spend a bit of time sitting with her auntie. Anyways, I been helpin' dig up some of the bulbs in the garden so when I come over, I tried the kitchen door first, where I usually go in, but it was locked. I knocked, but no one came. So, then I went and tried two other doors, the front and the east side, but they was locked too. I listened, but I heard nothin'—not a sound. Weren't nobody to be seen through the windows, neither! Then I went down these outside stairs to the cellar door, see. Elizabeth said she'd locked everything up tight last night because Esther was real worried. But that cellar door just swung wide open for me. I were that surprised! And there—there she was, see? Right down at the bottom of them inside stairs. I was so scared I couldn't even holler. Just run home and got Mort, and called for you. Even Elizabeth don't know yet—least-wise, *we* ain't told her. Lazy slug-a-bed always sleeps in 'til at least seven!"

Glad finally to have a distraction from the nails-on-chalkboard voice, Philip kneeled by the crumpled heap on the cold concrete floor. Her cane, which had evidently snapped in two in her fall, had caught in her skirt and left a long tear in the cotton house dress. Splinters also lay under her face, on which she was lying, one hand outstretched touching the rifle beside her. There was no blood.

Philip did not move from this position for several long minutes. Stillness, mercifully, had descended on Mrs. Henry's tongue. He stayed kneeling for an achingly long time, studying the lifeless form with a look of perplexity knotting his forehead. Then, deftly, he turned the body over. Glazed, wide-open eyes stared unseeingly back at him. *Just like the three hotel maids. There were the eyes again!* The face had a discolored mark on the temple and a few drops of blood had dried at the nostrils. There was no other sign of injury or wound. He looked up at the Henrys.

"This woman has not been shot."

Carefully, one hand on the back of the neck, he returned the body precisely to its former position. He then rose to his feet, brushed the knees of his pants and walked to the foot of the interior stairs, looking speculatively up the twelve steep steps to a closed inner door on the ground floor of the house.

"I suppose that door leads to the kitchen?" he inquired of the spellbound spectators.

"Yes. Did you—what do you mean she weren't shot?

Philip did not deem it necessary to answer. Thoughts and speculations were whirling around in his mind in a most dismaying manner. Gone was the old mental stimulus, the quick sarcastic response and a need to spring into urgent action. He felt only petulant annoyance—so many things to do, and here he was without help. An ache pulsed through his temples and he squeezed his eyes shut momentarily, placing his brow between his fingertips.

"Will you," he began, then as his eyes rested on the woman, he rapidly transferred them to the man—"will you see what has happened to Dr. Graham, please? And make some other calls as well. I want Anderson here if you can find him, and I think," he broke off to listen, "a car just stopped out there now. Hold on."

He started up the steps then turned back, motioning to the Henrys to precede him.

In the morning light, Wilfred looked shockingly ill. "Sorry to be so long," he said. "Nearly didn't get here at all. Flu or some such, I'm afraid. Esther's been shot as well?"

"No." Philip looked at the Henrys and felt stifled. Why such a seemingly inoffensive pair should have this contradictory effect on him, he really couldn't grasp. However, they must leave the premises or he'd never be free to speak or think freely. There were many more questions to be asked of the woman, but they would keep. Not too much danger of that fount running dry, thought Philip bitingly.

"Will you call Anderson please?" he said to them again. "And make sure Fredericton is on their way. Thanks for your help. I won't need to detain you any longer just now." He pointed toward the stairs. "Down here, Dr. Graham."

"But what about Elizabeth?" Mary Henry persisted. "Aren't you going to tell her? Find out where she is? Perhaps she's been murdered in her bed, with everything else that's—"

"Elizabeth doesn't know?" the doctor cut in, startled. "You— you haven't seen her yet?" If possible, the man's grim face turned several more shades of translucent green.

" Nope. Haven't had time. I think you'd better have a look down here before you break the news."

Dr. Graham's examination of the body was brief and perfunctory, his manner abstracted and disengaged in a way Philip knew, from scrapes and scraps of old, to be completely out of character. "You're right," he commented, straightening his back one vertebra at a time as he stood. "She certainly wasn't shot. Looks as though she fell down those steps. Her neck's broken. Notice that?"

"Yes. I did move her to examine the other side. Perhaps we should keep the broken neck to ourselves for now—not make it public. I was careful not to mention it to the Henrys. Wilf, what about this niece? How come she didn't hear anything, I wonder? And why hasn't she put in an appearance yet?"

Gruffly, the doctor pushed past him. "I'll look after her. She's my patient and she's not been well. I suppose another autopsy is inevitable?"

Philip stared for a moment. "Do you think? She didn't just accidentally fall down those stairs carrying the gun?"

"Hmm. Perhaps...Yeah, likely isn't at all necessary. Not feeling quite right, that's all."

Of course, Philip knew an autopsy would be called for but it was interesting to note the doctor's behavior and reactions. It was odd. The man now seemed to be sorry he'd blurted out the question. In the kitchen, which they had expected to find vacant, was Mary Henry, determination written fiercely on every ferocious feature.

"I'm going up with you to see Elizabeth. She's up *there*, not in her bedroom down here. And there's something wrong. I know. She should be up by now and even if she is all right, what would that poor, meek girl think if she was to wake up to find her room full of strange men? That's what I'd like to know!"

No doubt you would, you old wind-bag, thought Phil.

Dr. Graham suddenly became adamant. "Neither of you will go with me if I can prevent it. Elizabeth is not at all well. I gave her a sedative last night and I expect she's still sleeping under its influence. She's in a very nervous state. I'm not going to have her alarmed or upset any more than she needs to be."

"W-e-lll!" Mary Henry sneered. "So that's where she was last night while I was here. Now, why on earth couldn't she have just said so, instead of being all snooty-like and mysterious about it all. Sick, eh? Well that does explain a lot!"

"I'll go break the news to her," Dr. Graham said. He didn't look at Mary, but the loathing which she inspired was an almost solid tangible. He walked slowly forward, grabbing the top of the chair rail above the wainscoting to steady himself every few steps.

Impervious to snubs, remarkably unconscious of the feelings she engendered, Mary plowed on. "Yes, indeedy now. That explains a mess of things. Why, when Elizabeth did come in last night she looked like she'd been courted by a ghost! Not one word would she say, not even when we tried to tell her about the shot. Just looked right through us like we wasn't there a' front o' her own nostrils. Maybe if she'd knowed that was the last chance she'd have to say a word to her auntie… But nope! Not her! Into her bedroom she goes straight off, comes out again in a minute with her nightclothes all bundled up higgledy-piggledy under her arm, then—whaddaya' think? Up the stairs she marches! Esther and me, we hears her movin' 'round in the spare room up there. The *spare* room, mind. Ain't been used in I-don't-know-how-long! Why, Esther Grimball just sat there like she'd bin turned to stone!"

With that, Mary finally took in air, clapping her hand almost coquettishly over her mouth, but not having quite enough grace to entice a blush over her chubby cheeks. "Oops, guess I didn't mean that, exactly! I mean, poor Esther! Anyways, she was real took back. Looked at me and I just stared back, and the two of us couldn't pin the tail anywhere's near the ass's ass on that one. I'd a-stayed on with her for a while, but I knowed I should tell somebody about that shot so, mod'rate soon after, I went on home. But that's another reason I was early over here this morning, like—I wanted to find out what our Miss Elizabeth had been up to. And I ain't leavin' 'til I do!" Mary Henry stuck out her chest and pinned back her elbows like a squawking hen, then perched on the low kitchen counter as though every crumb under her other chubbier cheeks was a fragile yolk of gossip over which she nested.

Philip squeezed some sacrilegious syllables between his teeth, muttered something about 'disturbing the evidence', and escaped to the second story above, well after the tread marks of the good doctor's boots had settled in the dusty oak steps. It was all very well for Wilfred Graham to be dictatorial in his demands to see his patient alone, but especially since Phil had heard of her peculiar actions of the previous evening, a police officer might also prove an essential intrusion. As for Mary Henry, close on his heels... Well, to hell with it! He didn't feel up to coping with her.

Dr. Graham was sitting on the edge of the bed stroking his patient's hands and talking clearly but quietly. His profile was more the image of a doting parent than that of a physician making a professional house call. "Elizabeth! Come on, dear. Wake up!

Didn't I tell you that stuff would put you out? There, you're coming out now. Welcome back. Feel a mite groggy?"

"Yes I–I… It's so strange. Can't really… What are you doing here? Have I been ill for long?"

"No. You're fine. More than most of us, I dare say. You've just had a good old-fashioned slumber party all by yourself."

"But…I don't understand." Elizabeth rubbed her eyes, inching herself up in the bed. "Who's out there?" she asked, startled, looking toward the hall.

With a scowl the doctor turned and glared at the unwelcome duo outside the door, then squarely turned his back on them. "Elizabeth, I haven't time to lead up to this gently. There has been an accident. Your Aunt Esther—sometime during the night I guess, or early this morning—she fell. Down the cellar stairs. I'm afraid she's gone, Bethie. Dead."

"What? No! She–she can't be… Oh, my God! Then it's true— Grandfather *did* come! Oh, he shouldn't have! Grandpa, you shouldn't have done it!" Confusion and fear came over her terrified face as Philip watched from the door. Tears began welling in her eyes, but she blinked hard, shook them away.

"Elizabeth! Look at me! You're still asleep. Keep quiet, now. Rest."

"But, Dr. Graham! I saw him! He was in here last night. He sat right over there in his old rocker. He–he said…"

"She's the one off *her* rocker!" Mary Henry spat in a penetrating whisper. "Her grandfather's been dead must be close to twenty years, now! And there ain't no rocking chair *in* that room."

Wilfred Graham's body shrank visibly before them as the creases in his face deepened. He ran a hand over his own clammy brow. "Elizabeth, you were dreaming. The medication. Last night, you had a shock. I'm sorry. I was wrong to tell you when you were so tired and—and vulnerable. You realize you've just had some nightmares, don't you?"

"Yes." Her voice was so low the listeners in the hall had to strain to hear. "Yes, of course. But it–it seemed so real. He said he'd always look after me and see no one would hurt me. Aunt Esther—she fell down into the *cellar*? My God! She always said those stairs would be the death of her. I've heard—well, she's said it hundreds of times. Good Lord!"

"I want you to stay in bed today. I'll see about getting you some breakfast, but you must stay right here. Sleep all you can. You need it. Is there anyone you'd like to come stay with you?"

"No. No, thank-you. There's no one…" Elizabeth's voice trailed off as her eyelids began to droop.

"I'm going to leave you now, but I'll see you again soon."

"Yes. All right."

The doctor marched toward the hall. "Phil, it's about time someone was kind to that poor girl. Listen. I've got to go home and go to bed myself. Feel like an animal crawled in me and croaked. I'll try to get over again tonight to check on her. If I can't make it—and Marcia may well not let me—will you, you know, tread gently? Please? She's had a bad time of it."

"Fine. Go on along. I'll manage."

"But—about Elizabeth—she should really have someone to look after her today." The doctor turned to Mary. "Hasn't she a colleague from school maybe? Someone who would be willing to come in for the day, do you know?"

"Nope. She ain't. Always kept herself high and mighty above everyone else. I guess I'd know, too!"

"A fine thing," the doctor said, slapping his thigh impatiently. "Lived here all her life, helped so many. But not a goddamn friend to be had when she needs one!"

"Well, it's her own fault. If she woulda—"

"Oh, get out of my way, woman!" Dr. Graham thrust Mary aside as he reached the front door, struggling with the knob. It still appeared to be locked, so he threw back the bolt and exited.

Philip faced her and drew back his shoulders. Persuasively, he began: "Look here, Mrs. Henry. Someone needs to stay here at the house and I've got a million things to attend to. Could you not look after things here?"

"Not a chance. I ain't no nursemaid and I gotta get to work. 'Sides, you heard her. Crazy, she is! Right off her head."

"Yes, well, she admitted she isn't quite herself at the moment. I'll just tell Polly Jane you can't make it in today. It's Saturday, anyway—surely it's just sorting catalogues and things?" He suspected she didn't want to miss the opportunity to be behind the counter where her copyrights to the recent turn of events could be widely broadcast. It would be better if he could keep her out of the public eye for now, anyway.

"I ain't gonna get left here to be robbed and murdered for my pains, thanks very much."

"But—if you were never left alone? I can issue you your own personal guard and you know," he said, suddenly filled with a touch of his old inspiration, "there are bound to be reporters, photographers, policemen in and out all day and you're the one who heard the shot last night, and who discovered the body this morning. It's really *essential* that you be available here for questioning and interviews."

"W-e-lll," she hesitated, but Phil looked through the surface waters and saw her gills quiver as she rose to the bait. She was unable to conceal the pleasure with which this new prospect filled her. (Of course, she wasn't to know Philip wouldn't allow her anywhere near a reporter.)"Well, all right, I'll stay with Elizabeth. But mind, now,I ain't never to be left alone!"

"Fine. I'll arrange it. Now, I've some phoning to do. Where is it?"

"Ain't no phone here."

Philip thought perhaps he'd stepped off the earth onto another, less evolved planet. "I—no phone?"

"Nope. Esther always said she never needed no phone. You can come over and use ours, but—oh, here comes Mort with Chet Anderson!" Her strident voice persisted with barely a pause. "Mort, ain't you going to work at all today? You might as well. There ain't nothin' you can do here, and I ain't gonna be home. I've got my hands full, eh? Go on to the Burgess's, if'n they ask ya, fer yer dinner."

"All right," her husband said. "If Inspector Steele don't want me no more, I'll be off."

"No. Sorry to have held you up, and thanks for bringing Chet along." Philip turned to the startled-looking constable. "I'm afraid you've another busy day ahead, Chet. Come on in."

The two men entered the living room, Philip securing the door firmly behind them. Perpetual motion. That's what that woman's tongue was in, he decided. And now her ear would remain pressed against the sturdily paneled barricade which separated them, although it did seem like a fairly thick wall. He wondered if Esther Grimball had been the same kind of woman. In spite of himself, this case was beginning to pique his interest.

The living room's faded, peeling wallpaper was striped down to the heavily glossed chair-rail moldings, under which were more darkly stained and varnish-cracked panels from a by-gone era. Some brocade lampshades adorned two lamps, but the shades were iced with sugar-dust, as were the wing-backed, paisley upholstered armchairs. Phil waved at one.

"Sit down, Chet. There's a lot to be said, and I've got to get on the phone and get some action started." Philip related the events of the morning and, in a skillfully-abridged version, unfolded Mary Henry's description of the previous night. Anderson was quiet and pensive throughout. Phil concluded not many minutes later by saying, "The body we'll have to leave until our department's medical examiner has seen it and they've finished with photos. The gun can stay there too until it's been dusted for prints."

"What kind is it?" Anderson asked.

"Looks like an ordinary hunting rifle to me. An old .303, I think. Suppose it belongs here?"

"Could do. John Grimball used to hunt deer and moose every year." Anderson replied, leaning forward. "Of course, he's been gone a long while, now. But I expect his gun could still have been here. It was by the body?"

"Like to see?"

But Anderson shrank back suddenly. He supposed all policemen, no matter what their age, should be somewhat hardened to violent death; it would be a long time before he got over last night, however. Keeping company with a kid's corpse in the dark wooded hollow. He certainly didn't want to repeat the experience any time soon if he could prevent it.

"Uh, no. Wouldn't do much good, would it? I wouldn't recognize the rifle. My dad might, though. He and Grimball used to hunt in the same gang."

"Hmm," Philip said, "since Miss Grimball wasn't shot, it's only of importance I suppose, if it proves to be the weapon with which young Brock was killed. We'll leave that up to ballistics. Listen, Chet, I've got to get back on the blower, so I need you to stay here. There'll be a huge crowd from my force along presently, and you now know everything I do. If they get here before I return, fill them in for me, and keep an eye on things here, will you? Be sure that Henry woman takes Miss Grimball some breakfast, too; she's resting upstairs, under sedation." Philip thought it prudent not to elaborate further on that particular note. Anderson made a wry face then turned to join Mary in the kitchen.

Philip made his way next door to the Henrys' house to make his calls. Turner should be in charge at headquarters at this hour, unless of course he had personally dashed off, basking in supervisory capacity in pursuit of yesterday's bank thieves. Regardless, Turner resented him so much for his prominence across Canada, he was sure he would be put exclusively at the helm of the Victoria deaths because Turner knew that was the last thing Phil wanted. He grimly punched in the now-familiar numbers to Fredericton, expecting the worst. In its briefest form, he related the news, arranged for an autopsy on Esther Grimball, and asked that Zareb Woodbridge, the only man in the province whose work he both respected and with which he was experienced, be allowed to assist him. Since the irresponsible labeling done by Turner and his team on the recent Caswell murder in Fredericton, Philip felt there were few he could trust to work up to his —and thus his father's—highly professional standards. The Just State. He'd been raised on it, and couldn't have escaped it if he'd tried. Therefore, another request: Santana and his contingent were to be sent over to do the fingerprinting. Philip had considered that group to be the most meticulous. And Woodbridge was already in a squad car heading north before the two adversaries disconnected from their tense discussion.

Philip next telephoned several houses down to the parsonage, where Mrs. Baker was asked to arouse her husband in expectation of an immediate caller. Hurriedly, Phil trotted down the sidewalk, pressing his eyes between thumb and forefinger to rid himself of the dull headache which was dawning with the florescent sun.

The Rev. Baker himself opened the door, clad in a ragged olive green dressing gown. "Ah, Inspector," he said extending his right hand to Philip whilst making futile dabs at his ruffled hair with his left. "Sorry to be in such a state of disarray but as you know, I was forced to retire very late last night and—"

"And it's barely morning. I know, Reverend. Sorry, but it really can't be helped. I'm afraid a parishioner of yours, er– suffered a fatal accident during the night."

"Oh, gracious! Now what?"

"Miss Esther Grimball has fallen down her cellar stairs. Dead when discovered."

"Oh no! This is dreadful! Oh, dear!" The minister took a moment to gather his thoughts. "She was *not*, however, of my congregation. In fact, I barely knew her but—how on earth has this happened? Such tragedy in this little village in one day!"

Conveniently coinciding with my own much-needed holiday, thought Philip sourly. Aloud he said "What I really require of you is a list of boys within a year or two of Oliver Brock's age. I'd ask Elizabeth Grimball, but I'm afraid she's got rather a lot on her mind at the moment. I've hopes some of the young man's contemporaries know what he was up to while skipping school yesterday. It may facilitate our investigation, not only into his death, but perhaps into that of Miss Grimball."

"You–you think the two are somehow related?" asked the reverend, astonished.

Philip compressed his lips. "Too early to tell at this point, I'm afraid."

"Y-e-ss, I–I understand. You know, to be frank, I don't suppose you'll find much out from any of the local boys. Oliver had no friends, really—he was secretive— well, sly, actually. Also, he was stronger and bigger than most of the boys and inclined to bully them."

"Any girl-friends in whom he may have confided, then?"

"I hardly think so. But really, I suppose his teachers could tell you better than any. Certainly not his parents. They really knew very little of that boy's habits, sad to say."

"Still, perhaps I could begin with a list of as many cohorts as you can think of?"

"Inspector Steele." Pink-cheeked and hesitant, Mrs. Baker poked her head into the vestibule. "Would you—that is, I wondered if you might like a quick breakfast with us? It's all ready and I'm sure you've been far too busy to eat…"

• • •

Twenty minutes later, a much-fortified detective strode down the street supplied with the names and addresses of several boys and two girls which the community parish leader thought might have been in Oliver Brock's confidence. He arrived at 8:15 at the gray brick house of a family called Bancroft. He'd never heard of them. They must have moved here since my time, Philip decided.

After ten minutes of adroit questions, he had managed to elicit exactly zero relevant information from the tow-haired Billy Bancroft. Nor were the next four calls any more profitable. Oliver Brock's nickname had been 'Livvy', shortened apparently from 'Liverwurst' and not necessarily because of his given name. A typically undignified nickname which initially linked, Phil could only assume, to the various cold cuts in his parents' store. Or the habitual sandwiches the boy brought to school? Oliver had been strong physically, but hugely lacking strength in the mental department, it seemed, and he had made his teachers' lives miserable with his practical jokes and not-always-harmless pranks. His one passion, Philip was told by a wide-eyed female fittingly named Fawn, was hunting—and he had been 'awful mad' when they took his rifle away from him. He'd said he was 'gonna get even with 'em'. When asked to specify the identity of 'em', Fawn had shyly shrugged, then said that she supposed he'd meant his Pop, and the farmer whose cow had been shot. These and many other borderline irrelevancies Philip learned, but they added nothing to his knowledge of the events of the previous eve.

However, on his last call of the morning, he learned something which did disturb him. Although the interview had not begun well, Philip was finally able to exert all of his considerable tact and persuasive skills, (not to mention flat-out bribery in the form of a promised ride in a squad car, complete with sirens and lights) on the thirteen-year-old boy in front of him. Because Ted Watson had been so uncommunicative initially, Philip was not prepared for the stirring his sudden disclosure aroused in him.

"Yeah, well Liv came up from the gully after the game and asked me who'd won."

"Ah, that was you, was it? I knew that was the last time he'd been seen, at least —so, who *did* win?"

"We did, no thanks to him. He was s'posed to be playin'. He was pretty good too, but man! He always liked trompin' around in the gully better. Didn't care much for sports. But he always scared off the other team. He said—" Ted pulled a piece of what appeared to be grape bubble gum from his mouth and strung it out until it made a thin thread, glistening with saliva. Then, shoving it back in one flowing swoop, he asked for the third time, "You sure they'll let me ride in the front, with the sirens an'ever'thin'?"

"I'll drive you myself, Ted. Now, tell me what's on your mind."

"Wal…I dunno what he meant, 'sactly. But when Livvy come up from the gully he said he—he said he had to go. 'Cause he had a date to keep with Miss Grimball."

"A date? You mean—did he mean his teacher, or her aunt?"

Ted shrugged, bored and distracted by the Saturday morning cartoons from which he'd been interrupted. "Dunno. He just said 'Miss Grimball', man. That's all."

"And then you saw him head back down into the gully behind the soccer field?"

"I guess—he was… there was a squirrel an' he was pretendin' to shoot it with his finger, like—POW! You know? He was stupid, anyway. I didn't stick around."

"So he may not have gone back down into the gully right away?"

Again, the apathetic shrug. Philip discerned that the lure of the squad car had been dispelled for the time being. He called it quits.

So then, reflected Philip as he walked down the street, Oliver Brock had been going to the Grimballs' house after all. But why disappear at 5:00, and then the shooting not happen until after 10:00? What had he been up to all that time? Had he been planning some malicious prank against Elizabeth? She was, after all, the teacher who had failed him at the end of June, and perhaps now school was again in session, Oliver had been finding it difficult to repeat the eighth grade, staying behind in the remote village while his friends went off to the high school in Fredericton. Had Elizabeth actually encountered him just before his death? That might explain her peculiar behavior when she entered the house, going to sleep in the second-floor spare room well away from her aunt. She must have returned home just after the shot had been heard, according to Mary's account. But the doctor had said she'd gone to see him, and she would hardly have been toting a three-foot rifle around with her. There must be something else to explain why her nerves were so testy. And why, if the gun had been the same weapon that shot Brock, was it not found near him, but discovered this morning by the broken body of Esther Grimball?

Perhaps it was Esther with whom Oliver had had business. According to Ted, he said 'a date with Miss Grimball'. That, of course, could mean almost anything with either of the two women. It seemed absurd and yet both Oliver and one Miss Grimball now lay inexplicably but most assuredly dead. Had Esther perhaps found the teenager trespassing, taken the rifle out with her when she went to investigate?

And why was Wilf Graham, sick as he was, fluttering about like a mother hen over his patient? Did the good doctor suspect something incriminating about Elizabeth? *Know* something? Was he feeling guilty about his decision to treat her with sedatives? Perhaps he felt he had caused her to do something unforeseen…

But no, it was useless trying to speculate further. He must wait for the ballistics report. Also, he'd better get up to the old Sanderson house to see if the experts had arrived, and if they had the answers he needed before he made any more conjectures. Phil paused again in the brilliant sunshine, holding his temples as his headache throbbed on. Was it really just yesterday he'd been *enjoying* the intrusion of those bright rays as he'd explored his boyhood haunts?

CHAPTER FIVE

Mary Henry was happy. She was having her moment of glory, a Warhol fifteen-minutes of fame. Surrounded by reporters and police detectives she found herself being given more attention than she'd received from anyone, at least since her wedding day almost forty years before. Her tongue rattled endlessly on to anyone who would listen. She had showered more people with her wash of spittle than the forecast's expected rainfall for the month. The only trouble was, she decided, there were too many people to talk to at the same time. They were tearing the house apart, snooping in every room. The only section they had not turned upside down was the one in which Elizabeth was still obliviously sleeping.

At least, Mary supposed she was sleeping. Police Officer Sara Burns was standing guard outside her door, for reasons Mary could not comprehend. While she was given no information in return, she had told and retold everything she knew. And sometimes a little more besides…

On the other hand, a confused Chet Anderson was not pleased at all. Things were happening much too fast, were being taken out of his hands without so much as a by-your-leave. Admittedly, he knew he was unqualified and too inexperienced to manage these perplexing cases. It might have been considerate, however, if he'd been allowed to take part in the investigations instead of being ignored as soon as he'd finished briefing the officers. He was glad when Philip Steele returned.

"It was that gun which fired the shot, Phil!" he said, hurrying toward him as soon as he saw him heading down the front path. "They've found that out, but the only fingerprints on it were Esther's and Elizabeth's. A specialist inked her in her room just half an hour ago, but she barely opened an eye."

Philip nodded. It was nothing more than he expected. He grinned at his old friend. "Hell of a lot of reporters traipsing about. Can you keep them organized *outside* the yard?"

"God knows I've tried! They've been told nothing by us, but I defy any authority to prevent Mary Henry from opening her trap."

"Damn. Have you been keeping an eye on Miss Grimball upstairs?"

"I did, until your party of pros arrived and then they stationed a policewoman up there—more to keep Mary *out*, if you ask me."

Despite his headache and an even greater sense of impending doom, Philip laughed aloud.

Chet continued. "Elizabeth hasn't paid much attention to anything that's been going on, and frankly I have to wonder if either Dr. Graham gave her an overdose of the stuff last night, or if she's, I don't know, maybe faking it?"

Philip's lips compressed into a thin line. Laughter evaporated. "You may be right, Chet," he said, putting a hand on the other's shoulder. "I hate to think it, but we'd better go check. Any other fingerprints found about the house?"

"Only Elizabeth's, Esther's—and Mary's. Brother! You should have seen the fuss she kicked up for the benefit of the cameras when she was told she had to be I.D.ed to eliminate. Oh, yes, and a larger set of prints—a man's. I expect they'll find those are only Wilf Graham's, though. He's made quite a few house-calls recently to both Elizabeth and her aunt. From what I gather, anyway."

"And I suppose the older members of the family have been dead too long to have any prints left. All right, good to know."

Chet Anderson felt better now. Phil Steele had turned into a really great guy. Not superior at all, like Chet had imagined he might have been with all his much-publicized successes. And he didn't ignore a fellow the way those others in the house did. He made you feel included.

Now he said, "Well, thanks for holding the fort, Chet. I've made a number of inquiries about last night already. I'll fill you in later. Right now you'd better slide on home and get some breakfast. But come back. You'll be needed!"

A tall and burly black man, with a long nose, horn-rimmed glasses and an infectious smile approached him then and as Chet hurried away, Phil climbed the porch steps, hand extended. The man in sergeant's uniform shook hands with enthusiasm.

"Hello, Woody! You didn't waste much time getting here."

"Nope. Things are getting a bit hectic in this village. Was your holiday getting so boring you had to stir up all this excitement? Or did you just miss me?"

" Hmph. Was Turner pissed?"

"Putting it mildly, I'd say so, yeah. He was some burned that you asked for me, specifically. You know Turner. Can't be bothered with good dead folk when there are live baddies on the loose. He thinks he's hot on the heels of those bank crooks. 'When a shot rang out, get sharp after thieves', as Swinburne wrote."

"Er—wrong as usual, I believe, Woody; it was 'When a *look shot* out...'" Phil was starting to feel more comfortable now his new favorite sergeant was back at his side. Light banter at murder scenes was always frowned upon by civilians who may overhear it, but it cheered him up and he felt his headache dissipating.

"Whatever." Woody shrugged, unoffended at the correction he'd half expected as they turned to enter the darkness of the house. "How long d'you think you can keep me away from that prick Turner?"

"Frankly, Woody, I'm not sure how long I'll need you. We may have things wrapped up here fairly quickly."

"Quicker than the Caswell case?"

"Don't remind me. Nothing should ever be *that* quick. But we do already have a suspect."

An eyebrow on the sergeant's face shot straight up into his afro'd hair-line above the ridge of his glasses, while the other remained slanted comically over one wide-open pupil. "What? You mean, there's something in what the spitter says? That the sick woman upstairs is the one?"

"Good Lord, has Mary been running around *telling* people that?"

"Are you sure it's even possible? That weak little thing asleep up there looks as harmless as my Lanique's new kitten. And she's wasting away in bed, for God's sakes! I went up with Puro when he printed her and I saw her myself! Barely functioning!"

"That's the case today." Philip said. "We don't know what she was like yesterday, and I've been asking around. It seems hard to believe, I know, but—*hell! What do you think you're doing?*" The two men had turned into the living room to find some privacy in which to continue their discussion. However, cross-legged on the floor with papers and odd scraps of watercolor paintings spread out all about her, was a vibrantly adorned woman, wearing a jaunty red beret and a brightly patched peasant skirt, much absorbed in the paintings. *A transposed Flower Child?* thought Phil as he said, "Who the hell are *you*?"

"Hey there! Now don't freak out, man. I'm Jenny Connelly from the Moncton Monocle." She hastily gathered the papers into a brown workbook and stood up.

Beside him, Woodbridge snorted. "Never heard of it!"

"It's just started up this year. Give the new Times owners a run for their dough. And you are?" The young woman extended her hand, but Philip ignored it.

They gave their credentials, then Phil snapped "I think you'd better leave. NOW."

"I know, I know. Sacred property and all that." Rather reluctantly she handed him the book. "Still, it's better than listening to that ambassador of bad will in the kitchen and I've found out a lot more truths than I'm sure *she's* spouting!"

With chin stuck out determinedly, she marched from the room and Philip followed her, ushering her to the front door and locking it behind him. "Costello! *Costello!*" he bellowed into the cellar. "You down there? For Christ's sake, Robb—get up here and don't let reporters in! I've sent Anderson home for breakfast and anyway, he couldn't be expected to hold off that army of snoops all by himself. There're doors all over this place."

Joining Woodbridge again in the living room, he leafed through the workbook. "What is it?" the sergeant asked, trying to look over his shoulder with obvious curiosity. But just at that moment, several men came up from the basement, filing into the room to greet the man in charge. Hurriedly, Philip folded the book, thrust it into his inner jacket pocket, and turned to greet the newcomers.

"What have you found out?" he asked them, with an air of chatting over a bowl of popcorn rather than with the urgency he felt.

Santana, the fingerprint expert whose ancestors were originally from Havana, and whose nickname among his colleagues was 'Puro', spoke up to relay all Philip had already been told. He added that one of his staff had been sent over to the Grahams' house to 'ink up' the doctor. Verifying it was indeed the medical man's prints which were those found in several rooms of the house was crucial at this juncture.

Then MacCarrey, a stiff-faced Scot, chimed in to divulge that he would rather work with Turner (whom none of them particularly liked—one reason Phil had named this team) on the bank robbery, than to have to listen another minute to the chatterbox witness. After the chuckles subsided, MacCarrey filled his pipe and said, "I understood you thought there might be some wee connection between yesterday's heist and last night's shooting, sir."

"Possibly. But let's leave Turner and his men in charge of the robbery for now. We'll just concentrate on these two deaths."

The ballistics examiner Hastings spoke next. "I've got to go to the lab and run some more tests, but for now I can safely tell you that the rifle found by the body downstairs did kill that poor kid last night. It's a .303—an old one—likely kept around for hunting. But the cartridges are of recent manufacture. Easily traceable, I'd say. I suspect whoever fired the shot wore gloves. Parts of the Grimballs' fingerprints have been slightly smeared."

"Do you know how many rooms there are in this house, Inspector?" MacCarrey put in, straight-mouthed as he sucked on his pipe but with a twinkle above his ginger beard. "Twenty-three! And twenty of them look as though they'd nae been lived in for as many years. Och, it's an unco set-up we've got here. How do you think the old girl happened to fall down the stairs? And why did you want an autopsy?"

"It wasn't my suggestion, initially. It was made by Dr. Graham who was here with me first thing. But he's been taken ill and had to go home. He pretended he wasn't thinking straight when he blurted it out, but there's more to it than that. I'm not so sure her death was just a coincidental accident in the middle of the night. Besides, what was the gun doing there?"

"'Keep your rifle and yourself just so,'" quipped Woodbridge. "That's Keats."

"Nice try, Woody. Would-ya-believe: Kipling? What has Haley said? Was he here yet?"

"Haley breezed in and out right fast, sir." Hastings replied. "Said he couldn't wait to see you, but wanted to know what arrangements you wanted. He thought the body should be taken to the mortuary. Everything's been tagged and photographed. Haley agreed there were no indications of anything but accidental death. Her neck was broken, but whether before or after the fall, he can't yet say. He also suggested he might find alcohol, drugs, or even poison in her system."

"I doubt that, but we'll see." Philip, despite himself, was feeling more enticed by the complexities of the case with every new bit of information. "I've got to go find out what Dr. Graham is hiding, I think. But first, I'll fill you all in on what I've found out this morning."

When Philip finished his description of Elizabeth Grimball's odd reactions, of Oliver Brock's tendencies, and relayed the information Ted had told him in exchange for a squad car ride, Woodbridge was looking thoughtful.

"Do you suppose then, that there is some truth in the story the Henry woman seems to favor? That this teacher Elizabeth has gone off her head and turned homicidal? You know, there was a teacher in Georgia six years ago who killed off three of her students—"

"Woo-*dy*!" Phil raised a hand to stop his sergeant while the other men grinned at each other. They'd seen this double-act many times in weeks prior and rather enjoyed watching Woodbridge get corrected so frequently. "Woody, an acquaintance of mine was assigned that case. It was a nurse and she killed three of her elderly patients. And it was Virginia, not Georgia. *And* there's still some who believe she was of perfectly sound mind, practicing euthanasia."

Woody's long nose seemed to grow like Pinocchio's as he turned his profile away from Philip, shrugging. Not for nothing had the sergeant's early career in journalism been cut short by an irate editor, thought Phil, not for the first time. "Whatever. The point is, it's looking not too good for Teach at the moment. I mean, she couldn't have known the Brock kid would go around blabbing about having a date with her!"

"We don't know that's who or what he meant at all. Or even if he truly said it."

"Besides," Robb Costello interjected. "It's some far-fetched, isn't it? I mean, if every old schoolmarm solved her report-card hassles by putting a bullet into the mischief-maker, there wouldn't be much left of the younger generation, would there?"

"Right," Philip agreed, as he rose. "But the most ridiculous of all is to form assumptions before we have all the facts. I'm going to have it out with the Doc. If you're all finished here, get back to the city. Hastings, radio the mortuary and tell them we're done with the body. They know the way; they were just here last night. I want the rifle left here. It still needs to be positively I.D.ed. And Puro, leave your little ink-blot collection too, will you? MacCarrey, Sara Burns is upstairs. You can take her back as well. I'll make sure Miss Grimball has another watchdog."

"Well, that didn't give us many more plays to run with," Woodbridge said as he watched the others drive away. "You want me to go see this Dr. Graham with you?"

"Just let me think a minute, O.K., Woody? Lord! My mind is like a big old muffled tuba. All these booming ideas want out but they're trapped, you know? No, first I want to confirm whose rifle that is. We'll have to Clear-sak it and pass it around some of the village old timers to see if they recognize it. I wonder if Anderson's back from his brunch yet?"

He opened the door and walked into the living room, Woodbridge at his heels like a faithful retriever. The room, only moments ago jammed with active brain cells, now had no pulse at all, was virtually still. However, the massive furniture—solid walnut antiques mostly—gave it an oppressively crowded demeanor. It was musty from a lack of fresh air, yet smelled antiseptically clean at the same time.

"Cripes, I'd hate to live here," Woodbridge stated. "It doesn't have a feeling of life to it at all. In fact you can hardly call it a 'living' room, can you? Not a book or magazine, no old lady's knitting, no TV or radio—nothing. It's almost as though both aunt and niece not only slept in those other two hideous rooms on this floor, but spent all their spare time in them as well!"

Sounds of quiet footsteps descending cautiously down the stairs caused Philip to hurry to their foot. He had half expected to see Elizabeth's wan complexion but instead, the sheepish face of Chet Anderson appeared on the landing.

"You know, I feel like about all I'm good for is a bloody nursemaid," he complained. "I can't help thinking about poor Elizabeth up there all alone, wondering what on earth is going on, but I've climbed those stairs a dozen times today and she just sleeps on and on. I can't see that she's faking it in any way. Besides, she's not the type."

"Do you know her well?" Philip asked

"As well as anyone does, I suppose. But that's not saying much. She began teaching here at quite an early age. Twenty-one or two, I guess. She'd been so smart in university that she breezed straight through in a couple of years and came right back here. God knows why she didn't stay out when she had the chance!"

"What do you mean?"

"Oh, nothing really. I mean Victoria just doesn't hold a lot of promise for the future, does it? I should know 'cause I'm still stuck here too. But it must have been ten times worse for Elizabeth, living here with that old grouch all her life."

"You think she has generally had an unhappy life, then?" Philip asked, as out of the corner of his eye he saw Woodbridge pull out his notepad and pencil.

"Uh, I don't know—not really." Plainly, Chet regretted he had begun this line of conversing, and now mistrusted his own insinuations. "I've never really heard the aunt was abusive to her or anything. It's just, no one much likes—liked—old Esther too much. But I shouldn't have said anything. Still, Elizabeth's been through the wringer lately. Almost lost her job last year, and a young man she'd been seeing—another teacher at the school—died in a car accident in May."

"Jeez!" Woodbridge mumbled, dabbing the lead point of his pencil on to his tongue.

"Why did she almost lose her job?" Phil asked.

"Oh, there were just a lot of hog-wash rumors that she'd been staying around after school doing extra tutoring, helping kids with their homework. Unfortunately they were mostly teenage boys; that and the fact she was dating Percy Collins didn't sit too well with some of the parents on the board. You know what these small villages are like—gossip-mills, and not much else."

"Gossip and prejudice," said Zareb Woodbridge fiercely.

"But she was never fired?" Philip asked.

"Oh, I heard she eventually just got her knuckles rapped a bit. You see, Jake Brock's on the school board and he's always hated the Sandersons and the Grimballs. The way I understand it, his father used to work for Old Man Sanderson here at the house but he got laid off for some reason or another. Had four kids at home, and Jake's never forgotten it because his father turned to drink not long after that, then died of liver disease. Anyway, with a grudge like that, you don't want to step on the wrong toes. I guess Elizabeth inadvertently did. But other prominent people—like Dr. Graham or Genevieve Stroud—they like Elizabeth all right, respect her. They helped fight to keep her on."

"Why still live here, then, if it's caused her so much heartache?" Woodbridge asked.

Anderson shrugged. "Maybe she thought she owed her aunt something. After all, Esther did bring her up single-handedly and pay to educate her. But Elizabeth sure hasn't had much fun out of life."

"Why does she seem so unpopular?"

"I don't know if I'd say she was unpopular exactly. It's just she pretty much keeps to herself outside of teaching. In a tiny community like this, if you don't take an active part in a neighborhood's existence, you're looked on as rather strange I'm afraid."

"Or any other way you're a bit different," said Woodbridge and both men looked at him curiously. "I come from a small town west of Halifax. I know small towns."

"Well, you're right there. Some folks claimed she was just like her aunt. And her grandmother too, in her day. Hermit-like, stingy. She never did anything extra except for tutoring the kids. That only got her into trouble in the end."

"Thank you, Chet. You've clarified the matter of Miss Grimball considerably. I hope you don't mind if I ask you to carry on here. My Fredericton crew have gone, now and I did promise Mrs. Henry she wouldn't be left alone. You've heard the rumors she's put out already, I suppose—that Elizabeth's gone insane, killed the Brock boy and her aunt too?"

"Stupid woman," Anderson grumbled between his teeth.

"Yes, but *could* it have been that way do you think?"

A long pause ensued while Chet Anderson placed a toothpick in his mouth, plucking out his breakfast and his words with equal care. "From what I know of Elizabeth Grimball, she is not a violent sort at all. I've never even heard of her raising her voice to a student. Still, I guess any amount of brewing pressure under the surface can finally explode. I'm not saying she didn't, mind. Just that—well, anything is possible, I s'pose." He broke the toothpick in half, then plunged it and his hand into his jacket pocket, continuing with a stronger intensity than before. "Victoria's a bit like a soap opera on the T.V." He pronounced it with the emphasis on 'T', Phil noticed. "Look at the people who have grudges against Elizabeth already: Mort and Mary Henry are just ignorant, but Jake Brock is a naturally vindictive type. Even said he'd get me fired when I went to investigate the shooting of that damned cow a while back. I wouldn't believe a word any of them told me, that's for sure! I made damn certain Oliver Brock wouldn't get his hands on another gun for a long time. Huh, ironic, eh?" Anderson shook his head as if pondering the fateful mockery of the situation for the first time.

"Well, somebody definitely *did* have a gun. So, if you can manage to stay here a while longer, Chet, then Woody and I will get on…"

"Oh, wait. I haven't told you yet: while you were having your conference in the living room with your troupes, I brought my father and Roan Carson back here after my brunch. They were both old hunting pals of John Grimball. They positively I.D.ed that gun as his. Seems he always made two little nicks on his weapons, all in the same place. Oh, now—" Anderson held up his hands as if pre-empting their next words. "They didn't touch it, don't worry. And I took their official statements. Here."

"Terrific! That'll save us some legwork." Philip praised. "However, what we have to determine is how the hell that rifle got out of this house, where it went after Oliver's shooting, and why it appeared back here with Esther this morning. Woody, you'd better come with me for now. I'm off to see Dr. Graham, but there are several more things to which I'd like you to attend in the meantime. Chet, hold the fort here; we'll be back as soon as we can. Morgue fellows should be here soon to collect the body. God, it's nearly noon already! As soon as Miss Grimball seems awake and lucid, tell her I've a good many questions for her."

Pulling the door shut behind them, Phil repeated inaudibly, "A damn lot of questions." He clenched and unclenched his fingers.

"Talking to yourself again, sir?" asked Woodbridge. He wasn't surprised when no answer was forthcoming.

CHAPTER SIX

As Detectives Steele and Woodbridge marched briskly down the street, the sun winked through the tall russet-turning oaks on either side, dappling the sidewalk beneath their feet. Two women Phil didn't know were leaning over a well worn picket fence gossiping, but they stopped abruptly and both turned, staring rudely as the men approached. One woman's mouth even hung open a little, loosely hinged at her jaw.

"Ladies," Phil said, nodding at them with a courtesy he didn't feel. Neither woman budged but continued to gawk, bug-eyed.

After they'd moved out of earshot, Phil turned to his sergeant. "Do I have some unmentionable hanging out my nostril or something?"

"You have an unmentionable walking beside you," Woody retorted.

His supervisor shook his head. "I'm sorry, Zareb," Philip said, intentionally calling his sergeant by his first name. "How you can stand it, and so patiently, is beyond me."

Woody shrugged. "It was worse when I was a reporter. The venom they used to spray at me, sometimes literally."

"And I suppose people you were interviewing for facts would just clam up?"

"Just like now," Woody agreed. "It's why I quit."

"Oh, is that why?" Phil smiled. "I thought it was because you couldn't get a quote right."

"'I refuse to accept the view that mankind is so tragically bound to the starless midnight of racism'…I don't get *that* quote wrong," declared Woodbridge staunchly.

"No, and that spring day three years ago is one which still makes me want to vomit."

"Mr. King *was* the king. No question."

There was a pause while they both contemplated the great man and his fate. Then Phil spoke up again.

"You know, Atlantic Canada can be especially hard for anyone new or 'different'. The older and smaller a place is, the harder it is for them to accept change, it seems. Even Caucasians who have been here for decades are 'come-from-away'-ers."

"Yup. Despite a whole passel of us black folk in Halifax, they still call us 'darkies'. And that's when they're being pleasant!" Woody kicked a large pebble into a hedgerow, then shoved his hands into his pockets.

"Santana told me once that his family had been here for *centuries*—as far back as the 1700s when the sugar and cod trading was going on. Yet, to this day people call him a 'Spic' and 'Wetback', as if he'd just arrived here."

"My poor Mama's name was Ginger. Rearrange *that* anagram and imagine what she was constantly called!"

Although somewhat reluctant now to dispatch his sergeant to the questioning of yet more village teens whose general penchant for keeping mum would only be heightened by their blatant studying of his ebony face, Phil sent Woodbridge on his way with a few addresses and names, then continued to the doctor's house on his own. As he opened the intricately-wrought iron pedestrian gate, he was amused when confronted by a spouse whose rubber gardening apron might as well have been a suit of armor and the spade she brandished, a piercing lance. Marcia Graham rose to a militant stance, determined that no one—and that included policemen of any rank—would disturb her slumbering husband.

She admitted him into the house, chatting lightly as she scraped mud from her boots, told their Boston terrier to go lie in his bed, and settled Phil on a bench in the harvest gold kitchen with an orange mug of coffee in front of him. But her ultimatum was clear: under no circumstances would he be questioning Wilfred that day.

"He's running a temperature of 101," she said. "He's been vomiting and admits to feeling faint, which is one of the few things he *never* complains about, so I know he's truly ill. I'm sorry, Philip. But I absolutely can't disturb him again. Someone was already here fingerprinting him, for God's sake! However, if there's any way *I* might be able to help…"

"Well, yes. Perhaps you could enlighten me a bit. Do you know what time Elizabeth Grimball left here last night?"

"Elizabeth? About 9:30, I think."

"And can you tell me why she came to see Wilf at such a time?"

"Well, I can only tell you what I know, of course. And you mightn't get much more of Wilf, anyhow. He's a stickler regarding doctor/patient confidentiality, and Elizabeth has long been a favorite of his. I know this whole thing has him incredibly upset." She paused, sucking an end of her wispy hair as if to debate further disclosure.

"Please go on," urged Philip, knowing the bribe of a squad car ride would not help in this instance.

"I suppose I should know Elizabeth well. This is such a connected village, and she taught both of our boys. But, until last night, she was really only someone I'd exchanged a few polite words with in parent/teacher interviews, or if we passed on the street. Last night, though, a lot came out. I mean, a lot *I* didn't know, anyway. She came here very upset, almost in tears from lack of sleep and worry. I comforted her for a while because Wilf was on the phone in his study. I think he was talking to your people in Fredericton. A Turner someone-or-other had called, so he was answering questions about the extent of Ouellette's injuries during the bank robbery."

Philip smiled. Even though he'd not been on duty last night, it was typical of Turner to rush to conclusions. He looked Marcia straight in the eye as he asked, "When you first saw Elizabeth, was she by any chance carrying anything? Perhaps a long parcel?"

"No. She had nothing in her hands when she arrived and when she left, she carried only a small sample package of sedatives which Wilf keeps around for just such emergencies."

"Fine. Please continue. She was distraught, would you say?"

"Very. I–I don't know how much you know about Beth's history..."

"Practically nothing at all."

"Well, I should start with some of that, just so you understand her mentality."

"That would be ideal, as I've yet to speak with her. Except for a brief meeting yesterday." *When the morning was yet young and full of hope.*

"Yes, Wilf mentioned she was still fairly doped-up, poor lamb. Well, Elizabeth's father was Esther's only brother. The Grimball side had little money, but their Sanderson grandfather, Sam, paid for Jack to go away to the university—but not Esther. I suppose that's part of what made her bitter all her life. Jack met Elizabeth's mother, Camilla, at school. When they eloped, both sides of the family cut Jack off completely. However, six years and a daughter later, Jack and Camilla were killed in a car crash. So her grandmother, Patricia Sanderson Grimball, and her husband John Grimball, living there at the house with Esther, took poor Elizabeth in. Patty died shortly after that, then John only two years later when Elizabeth was about nine. Her Aunt Esther took over then, and for all these years it's just been the two of them there. You never met Elizabeth when you were here as a kid?"

"I don't think so, no. I don't suppose the McKinley boys and I much cared about a little girl when we were turning the neighborhood upside down in our teens! Still, I do remember now hearing something about that accident. It must have happened during one of my summers here, because it created quite a stir around the post office. Do go on with the story."

"Well, I never had much to say to Esther Grimball and although she was a patient of Wilf's, she was one of the few he heartily disliked. She was all the things spinsters are often claimed to be, but seldom really are: acid-tongued, uncharitable and narrow-minded. Now, knowing what I've learned since, I marvel that I never really considered the drab existence Elizabeth must have had. She was always just too quiet to encourage interferences from other people, I guess." There was some more sucking on the split ends. "I suppose I figured maybe the influential but stingy Sanderson blood had just been passed on to yet another generation. You see, Victoria has never much liked that founding family since old Sam Sanderson died. He'd promised to leave a good part of his estate to the town—the church and school board, especially. But Patty, Esther's mother, inherited everything and never made a gesture toward any of the organizations her father had patronized. Esther just followed along in her mother's footsteps, except she became even more bitter and tight-fisted as the years wore on. She never married and has done her utmost to keep Elizabeth from even dating, although last year she went out with a teacher, Percy Collins, who was killed when he lost control of his car, sideswiping to avoid some cows out on the River Road."

Philip nodded. "Yes, and I've heard she nearly lost her job by spending too much time at the school helping students?"

"Well, if you were Elizabeth, would *you* want to hurry home? And of course the school board has never forgiven the Sanderson/Grimball families for not helping out financially. Especially the Brocks, who have always had something of a vendetta against them. I suppose it wasn't particularly smart of lovely Bethie to shut herself up in classrooms after hours with boys just entering puberty and to be seen walking about the school grounds with Percy, but really she was only trying to be helpful to some struggling students, and what other chance could she get for a social life?"

"What I don't understand is why she allowed her aunt to dictate to her? Why not just leave?"

"Ah, that brings us to what was just revealed to me last night. This is what's been troubling Wilf so much. I know I should tell you, but I'm afraid my husband would be angry if he—"

"Marcia, if you or he suspects poor Elizabeth Grimball of killing her aunt and the Brock boy, it's what everyone else in the village is thinking, myself included, I'm afraid. What you tell me may make things clearer but it won't, I assure you, make you responsible for any future developments."

Marcia Graham stared at him with a twinge of violence sparking her sea-green eyes. "Good Lord, Phil! You don't suspect Bethie, *surely* not! Why, that's the most ridiculous thing I've ever heard; Wilf would be beside himself if he knew this. Oliver Brock was one of the children she tried to help the most. That was one reason his father was so against her. He didn't think it was proper, and felt his kid was 'smart enough'. And as for killing her aunt— well, *really*. It's preposterous!"

"All right, Marcia. Take a deep breath. I apologize for upsetting you, but you'd better tell me everything you know if you want to convince me otherwise."

Marcia's pause as she glared at him chilled the air by several degrees. "Elizabeth got here at about quarter to nine last night. I know, because I was just about to tune the radio in to 'As It Happens'. As I already told you, she was here for at least three-quarters of an hour, crying most of the time. When Wilf finally got off the phone in his office, he came and ushered her in. He started to close the door, but Elizabeth asked for me as well since I'd been comforting her for quite a while. Elizabeth has always been slender, but lately she looks emaciated; dark circles under her eyes, twitchy hands, pulse erratic. Wilf had just examined her a few weeks ago but he was shocked by her appearance now, as was

I. She complained of insomnia. Wilf assured her he had some sedatives which would help her to sleep, but that first he wanted to get to the bottom of her troubles."

The doctor's wife took another deep breath, a sip of coffee, and went on. "In the beginning, she was as reticent as she's always been, but when my husband told her she really needed to get away for a few months' rest despite summer just being over, she broke down and said she couldn't possibly. Said she couldn't financially afford to stop teaching even to take a sick leave, and that she couldn't leave her aunt. Wilf and I assumed the first reason was just standard Sanderson miserliness, but he pressed her hard about leaving both the Victoria school and Esther, saying surely there was no good reason why she couldn't go off on a cruise, or relax at a spa, or some such. If it was under doctor's orders? She must have seen the disbelief in our eyes, because she told us how much money she spent per month, and how much was saved. She said she has always given seventy-five percent of her earnings to her aunt, supposedly for groceries, to pay bills, to keep house, things like that. Apparently she's been under the impression all the Sanderson fortune had been lost, except for the house and grounds. Her grandfather John Grimball had, according to Elizabeth, managed to dwindle it into nonexistence. She didn't know how exactly, because Esther was always so painfully venomous when the subject was broached. But Elizabeth had dearly loved her grandfather and she was sure it was nothing but an error in judgment on his part."

Philip, remembering the rocking chair apparition which Elizabeth had thought she'd seen last night, wondered if subconsciously she didn't blame him for more than she would admit.

Marcia continued. "Elizabeth said they lived only on her small salary and had shut most of the house off to keep the bills to a minimum. She told us candidly that the only reason she had returned to Victoria after university was because of a sense of duty to her aunt who had paid for what education her own scholarships had not. It had always just been understood that as soon as Elizabeth was able to return the favor, their roles would be reversed."

"But couldn't they have sold the house, moved somewhere smaller, cheaper?"

"Elizabeth suggested it many times, apparently. Esther would not hear of it. So one day a few years ago Elizabeth said she would move out. She'd been offered a good teaching position at a city school in Moncton. She told Esther she would continue to send her money of course, but that she could no longer bear to live under the same roof. 'And so why didn't you, then?' Wilf asked her. She said 'Well, that was about the time you told her about her heart.' 'What about her heart?' Wilf demanded. Elizabeth just looked at him for a minute. Then she whispered, 'You—you said she had a heart condition, she needed care. You said she–she might die at any time and that if I left, she'd have to go to a nursing home. Well of course I couldn't do that to her. So I turned down the Moncton job right away.' Wilf leaped up from his desk chair and practically shouted: 'I've never told that woman any such thing! There's nothing wrong with her heart at all; I'm not sure she even has one!' He stopped for a minute, looked a little sideways at me, then added, 'and legally, I really shouldn't be telling you this at all, but your aunt is far from broke. I witnessed a new codicil to her will only a month or so ago. I didn't see much of it—she kept me busy signing some copies—but what I quickly saw is enough to know your grandfather most certainly did not lose the family fortune. For God's sakes, Beth, you do *not* have to stay around to look after Esther Grimball! Count on it!' Then he gave Elizabeth the sleeping pills, told her to go home, to take one with warm milk, and then to get the hell out as soon as she could and not waste any more time."

Philip sat immobile, intent on the keenly empathetic face before him. As the pause to her concluding words lengthened,

Marcia stirred restlessly. Philip realized that only then did she absorb the fact that, rather than helping Elizabeth's cause, she had just established one or more motives.

He spoke only to reiterate, "And that was at 9:30. You're sure?"

"Maybe a bit after."

"How long do you think it would take her to walk home from here? Less than five minutes, wouldn't you say? Yet it was 10:30 when she arrived, according to Mary Henry who was there." Philip remembered Mary spitting: *'Not one word would she say, not even when we tried to tell her about the shot.'* He could well imagine the anger and grief Elizabeth must have felt, after all those years pinching and scraping then being falsely manipulated into staying. No wonder indeed she had gone up to the second floor to sleep! It wouldn't have surprised him to learn that she'd also taken more than one sleeping pill.

The doctor's wife would not resort to speculation. "I don't know where she went after she left here. But I'm sure she wasn't down in the gully shooting one of her students! She had a good deal more important things to worry about."

"Perhaps. Then again, she may have been filled with hatred for everyone. All I know are facts—that rifle came from her home. The boy bragged of having 'a date with Miss Grimball'. Her aunt fell down cellar steps in the middle of the night."

"Oh really, Philip! I knew that Oliver Brock! He's the same age as Carter, our youngest boy. Carter's living with his cousins in Fredericton to go to high school now because he's in Grade Ten, where Oliver should be. Except Oliver's failed Grade Six and Grade Eight both. Carter always said Oliver had had a crush on Elizabeth for a long time. That was part of the reason for Jake Brock wanting her out of the school, no doubt. Jake wouldn't want his son to show sentimental tendencies! That family is the antithesis of 'make love, not war'."

"But Marcia, their kid is dead. *Some*body shot him. And unless someone has an alibi for Elizabeth Grimball between 9:30 and 10:30 last night, things are not looking good for her. Maybe she was out walking in the gully, perhaps Oliver met up with her, tried to persuade her to do something for him, maybe even kiss him? Maybe she took him back toward her house, got the rifle and—"

"No! No way, Phil! It's absurd. Listen, does anyone know when that gun was last seen? How do you know it wasn't taken weeks—even months—ago? Oliver's one passion was hunting and weapons. He's had his own gun forcibly removed this summer. If he ever had a chance to get hold of another, he wouldn't hesitate a moment."

"Yes. I had thought of that, but... Marcia you seem to feel I'm deliberately trying to implicate Elizabeth Grimball. I'm not. Actually, I really feel badly for her situation. I'm sure she's had a helluva life. Still, I must get at the truth. And justice must prevail. You know that." There went his father's doctrine pecking away in his head again, Phil thought.

To avoid sounding too condescending, he followed hurriedly with, "Perhaps she did have nothing to do with young Brock's death—maybe her aunt's *was* an accident. Though you can hardly say there was no motive there! But there is one thing maybe you can tell me: why would Wilf have assumed an autopsy was necessary on Esther if he didn't suspect foul play?"

"Heaven only knows. You've got to understand. Wilf hasn't been well for days. I guess the flu bug's been going around and he's treated one too many cases of it. Besides, he feels personally responsible for the things he told Beth last night. Maybe he did go too far; mentioning she had no heart condition was shock enough, but for Elizabeth also to find out that he'd recently seen Esther's will and that she was still extraordinarily rich, when all this time poor Bethie has had to use old Sears catalogues for toilet paper…"

• • •

Softly, Philip entered Polly Jane's house. She was still at work in the post office, ridiculously busy for a Saturday. He was fairly sure she was mostly giving and receiving information on the village's most recent excitements, and he had no desire to discuss them with anyone at that moment. He knew from experience that his godmother would eventually tell him anything he should know, first tossing aside whatever she considered inconsequential hyperbole. The woman could sort fact from fiction as efficiently as she sorted the mail from the flyers. Tip-toeing, he made his way straight to his own room and sank into a chair in front of the dormered window overlooking the tall English garden in the backyard. He closed the glass, shutting out the sounds of the now-busy street which carried even to the rear of the cottage. With both door and window closed, he was offered the silence, the solitude, his mind craved.

From his inner pocket he withdrew the workbook he had surreptitiously placed there earlier in the morning—the one with which that hippie reporter had been so intrigued. It hardly seemed a vital piece of evidence at first impression; a typical brown soft-covered notebook with the words 'Social Studies—Miss Grimball's Copy' printed in careful black felt-tipped marker on the front, it was now slightly dented and curled from having remained tubular for several hours. However, as Philip carefully leafed through the pages of reminder lists, scribbles and a few sketches of still lifes, he found near the middle a variety of dates and entries resembling a diary.

The room became hushed. Only the quick, light breaths he drew and the faint rustling of the paper broke the absolute serenity. Mesmerized with intrigue, it was many minutes before the fifty-some pages which purported to be school notes were transcribed into the humility of a life's-worth of emotions. Also shoved loosely between these diary sections were several stiffer pieces of watercolor paper with artistically interpreted bowls of fruit, flowers, and everyday household objects.

Elizabeth Grimball, it seemed, was a woman no one had yet described to him and since he still had not had the chance to interview her, this was the next best thing. Perhaps even better, as it cut quickly through the formalities to her innermost thoughts. This shy teacher who unobtrusively stayed away from neighbors and friends was actually a creature of passion and flame—and painful torment. Samples of her writing described her growing attraction for Percy Collins: *"there has never been a kinder man besides Grandpa, in all the world...Percy meets my eyes across the hall and I feel a sharp gasp rise to my throat. His soul is deeper, his understanding more empathetic than ever I could imagine...Today I told Percy about Aunt Esther's heart condition, and he held my hand tightly, saying he hoped he could make it more bearable for me to remain in Victoria."*

Then, upon his death, her writing grew rambling, negligent, with tear stains smearing much of the inky scrawls: *"How can this have happened to such a fine person? And why has God done this to me again? Another car crash taking the third real love from my life..."*

There were also many words of anger toward her aunt: *"I can't bear it—she's done it again! I tried to order a new yellow suit from the catalogue today, but she caught me and threw out the order form. She said I didn't need new clothes and if I did, navy blues and browns were the only respectable colors for a spinster schoolteacher...How dare she! Then, when I got angry and threatened to move out again, she clutched her heart, begged me not to. Saying she must lie down. I helped her to her room and then went over to Genevieve's for tea and talk..."*

This was the first indication that Phil's 'suspect' had had any close friends other than her brief relationship with Collins. He read on, not at all embarrassed to feast upon a stranger's private words. Her writing skills were so simplistic, her emotions so honest, so volatile, and her summing up of others' characteristics so shrewdly amusing, (also, so sardonically like his own!) that he in fact could no longer think of her as a stranger. "*Genevieve has an uncanny mastery of the human mind,*" she wrote. "*She thinks Aunt Esther is jealous because Grandpa loved me more than her, and because I got an education and she didn't...She also said it's 'because of the virginity thing'. But I'm not sure I follow...*"

In another section she jotted a note to herself: "*Reminder: never get up earlier than necessary. Marblehead Mary and Aunt Esther are two forces not to be reckoned with on an empty stomach! Frumpy and Grumpy were out weeding the garden at six a.m....*"

At night when the world slept, this poor creature had come alive, Philip reflected. Not only had she taken herself to wonderful places she'd never been and met interesting people she'd never meet, but she made herself beautiful, attractive, funny—all in her imaginary 'social studies'. Philip rose, stretched and walked about the room, knowing he should grab some food and head back to question Elizabeth in person, but somehow believing everything he needed to know lay right there between those rumpled brown covers.

He soft-treaded to the kitchen to root about in the cupboards for some nibblies, but Polly Jane heard him from the front room despite his best efforts.

"Phil? Are you managing? I made you some sandwiches. They're in the fridge."

"Oh, perfect, P.J.! Thank you! I'm doing some paperwork in my room, so I'll just hustle back with those. Mmm. Egg salad, you know I love it!"

As he was obviously trying to avoid questions, she only said with her usual tact, "Are you all right? Do you need some oatmeal cookies to go with those?"

He gave her a quick squeeze around the waist. "When have I ever turned down one of your home-baked creations?"

She went to the cookie jar above the old Hoosier, took off the whimsical lid with a swirling rooster's tail on its handle, and offered him the wide opening. He grabbed three raisin-dotted biscuits, added them to his sandwich plate, said, "You're a peach, God-Mum. I'll see you tonight—for supper, I hope!" He moved off swiftly, but could feel her eyes watching him, partly curious, partly concerned.

Philip resettled himself in his chair and read more rapidly. A sudden feeling of urgency possessed him as the context of the diary began to change. There was gradually less humor, less sarcasm, greater despair. As he took a bite of his sandwich, he turned a page to an entry with "2 a.m. Friday" signed off at the bottom of it. She must have stayed up most of Thursday night writing, judging by the length of the entry:

"I am such a fool! An idiotic weakling! I despise myself. Oh God—if there is a God—please help me! I've killed the only thing I had. Killed it deliberately—by choice—because I was afraid. I thought this fantasy world would come true someday but now it never will. Why have I struggled against it? It didn't mean I was crazy…Only that much closer to truth and sanity. And yet I have fought it off. My painting used to help the transitions between the real world and the fantasy…Now I can no longer bear to pick up the brushes, to look at the even muted colors. My world is black and white—mostly black. Yes, today I threw my watercolors away. I will never seek creativity again—besides, who the hell cares about fruit and flowers in crystal and pottery? Still Lifes! If I can't have the real thing with the full spectrum of color and movement, then I will never paint again. Nor do I feel I can ever write again. I am so sick. I just need to sleep. Forever would be

nice. I just wish—Oh, what's the point? Wishes are for children and falling stars, not old maids shut up in prisons with their aging aunties..."

The writing ended abruptly. There was nothing written the previous night, Friday. Poor Elizabeth Grimball. He loved the name 'Beth', which her most sympathetic neighbors seemed to call her. 'Elizabeth' had so many variations: 'Liz, Eliza, Lisa, Betty, Ellie, Beth'... But the woman behind the name seemed unable to progress beyond 'Elizabeth'. What did she call herself, he wondered. He remembered his mother playing 'Variations on a Theme of Paganini' on her violin. What variations on a theme of 'Elizabeth' were there? Could she really be a murderer? And 'Grimball', what a horrid-sounding surname. Her name haunted him. Her face haunted him. He thought he understood her now and also understood Wilf Graham's over-protective attitude toward her. Here she was: lonely, unloved and fighting a grim battle against circumstances which revolted every fine thought and desire she might have. Did he not feel the same? Had he not tried his best to get out of what he considered a bad situation in his life only to have it thrown back in his face? Was he not angered by the unjust cruelty of human nature; was he not driven to almost-violent tendencies by the ridiculous and the banal?

He knew this woman, this Elizabeth Grimball. Knew her to be an intellectual and clever woman, knew her to be loyal, dedicated and true.

And yet knew her to be capable, he was now fairly certain, of murder.

CHAPTER SEVEN

Sometimes it is something catastrophic, dramatic, sensational—a world war, an epidemic, a global depression—which will completely alter the ordinary affairs of ordinary people. Other times, it is something so infinitesimal that it seems absurd that such a small activity could culminate in disaster.

It was 2:00 p.m. when Chet Anderson ran out of cigarettes. He had even puffed the last butts from his car ashtray and had then graduated to chewing up the remains of toothpicks left in his pockets. He was alone in the living room of the Sanderson house, waiting for something to happen—*any*thing! After the last twenty-four hours of non-stop activity, he was now bored silly. He was the recognized constabulary of this village. Yet, what was he doing? Baby-sitting an invalid and a dotty old gossip. He could hear Mary now, bustling about in the kitchen, washing up Elizabeth's breakfast tray (which she had until now neglected to do lest she missed any of the activity involved in the removal of the body of Esther Grimball). Aside from the rattle of dishes, there was no other sound in the closed-off house. Upstairs, lying on her back with pale lips slightly parted and barely-audible sighs escaping them, Elizabeth Grimball maintained her semi-comatose state of exhaustion.

Although it was such a warm fall day, the house was cool and damp. Restlessly, Chet strolled from empty room to room, curiously turning up the corners of the dust sheets and plastic from various pieces of furniture to see what lay beneath. The urge for nicotine was growing increasingly more urgent. Finally in desperation, he sought Mary Henry, asked her if she thought Mort would mind if he went next door and borrowed a few smokes. He was informed, with great emphasis, that 'Mr. Henry don't smoke', that 'nobody would never find tobacco' in *their* house. Chet didn't feel like arguing with her. Of course Mort *did* smoke but apparently never anywhere where his wife might catch him! Well, very soon now he expected someone to come along to relieve him. Then he would head off down to the store.

The afternoon dragged on. Mary was almost as restless as Chet. She had been promised an exciting day but for the last two hours there hadn't been a soul around. At 4:30 she finally announced plaintively, "Guess I might as well start supper. It'll be gettin' dark afore long and I'll have to go home and start something up for Mort to eat too. Or I'll make something extra up here and then tell Morty to come over. That way, at least I can make something substerancial. 'Cause that little bird upstairs sure don't care to do more'n pick at *her* vittles! You care if we eat early?"

Chet did not care; there was only one thing which he now wanted in his mouth. He stood at the window, gazing gloomily out at the darkening sky. Looked like maybe a storm was on its way. The lights were on in Brock's store. Sam Wiley must be behind the counter. One thing was sure—Jake and Rosie wouldn't be around. Hmm… A fellow could get waited on quickly today. Sam didn't take to idle gossip and unnecessary defamation like his employer did, so he could whip down there, grab a pack of smokes and be back in under five minutes—before Mary would even know he'd been gone. First though, just another quick check on Elizabeth.

She was now lying on her side, an arm flung over her face covering her eyes. Her breathing was quieter than before, but deep and regular. Never in his life had Chet seen anyone sleep so much!

She must not have slept for at least a week to need this much time to catch up. He'd just scoot now while the going was good.

The five minutes had stretched to nearly fifteen by the time Chet Anderson returned. Jake had indeed not been in the store to hold him up, but damn near everybody else in Victoria seemed to be. Oh, the impertinent questions!

He quietly opened the front door, panting from the haste of sucking back a cigarette while hurrying along the sidewalk. Inspector Steele would be pissed if he'd returned to find him gone. But as he entered the Sanderson house, all was as before. Dead quiet. Still.

The kitchen was fully lit now, and something was baking in the oven. But Mary wasn't there. Probably slipped over next door to tell her husband supper was nearly ready. Once more, for at least the fortieth time today, he mounted the stairs. Opening the door of the now near-dark bedroom, he could discern the slight form huddled in bed, on her back again. Her breathing sounded more rapid. Maybe she was finally about to wake up? It didn't seem natural for her to go on like this and besides, a lot of people had a lot of questions for her. She couldn't just keep avoiding them.

Downstairs, silence still prevailed. Chet switched on the living room light. He lit another cigarette, then went to the kitchen to empty the chipped saucer he'd been using all day as an ashtray. Mary was still absent. He glanced about for the garbage container—there wasn't one under the sink—and for the first time he noticed the door leading to the cellar was not quite closed as he'd last seen it. He'd just put another log into the furnace a half-hour ago; he knew he'd shut it tightly. Was Mary down there snooping around again, blasted woman? Disturbing evidence, he'd wager. She certainly didn't need to be down there stoking the fire yet. Oh hell, maybe she was only looking for a jar of beet pickles or some such in the cold pantry. He opened the door wide and yanked the string which lit the bulb at the top of the stairs. He listened.

"Mrs. Henry? Mary? You down there?"

There was no sound. He started down the stairs but on the third, he stopped. He could see part of the cold cement floor below. As much as he needed to see. More—much more—than he wanted to see…

He saw the body of Mary Henry.

PART TWO

"A maiden never bold;
Of spirit so still and quiet
That her motion blush'd at herself"
–Shakespeare, *"Othello"*

CHAPTER EIGHT

How strange to waken so effortlessly, to travel from deep slumber to full consciousness and to feel so well, so alert—so *whole*. Slowly, she rolled over, opened her eyes.

The chamber was filled with lucid morning light. It fell on the streaked bare walls, the narrow bunk on which she lay. What an interesting painting those long shadows would make, she thought. But no, she didn't do that anymore. At least not without life and movement and color. She had promised herself that. An elbow, propped on the feather pillow—(yes, *feather*!)—supported her head as she looked about. Her hair, which was straight, thick and a deep rich brown, no longer required pinning up or braiding. She could leave it loosely winding its way down her back if she felt like it. A chair was drawn close to the bed. Over its back was draped a navy blue dressing gown under which waited a pair of sensible brown slippers. Soon she would find some pastel colors in shiny satins with which to exchange those. Surely the Sears catalogue had something? And on the seat sat a brand-new, velvet-lined box with a matching yellow comb, brush and a small acrylic hand mirror.

The thin woman sat up, shivering slightly in the cool autumn damp as she reached for the robe. Comfortably clad, she grabbed for her new—and first ever!—cosmetic bag, then lifted the tiny mirror and began an intense study of the face it reflected. Two pale cheek bones sticking out too prominently, she thought. But still a spark of light in her eyes which she'd never noticed before. When she laid it down again, she picked up the brush and began methodically stroking her heavy hair.

Suddenly an idea came to her with a surge of excitement. Today she would cut it! That is, if they would let her have scissors. They probably would, as long as a guard remained in the room. They had denied her nothing yet, after all, though she did notice the mirror was obviously made for a child. Some sort of reflective plastic? Yes, Mrs. Quigley was especially kind for such a robustly uniformed sentinel; she might even offer to help her with a new coif. She wouldn't cut it off short, just about shoulder length, perhaps and would add some bangs over her forehead to cover up some of the wide, wan-looking temples. It would look so much better, would literally lighten a weight from her back! And wouldn't it look smart with the new yellow pantsuit which someone had dropped off for her yesterday? It must have been Genevieve—or perhaps Marcia Graham?

Ahh, at long last she had a room of her own. Even her few short years in university had been spent in a crowded residence with other girls who, although older than she, had been far less mature. But now—privacy at long last, with a key for the door, even! The fact that the room was locked from the outside only, troubled her very little.

Yesterday morning at this time she had been almost nauseated with fear. What if Dr. Haldrick thought she was not sane? But her worries were unjustified as he hadn't seemed to think this at all. Everything he'd said had been so interesting! At first she had mistrusted that sympathetic curiosity, but Inspector Steele later assured her she had not been deceived. Haldrick was a well-respected and understanding psychiatrist, he claimed. Apparently, they'd often worked together in other areas of Canada.

Philip Steele. Quite an enigma, thought Elizabeth. An attractive, freckled, open-faced one, no doubt. But a mystery all the same. How a jailer could be so unexpectedly thoughtful…Really, it was almost as if he knew her inner desires. It was he who had insisted on the feather pillow, and the new cosmetics case. He had told her she must look her best for court appearances or when being interviewed by psychiatrists and teams of solicitors, or for photos for journalists as she went in and out of the courthouse. No, whatever happened to her, she would never blame Philip Steele.

Elizabeth curled up on the tiny bunk, thinking it would be delicious to just fall back to sleep. But she mustn't. She had been sleeping far too much; that had been what started all this trouble in the first place. Was she being held on suspicion of just the two murders? Or three? She couldn't seem to take it all in yet… And was she being held on 'suspicion' or was she actually *charged* with murder? Inspector Steele had read her her rights; she remembered that. But what did that mean, for goodness sakes?

She had been here for three days. Was that right? On Friday evening, she remembered seeing Dr. and Mrs. Graham at their house. If only she had consulted the Doc fully before! Why had she waited so long? Why had she never wondered about those visits Aunt Esther often made to Beaufort Bromley, her lawyer? She was such an idiot not to have realized that had they been as impoverished as her aunt claimed, there would be no need for regular visits to a legal firm, nor money to pay them for their services. All Elizabeth had ever cared about was that she had the house to herself for a few hours to paint or write in her journal.

How was it Esther had kept money which neither Grandfather nor anyone else had been allowed to touch? Was it Sanderson money and not to be shared, even in marriage? How *could* that beastly woman have been such a stingy miser all these years? *And how dare she lie about her health just to trap me?* Elizabeth thought, now experiencing a rise in temperature as these emotions swelled.

She was saved from getting overly riled, however. Mrs. Quigley came to the door of her cell. "Someone to see you, Miss," she said, courteous as ever, as though she were a household butler. "You decent? It's that nice Inspector Steele again." The motherly guard flashed a brief glimpse of crooked yellow teeth, then waved and disappeared. Moments later, Philip arrived, key in hand.

"This is the strangest prison I've ever been in." He laughed to put them both at ease. "Do all villages have these silly little cells with a guard who makes tea every few hours?" Phil was about to compare the similarities to the set on Andy Griffith when it dawned on him that Elizabeth had likely never watched a television show. "Because let me tell you, you wouldn't get this type of treatment in the city, even a small one like Fredericton." Which was why, although he didn't say it, he'd pulled a good many strings and hop-scotched over a great deal of red tape to keep her here in Victoria.

"I bet they wouldn't let me keep my own clothes in the city, either. Or let me sleep in pink pajamas with violets on them!"

Phil had noticed some of the pink peeking out from the neckline of her dressing gown, but didn't mention that he thought it reflected a lovely rosy glow on to her cheeks. *Stop it*, he admonished himself. "We have to go over some basics again," he said instead. "I know you've told me some of these things already and I'm sure you repeated a good deal of them to Dr. Haldrick, but we're back to square one. No one else had motive or opportunity for all three murders and only your fingerprints and your aunt's were on that gun."

Motioning for Phil to sit in the chair, Elizabeth nodded, folded her legs underneath her on the bunk, and leaned back against the wall. "My aunt used to take the gun out of the cellar every now and again to clean and polish it. She always said it would be worth some money if we needed to sell some valuables. Naturally, I believed her. I didn't like handling it but a few times she asked me to hang it back up so she didn't have to go in the basement again. She claimed the stairs were hard on her heart."

"Why would she keep it loaded?"

"She didn't."

Philip raised his eyebrows slightly as he took out his pad and pen then scribbled a note. "Who else knew the gun was there?"

"No one, that I'm aware of."

"Who else was ever in your basement?"

"Oh. Well, that's different—I see what you mean. Aunt Esther and Mary often went down through the cellar stairs from outside when they were gardening in the mornings. Our old garden shed collapsed years ago, so most of the tools were kept down there, and the outside steps lead right up to the back yard."

"Any other people?"

"Well, in the summers we used to have hired help to do the lawn and hedges and to paint the back fence and arbor."

"Who were they?"

"Oh, let's see. Once Jamie Crenshaw came, and Kurt Powell, and Cindy March did some trimming and—oh!"

"What?"

"Um. Oliver Brock cut the lawn a few times this past summer for us, when Kurt was on holiday at his cottage."

Philip, who had been scribbling names, now looked up and paused. Elizabeth glanced his way, smiling shyly.

"I thought you were supposed to be questioning me about *my* activities—not trying to find out if someone else might have done it."

"You're right. Shame on me. But one way or the other, I'll get my answers and it's all part of the same job. By the way, P. J. sent you this pumpkin bread, fresh from her garden."

"Oh! Tell her thank you! Has she started her harvest moon dance yet?"

"Good Lord! How do you know about that? She's always told me that was a secret only I knew."

Elizabeth blushed. "Well, I like to go for a walk before bed to clear my head. I'm afraid when the moon is full, I've often taken a peek into her yard. Creepy, I know, but her garden is so lovely.

So full and lush! Really colorful, isn't it? And P.J.'s so graceful, even at her age. I've always been impressed. I didn't know it was a secret—lots of people know, I think. I mentioned it once to Genevieve and she agreed with me, about P.J. being graceful, I mean. Also, Mary Henry was bragging once about how Mrs. Whistler had been the Harvest Hunt Ball Queen two years running. During the war, wasn't it? And how she still, to this day, 'practiced her turns'. I get envious every time I watch her, because of her–her utter joy and freedom of movement. Of self-expression."

Philip tried to avoid the pain in her eyes, saying lightly, "Yes, P.J.'s always done exactly what she wanted in this lifetime and tends to not care what anyone else thinks or says about her."

"I'd love to be like that!"

"Tell me again about Friday night. From the time you left the Grahams."

"Well, I was too upset and—um, stunned, I guess—by Doc's revelations, to go right home. Like I said, I often walk before bed, normally. So I–I walked around the village for a while thinking maybe I'd ask Genevieve if I could spend the night at her place. She's really been my only friend through these last years. But I guess she'd already left for her business trip to Halifax. You say she's not expected back for a few more days yet?"

"Not until Thursday, they thought at the brokers."

"Well, there were no lights on at her place, so I just kept walking until I was exhausted and then I headed home. But as I passed the fairgrounds, I heard a shot. I only *remembered* hearing it though, after you told me Mary Henry had been visiting with Aunt Esther that night. Mary was blathering on about something…Sorry to be so vague but I'd already had one sedative while I was walking. I hardly remember dragging my things up to the second floor. Then I took another pill right away and fell fast asleep. I wish I'd seen my aunt's face when I went up there!"

"But you did hear the shot? And you now remember Mary asking if you'd heard it?"

"Yes, but I really think they thought it was just a car at that point. I guess I thought so too."

It was her imprecise ambiguity which was the real reason Phil had come back today. He hoped her story would be consistent with the first time she'd told it to him Saturday after he found her awake in bed, having responded to Chet Anderson's frantic pounding on Polly Jane's side door to tell him Mary was dead. Had any of this changed, he would be even more worried than he already was. Even at this point, she was still the only possible suspect and Stafford was adamant she be kept locked up. The amazing thing of it was that Elizabeth didn't seem to mind; in fact she rather seemed to blossom under all the attention.

And that's what scared Philip most.

•   •   •

The same autumn sunshine which fell through the barred window in Elizabeth Grimball's jail cell also fell on the tiled floor of Polly Jane's cozy kitchen. Although it created an atmosphere of optimistic cheer, Philip, when he entered for breakfast, knew it was spurious. The promise of winter was just around the corner and he felt anything but cheerful. Every time Elizabeth opened her mouth, the case against her looked worse.

He still felt guilty. Not for reading her diary that day; it was his job, after all. But for taking most of the afternoon to do it while Woody had been off questioning townspeople and poor Chet Anderson had been left on his own. Left to deal with yet another murder under his very nose. The poor guy would never live that one down, not in this village. Had Phil been wrong to yield passively to the circumstantial evidence, reinforced by the pressure of public opinion? For, when the news that Mary Henry had been strangled to death had run through the village in that rapid fashion so common to tragic news, it had resulted in a mob-mentality delegation arriving on the porch of the Sanderson house, demanding Elizabeth Grimball be arrested immediately. Of course, Jake Brock had been at the head of the crowd of shopkeepers and small businessmen, urged on by hysterically sobbing wives and excited teens behind them.

Beth had made no demur at the prospect of being taken into custody. Indeed, her removal was as necessary for her own safety as it was for the satisfaction of the villagers. But even at that time when he was as certain and sad as a man could be that she was guilty of the crimes, he had hated what he was forced to do. She had looked so frail, so tragic, looking up at him with violet-shadowed eyes, begging for escape. And what had he offered instead?

Philip pushed his plate away. He could not finish the scrambled eggs and English muffins before him. Grimly erect, P.J. sat across the antique drop-leaf table from him. Her breakfast, too, was essentially untouched.

"Phil," her voice wavered, but there was determination in it as she cleared her throat. "Did she eat the pumpkin bread?"

He looked up and gave her a half-hearted smile. "I think she was tearing into it as I left."

"Good. She needs meat on those bones! Won't you please tell me what's going on? Wouldn't it help to talk it over?"

Phil played with his knife, drawing circles in the butter on his muffin. As he remained silent, Polly Jane forged on.

"We've always talked over your cases on the phone, or if I've been out visiting you."

Her godson made a small grunt. "This is different, P.J. These are your own friends and neighbors."

"If it's confidential, you know I would never repeat a word. And you do know I'm usually on the receiving end of news, not on the reporting end of it?"

"I know. It's just that—oh, God, P.J.! What if it's all a terrible mistake? There's no proof, really, for or against. No actual fingerprints on the trigger, no marks on the bodies from a murderer's hand. No unidentified hairs. It's the strangest case. Elizabeth doesn't *seem* mentally unbalanced, yet…"

"She hardly seems like a cold-blooded multiple killer."

"Right. And considering multiple murderers aren't that common, anyway—certainly not in Canada—I hardly think a timid female village schoolteacher will be one of the first."

"So, she doesn't fit what you've seen before?"

"Well, there've only *been* three multiple killers this entire century so far, in our country. Having just finished with the Chambermaid Slayer, I'm up to speed on them all now: all three murderers have been men and all three belong in psychiatric hospitals. Archer, especially, was completely deranged. And obnoxiously confident. Does that sound like Elizabeth Grimball to you?"

"Nope. She's genuinely a soft, gentle soul whom I'd have thought couldn't hurt a mouse if she caught it in her porridge."

"I'd love to believe it. And I always thought I was a half-decent judge of character."

"No question about that!"

"But there just doesn't seem to be any other explanation, and until I find one…"

Polly Jane looked at him strangely for a moment. "Have you spoken to Genevieve Stroud yet?"

"She's out of town. Why?"

"Just that she might have some answers for you. She knows Elizabeth quite well, I think, and is a shrewd judge of character herself. And don't forget, she sells *life* insurance."

Philip stared at her. "What are you saying? P.J., do you know something?"

But his godmother shook her head vigorously. "No—no. But remember, I told you, I'm usually on the receiving end of news, and little tid-bits, well…"

"If you even *think* you might know something about this, P.J.—so help me, this isn't one of your murder-mystery movies to see which one of us solves the case first!"

"Really, Philip. I don't know any more than you do. In fact probably a lot less, as you don't seem inclined to fill me in. But even if Beth had motive to kill Oliver and Esther, what possible reason could she have for strangling Mary Henry?"

"The neighbors seemed to think she did it because she was already half out of her mind. Maybe because Mary was running around telling everyone that Elizabeth must be guilty."

"And this makes sense to you?" Polly Jane cocked her head sideways at him like a confused kitten.

"Of course not. I saw Elizabeth a few minutes after she was supposed to have killed Mary Henry and, after all my years on the force, I could see there was not a hint—not even the slightest suggestion—of recently-suppressed passion or crazed emotion. She truly did seem like a woman who had just awakened from a long, drowsy sleep. But Chet had noted that when he checked on her, when he came back from the store, her respiration was up. So I just don't know."

"Well, who else might have slipped in while Chet was away at the store?"

"No one, really. They'd have had to have known Chet wasn't just strolling about outside for a few minutes. For them to know there was just enough time to risk it, I mean. It had to be someone *in* that house who heard Chet complaining about being out of cigarettes, someone who could count on at least a full five minutes because he was going to the store. Elizabeth was the only other person in the house."

"How do you know that?"

"*What???*"

"Well, think about it—all those empty rooms. Unlived in by the Grimballs for years…"

"But Chet told me he'd toured around that afternoon being nosy because he was bored. No. No, it's impossible. There were so many cops in and out most of the morning and early afternoon. Someone would have found a stow-away. Also, Elizabeth admits she was awake when she heard the front door open and Chet leave. All I can think of is that she looked out the window, saw him head to Brocks', then ran downstairs to silence the Merry Mouthpiece. There simply isn't another alternative."

"But you're going to look for one anyway, aren't you?"

"Of course. I have to."

"Because it's your job?"

"No. Yes. I–I don't…"

Polly Jane held up her hand to stop his sputtering. "But I do." And she smiled.

• • •

Elizabeth settled back on her bunk for a nap later that morning. She didn't really need to sleep, but it gave her a chance to think with no distractions, her eyes pressed closed, her mind churning through events of the previous years, the previous days, over and over again.

She thought about Oliver Brock. She'd never particularly liked him, but she'd felt sorry for him and had tried to tutor him, to help him pass Grade Eight. Her efforts were in vain. When Oliver did remember to show up for a session, he spent most of the time mooning over her, telling her she was all he ever thought about, saying he wanted to run away from home and she could go with him. Looking at her with those silly puppy-dog eyes. Percy had told her once if Oliver persisted in harassing her, he would demand to be present in the classroom when she tutored him. Darling Percy, of course, had always been there to offer her anything she needed. But what she needed most was *not* to need anything. Or anyone. What she needed most was her independence. And now, ironically, she felt as if she had it.

"Sue her!" Wilf Graham had said last Friday night as she sobbed in front of him and his wife. "Sue your blasted aunt for breach of promise or libel or whatever. You deserve it."

Well, perhaps she did. But she *was* sorry Oliver lay dead. He hadn't deserved that nor, no matter how much she despised her aunt and Mary Henry, had *they* deserved to die.

She wished she could remember more, but she'd been so upset, feeling almost suicidal, ready to scream, ready to tear out her hair with frustration over the lost years, the wasted time. After Dr. Graham had told her the shocking pieces of information, she had walked for almost an hour then had, with some determination, decided never to bow to her aunt's wishes again. Upstairs there was a large, spacious room with a comfortable bed and a real walnut desk, not the puny table she'd had to use downstairs all these years. Her aunt didn't need her on the main floor! She could be alone up there. On a bed with fine white sheets and several fluffy pillows, reserved for the mythical guests who never came. To sleep in that room behind a proper locked door, to luxuriate in the feel of thick cotton and eiderdown bedding, to leave a light on all night if she chose, had seemed a wonderful beginning to her new life, a gesture of delicious defiance.

She had melted instantly into a relieved sleep that night—and then Grandpa Grimball had come to her. This dream was so memorable, so vivid, that she still felt it must have actually taken place. Suddenly there he was, looking exactly as she remembered him: the same baby-blue twinkling eyes, the grizzled gray beard, the same subtle aroma of sweet pipe tobacco. He sat in his old rocker in the corner and comforted her just as he used to do after her parents had died. How could she have ever believed he had lost the family fortune? It was ridiculous! She was sure he'd meant for her to be looked after always. Hadn't he told her she need never worry about money?

Dr. Haldrick had been too keen on that dream, though he had explained its implications soothingly. It was natural that, while her grandfather was fresh in her mind from Dr. Graham's disclosures, she would wish him nearby to apologize for ever blaming him and to feel comforted by her only childhood support system. Grandpa had been unjustly accused, just as she believed herself now to be.

Dr. Haldrick had asked her if she had ever been known to walk in her sleep. He'd said that often people who have vivid dreams, especially under sedation, will rise and carry on many duties without realizing it. She didn't think she was capable. She told him so. She told Philip Steele the same thing. But did they believe her?

Once again Elizabeth lived through the horrible terror of that last evening at home. Of course, of the day, she remembered little. Her sleep had only been occasionally pre-empted by the obscure soft step of many visitors, most of whom she was also certain she was dreaming. She remembered someone rubbing her fingers, holding a cool hand to her forehead, peering under her eyelids, opening her mouth, putting in bits of warm mush. She did recall Dr. Graham had come with the astonishing news that Aunt Esther had met her death. Somehow, she had connected that death with her grandfather. How unreliable the mind could be when one really needed it! Another time—or was it the same?—she had opened her eyes to see a strange yet vaguely familiar face gazing sadly down upon her. And once she had wakened, feeling more rested and slightly less dazed, to see Chet Anderson leaving the room. She was then conscious of him tip-toeing up to the third floor, then back downstairs and opening the front door.

These events, however, could not be pieced together in any real sequential order. She did remember—quite clearly this time—how suddenly doors opened and closed loudly, how the room seemed to be flooded with light from the bare bulb in the ceiling, how now-hurried footsteps clattered harshly on the hardwood stairs. A plaintive voice kept repeating: "*Dammit*! It's my fault! I never should have left. I never should have left the damned house!"

Slowly, laboriously, she had climbed from the bed rubbing her stiff muscles, then beginning to dress. She had managed to pull on pants and a camisole, but had sat back down on the bed again, dizzy and exhausted. It was at this stage of partial undress that the door had flung open; a cacophony of uproarious voices carried up the stairs behind the three men who barged in. As she hurriedly pulled a sweater over her head, questions were flung at her from the tall freckled man she now knew to be Inspector Steele, as well as from Chet Anderson and a bespectacled, burly black man with a long, pointed nose. Dully, almost apathetically, she kept repeating that she knew nothing.

And then— the *real* invasion. The front doorstep was suddenly filled with angry people: men who shouted, women who glowered, parents of some of her students who demanded she be taken away. She remembered Chet and Long Nose pushing them back outside and she could clearly envision Philip Steele's hand as he took hers to help her rise from the edge of the mattress. He read her her rights and, with a hand gently but firmly on her back, led her out to his car, past the gesticulating mob on her front lawn, and drove her the five blocks to the little 1800s two-cell jailhouse.

She remembered the bald-headed magistrate at the courthouse in Fredericton, where Philip had driven her the next morning. She remembered meeting a weak-kneed petite man who said he would 'represent' her. She thought back to her first meeting with Mrs. Quigley and her charming yellow teeth and ample chest, her cups of tea and her humming as she worked at her jailhouse desk. But she also recalled the night warden—a bitter, abrupt man whom she knew to be a cousin of Jake Brock's. He had spat through her cell door at her and raised a corner of his mouth in a smirk.

All these pictures were engraved on her mind, no longer part of the still life of fake fruit and parched petals which had made up her previous paintings. Though these many images were fragmentary, chaotic and in some cases startlingly violent, they were at least real. *Alive.* They were at least paintings with color and movement and action.

And at least—at last—they were happening to *her!*

CHAPTER NINE

It was Marcia again who greeted Philip at the front door of the Grahams' house that morning, soon after his breakfast discussion with Polly Jane. It was again Marcia who presented an air of cold but polite hostility as she ushered him into the hall.

"You know, Phil, you aren't exactly popular in this house at the moment."

"What have I done?"

"I'd say it's more like what you haven't done. I realize you've only been doing your duty by arresting Elizabeth. And of course I gather you were ordered to do so. But haven't you been shirking your investigative skills a little? Why haven't you found the *real* murderer by now?"

Philip grinned in spite of himself. "That's exactly what I'm here for today. Not to mention, my assistant Sergeant Woodbridge has been diligently tracking down minutiae for days. We're doing the best we can, Marcia."

The doctor's wife looked him up and down for a moment, glaring. "I sincerely hope you mean that. You know capital punishment is still legal in this country."

"It won't—it will never come to that."

"You're accusing her of three murders, aren't you?"

Phil blanched and stood firm. Marcia relaxed her face into a prim smile. "What can we do for you?"

"How is Wilfred?"

"A bit better. He's sitting up in bed but still too weak to get up."

"O.K. if I talk to him? Oh, and Polly Jane sent over this cheesecake as a peace offering on my behalf."

"Ah, lovely. I've been dieting like a fiend lately, but as soon as Wilf's a bit better he'll absolutely adore it! I guess everyone in town knows what a sweet tooth he has. Half of his patients pay him in home-baked goodies." She laughed as she took the carefully sealed parcel. "No wonder I'm always having to watch my weight! Come on ahead. I'm sure he's got some questions for you as well as vice versa."

Dr. Graham was propped up against his iron headboard with pillows and cushions, quietly reading the newspaper. Scowling ferociously as Philip entered, he set it aside.

"I'm glad you're feeling well enough to shoot daggers at me like that, Doc! Marcia's already put me through the test but suppose you get your two cents in as well." Philip let out an exaggerated sigh as he sank into the armchair pulled up near the doctor's bed.

"I just think you might have consulted with a psychiatrist before you dragged that poor girl off to jail. It was the worst possible thing anyone could have done to someone in her fragile state. I don't care *what* she's supposedly done; she was in no shape for anything but a hospital."

"What would you say if I told you our Miss Grimball is feeling perfectly well, looks ten years younger and told me herself she infinitely prefers a private cell in her village prison to a noisy unit in the hospital?"

There was an audible indrawn breath and an uncertain hesitation as the doctor spoke. "She said that? You mean you gave her an option?"

"Pretty much. She was rather in shock when we discussed it, but she's comfortable and seems fairly content where she is for the moment."

"And you can keep her in Victoria? I mean, she doesn't have to go to the penitentiary in Fredericton or somewhere?"

"I cleared it with the judge."

"And she's safe? The village idiots aren't going to lynch her?"

Philip smiled. "My sergeant, Woodbridge, all six feet, two inches of him, took down the names and addresses of everyone who was part of Elizabeth's bon voyage party that night, then told them he would personally escort them from their homes with silver bracelets if he heard that anyone had been within one hundred feet of the jailhouse. Of course, it won't make him any friends here, but this place already seems to have a predilection to racism. Besides, you know Trudy Quigley? She's taken the prisoner under her wing, completely at Beth's beck and call."

Dr. Graham relaxed back against his pillows. "Well, thank God, at least she'll be O.K. for a while then. And she's truly better? No crying spells? She's sleeping? Doesn't seem suicidal?"

"Stan Haldrick's done a thorough examination, Doc. He had flown into Fredericton for a conference this week, so I asked him to see her, as a personal favor."

"Stanley Haldrick? Well, you *do* know some big-wigs!"

"And he's deemed her sane and at no risk to herself. Now listen, Wilf. I'm in a hell of a predicament. This is turning out to be the most unorthodox case in which I've ever been involved. That even includes one out near Lunenburg which they warned me was Oak-Island cursed! In the beginning, this all seemed straightforward enough. But now, I just don't know."

"You mean you've gotten to know Elizabeth better and you know damn well she couldn't have killed three people?"

"We still don't know for sure that Esther Grimball *was* killed. And I think Elizabeth *could* have done it, yes. I guess I'd just like to believe she didn't."

"If Esther Grimball fell down those stairs accidentally then there's even less reason to believe Elizabeth's guilty of anything, isn't there? I mean, why the hell would she kill just Oliver Brock and Mary Henry? Plus, couldn't two or three people have been involved? Why does it have to be one killer? Just because this town hasn't had a murder in eighty-three years doesn't mean a few different people didn't decide to get in on the action on the same day, does it?"

Phil gave the older man a 'come-off-it' look with his head tilted to the side, his mouth twisted into his dimples. The doctor shrugged.

"Wildly unlikely, but yeah, so you see my predicament, Doc. And if Esther Grimball accidentally tumbled down her cellar stairs, then what was she doing with the rifle that killed Oliver Brock?"

"She caught him trespassing that night and shot him. Then she was going to put the gun back where it belonged and fell. Simple."

"And Mary?"

"Maybe her husband killed her. Could you blame him?"

"Listen, Wilf. Elizabeth had opportunity and motive in all three instances. I do not blame myself for arresting her. I don't even blame Jake Brock and Mort Henry and the rest for getting scared, believing she'd gone crazy. But there's been something bothering me: Marcia briefly mentioned you'd witnessed a new will for Esther not long ago. Who was the other witness?"

Wilfred Graham bit his lip. "Shouldn't you be talking to Esther's lawyer?"

"I've been trying to get a hold of him. He hasn't returned any of my calls."

Wilf shook his head slowly. "Well—it was Mary."

"*Mary Henry* was the other witness?"

"Yes. Esther and she were usually together every morning, often in the evenings too. Esther had called me to come by to check her blood pressure, but that was just an excuse. Instead, we signed several copies of a new codicil of her will which she'd drawn up herself. But, though I saw a few figures, I don't really know what was in it. I rather doubt that Mary Henry did either!"

"You didn't actually see any of the contents?"

"Not really. Just enough to know there was no way Esther Grimball was nearly as broke as she'd been making out to Elizabeth all these years. And I don't know who her new beneficiaries are, so don't ask."

"Elizabeth would presumably have been the only beneficiary before that point?"

"Who knows?" the doctor shrugged. "I would guess so. I wish I'd never mentioned seeing that damn will to Elizabeth. Or to my wife!"

"You did what you thought was right to help Elizabeth out of a terrible predicament."

"And instead, I seem to have landed her in a worse one."

"Not necessarily. As soon as you're better, I'll take you to see her."

"What does Beth say about it all?"

"Just what you'd expect. That she had nothing to do with the Brock kid's death, that she wouldn't have known how to use that rifle if her life depended on it, that Esther would never have dreamed of keeping cartridges for it. She says what regard she had for Mary Henry wasn't strong enough to be called anything; she was merely indifferent to her. She admits hearing the front door open and shut when Anderson left the house, but says she didn't know who was out or who was in at that point. As for the death of her aunt, she admits she took two of the pills you gave her and sleep came almost immediately. You know she dreamed of her grandfather but thought it was real, so it's entirely possible she did some sleep-walking as well. And *one* of those pills, she took right after she left here while she was wandering about the village in a daze. So who knows about the Brock incident behind their house that night? Maybe she honestly doesn't remember."

"Don't be absurd, Philip! They're only sleeping pills. Not magic potions," said Wilfred Graham.

"Well, the Crown Attorney is still going to find it a fairly easy job at this point. Oliver Brock was harassing her with hormonal-driven objectives, she'd just found out her aunt had been lying to her for years, trapping her to live in poverty and depression, and Mary Henry was telling everyone she was a murderer. As you say, they are only sleeping pills, so is it really possible she could have slept straight through for almost twenty-four hours without being a *bit* more aware of goings-on?"

"I told her to take one—not two."

"Even so, the prosecution will maintain either that she didn't take both, or that she was faking being asleep or drowsy all that time. They won't even need to be hard on her. They will come across as mildly sympathetic, suavely apologetic—and absolutely deadly. They'll make her look guilty as hell despite herself. After all, I've given them all the evidence and motives with which to do it. A jury will lap it up. I'm not enjoying the prospect, by the way. I've just got nothing else to go on."

"Do you believe her when she says she went for a walk, then went home and right to bed?"

"Yes. Yes, damn it, that's the trouble. I think I do believe her."

"Then take it from me. She didn't do any sleep-walking. A second one of those pills not only would put her right to sleep, but two would have made her so relaxed in every nerve she couldn't have called up enough energy to walk no matter how much she wanted to. I'll testify to that. You saw for yourself the next morning; she could hardly function. What's more, she would never have had the strength to strangle as wiry a woman as Mary Henry."

"But there's no proof she actually *took* those pills, Doc. Perhaps she's a talented actress. Maybe even this appearance of candor is cleverly assumed. She could feasibly have been filled with such rage when she left here that she might have committed ten murders! And rage gives one a superlative strength."

"You seem to be working against yourself as well as Elizabeth. Why aren't you looking for someone else that had motive and opportunity?"

"What do you think we've been doing?" Philip cried out bitterly. "Woodbridge and my team have had no sleep for three days. We've been over everything. What should I do next? Plunk a deerstalker on my head, go about the village with a magnifying glass? We just keep coming up empty. Or worse than empty. Anything we've found points more and more to Elizabeth Grimball being the guilty party. All right, I've got to get going. I'll try to get by tomorrow to see how you're feeling and if you're better, I'll take you to see your imprisoned patient. By the way, if she asks... you and Marcia dropped a parcel off for her yesterday—a yellow suit which she'd had her eye on from the catalogue. And some cosmetics."

"Marcia did that?"

Philip blushed. "You will say so."

"What the—why you devil! You crazy bugger! I'd like to —"

"You'd better sit back and rest there, old man. Or you'll never get over that fever. Try not to excite yourself." With a mischievous wink, Philip raised his hand in farewell and let himself out the front door.

●　　●　　●

Upon returning to the salt-box for lunch, Philip found Polly Jane in a dither.

"Look at this! Will you just look at this, Phil? I'm sure they're only trying to help, but they've really made it worse, haven't they?" She flung a newspaper in front of him in a state of high agitation, wringing her hands and brushing off her apron. "You read it over your sandwich. I made you one in the kitchen. Now then, I've got to get back to the counter. I'm training a new assistant, you know. Young Carol Caribou. Oh, and there're some messages on the table in the hall.

Philip scanned the article which his godmother had circled in red pen. Even had she not highlighted it, the headline was glaring: "VICTORIA WOMAN MURDER SUSPECT IN DEATH OF HER TORTURERS". The by-line was that of one Jenny Connelly, Moncton Monocle. The journalist who'd been caught inhaling Elizabeth's diary! Although yesterday's Fredericton Daily Gleaner had had a short article based primarily on the events of the weekend as noted from their brief court appearance, this story was a tabloid-worthy half-page soap opera. The over-zealous reporter had completely misrepresented the details of Beth's life, apparently in an effort to take her side but obviously only adding fuel to the fire. She made Beth sound like a thwarted martyr who'd put up with various forms of harassment from many of her students and the school board (especially the Brocks) and who'd literally nursed a bed-ridden, miserly aunt while they both lived an impoverished life. Mary Henry was the only character in the fairy-tale who came close to being described accurately: "*The third death was that of a libelous neighbor, Mrs. Mary Henry, 72, who spat in Elizabeth's face*" (the journalist failed to mention that Mrs. Henry inadvertently spat in everyone's face!) "*and abused the young school-teacher with degrading name-calling and false accusations.*" The article went on to describe the 'witch hunt' group who had gathered outside Beth's house, screaming that she be burned at the stake while the frail schoolteacher lay ill in bed. Shades of The Crucible, Philip thought as he tossed down the paper in disgust. It would do Elizabeth no good to read any of that! With a tuna sandwich in one hand and the telephone receiver in the other, he quickly dialed the now-familiar number of Mrs. Quigley's desk to request Elizabeth not be shown any newspapers. Next, he picked up the messages P.J. had left for him. The Fredericton precinct had called; he was to contact Fred Turner immediately. Also, Greg Armand, the lawyer assigned to defend

Elizabeth, had rung up, saying he had some shocking news from the Crown Attorney. Putting off the inevitable, Philip chose to call the latter first.

"Greg? What's up?" he queried eagerly as soon as the receptionist had put through his call.

"You're not going to believe this: Roland Sasback and his team have dug up some suspicious-sounding dirt. I don't know if it will help Miss Grimball or make it worse for her."

"Oh, great! What now?"

"Well, apparently they were digging around for more solid motives for Elizabeth killing the Brock kid. They looked into his school records and his delinquency reports with Chet Anderson then they questioned the farmer whose cow was shot back in the spring."

"That's when his rifle was taken away."

"Right. Only Anderson didn't actually confiscate it. He just turned it over to the father, Jake Brock, who supposedly has kept it hidden. But that's beside the point right now. The stunner is that Percy Collins, the teacher Elizabeth was dating, didn't just have a car crash. He was heading home after school one day and almost hit a whole herd of dairy cows scattered across the highway. He lost control of his car, slammed into a telephone pole. The cows belong to the same man whose Holstein was shot by Oliver Brock not long before the occurrence. And Sasback checked—the Brock kid had skipped his last two classes that afternoon."

By the time Philip had absorbed this information and thanked Greg for calling so promptly, he realized he'd obliviously gulped down his sandwich. He wasn't sure what this new bit of evidence could mean. But it meant *something* he was sure. The problem was, could it help Elizabeth or only point yet another stiff finger at her? He would have to get Woody on this right away.

Dreading the next call, he dialed Turner's office directly. Thankfully, the despised inspector was out, but one of the men on the bank robbery case told Philip eagerly that the getaway car, a

1967 Plymouth Belvedere, had been found in a ditch forty miles south of Fredericton, near Three Tree Creek. None of the license numbers had matched the original description given, but the car, registered to a Howard Ingalls of Nackawic, had been stolen from his farmyard the morning of the heist. They had, as yet, no leads as to the whereabouts of the thieves, but Turner had wanted Inspector Steele to know that a crumpled pantyhose package had been found under the front seat. The price tag was still stuck on the cellophane wrapper. It read sixty-nine cents, and then in tiny letters below it was stamped: 'Brock's Bakery and Convenience'.

CHAPTER TEN

"Wasn't it Samuel Johnson who said 'truth, sir, is a cow. It will lead skeptics to the milk'?"

"Something like that," Philip said curtly. He didn't feel like playing along right then. "Woody, get that sheet of paper out again, will you? Do we turn left after the right-angle bend or right after the curve to the left?"

"Right after the right-angle bend. The laneway is to the left. There it is: 'Guthrie', on the mailbox. That's it!"

Philip stepped on the brake and swung into the long gravel-bare, pot-holed drive up to the farmhouse. Pastures on both sides were filled with grazing Holsteins and ahead, beyond the house and barns, the detectives could see many men throwing the last bales of stacked hay onto a wagon. "Do we have to traipse way out there?" Woodbridge whined. "I thought Sasback was going to tell Guthrie to expect us."

"He did. I'm sure he's just in the house."

The red-faced, pot bellied farmer appeared at the door and motioned for them to come into his office which was full of spattered mud, leaping Labrador retrievers, and ribbons and trophies from fall fairs. They introduced themselves, sitting on the two chairs while Paul Guthrie leaned against his desk, arms folded and resting on top of his swelled stomach.

After initial preliminaries and niceties, Philip said, "Now, apparently the Brock boy has bothered your herd a good deal in the past? Do you know why he would have anything against you? Or your cows?"

"Nope. Just a damn-stupid, spoiled kid, if you's to ask me."

"But why was it always to *your* farm he came to target practice, or whatever he was doing?"

"Well, I s'pose I'm closest to town, an' also—I don't like his Pop none. Talks too smart-ass for me, an' I do my grocery shopping elsewhere. I s' pose that pisses his old man off. Prob'ly sicced his kid on me."

"Oliver shot your young heifer in the early part of May, is that right? And then your cows got loose and a couple was killed on the road in the latter part of the same month?" Woodbridge asked, consulting his notes.

"My cows didn't 'get loose'. I keep my fences real good. They was *let* loose. On purpose, like. I found later where a couple sections had been hammered right outta the posts."

"And you believe Oliver Brock was again the guilty party?"

"I know it. Who else would do such a durn fool thing? Killed that young schoolteacher and damn near killed one o' my hired help. Tim come 'round the bend too fast and hit two o' my prize-winnin' ole pets."

"Did Percy Collins live nearby?"

"Yup. Just two farms down, as such. Lived there with his pop and uncle. Helped 'em on the farm in summers, like, when he weren't teachin'. He were a good guy. Swerved to miss my cows." The implication seemed to be that because Collins had swung away from the herd and hit a telephone pole instead, he was a better man than the hired hand, who had not had the same presence of mind.

"You didn't notice the cows were loose? And no one saw anyone chasing them?"

"I were in the back fields plantin'. My man Tim come and got me. Told me he'd hit the old girls and we'd need to go shoot 'em outta their pain. And that must'a bin when Perce come round the bend. It were the time he usually drove home. You could set yer watch to him, like as not. He always come straight from school to help with chores." Woodbridge glanced at Philip who remained nonchalant despite the fact this was exactly the sort of information they'd been looking for.

"Why didn't your hired man try to put the rest of the cows back in the field?"

"Told me he tried. But they was spooked by somethin' and runnin' all heltery. Mebbe 'cause of the dyin' cows in the road, mebbe 'cause that young jack-ass was chasin' 'em with a cattle prod or some-such. My man didn't see nobody around, mind. But I know'd he was there somewhere. Hidin' in the ditch, mebbe or behind some brush."

"Well, thank you Mr. Guthrie. We'll just go on down to the Collins' farm, if you'll be so good as to point the way." Philip, berating himself again for his formal starchiness in these instances when he'd rather toss in some heavy-handed sarcasm, stood to end the interview. At which point, a Lab hurled himself on him with enthusiasm.

"Down, Jethro! Git down, now! Well, I hope I was some use to yous. Can't say I'm sorry that Brock brat is dead. I'm thinkin' whoever shot him did me and my herd a right favor. I didn't get much milk from my girls for *days* after them accidents. But Clementine, she's gonna win big fer me at the fair next month. That's her, there; she's that—"

"Well, thanks again, Mr. Guthrie. That's the Collins' farm two lanes down on the left, is it? We'll be in touch."

Once safely in the car, Woody distastefully wiped mud and muck from his leather shoes and picked several long dog hairs from his uniform cuff. "Christ, I thought my daughter's kitten was shedding badly! So, you think Brock planned for Percy Collins to have an accident?"

Philip glanced sideways as they drove down the road. "Seems obvious, doesn't it? The problem is, that only makes the case worse for Elizabeth. If she somehow *knew* that Oliver had been at fault for killing the man she loved, then that establishes an even better motive than just that he was harassing her. What if Oliver bragged about it to her?"

"Well, maybe the father and uncle can bring 'truth to light. Murder can't be hidden long,' you know!"

"You've used that one before, Woody. And Launcelot Gobbo wasn't already in jail awaiting his fate when he said it."

"Still a good one to use most times, in our job."

"You remind me of him, you know. Full of grand words and quotations, but always misapplying them!"

"I *say*, old chap!" Woody objected in his best 1930s Brit-wit. Then, reverting to a Cockney descent: "Oy, 'e weren't black, were 'e?"

"Shut yer Gobbo."

Both men grinned in spite of themselves.

As it turned out, the two Collins had nothing much to add to the sad story of their Percy's death. They did not suspect foul play they said, despite the rantings of their long-time neighbor Paul Guthrie. They thought he'd been making up excuses because his fences had needed repair. They had never had the opportunity to meet Elizabeth, but had heard from Percy that she was a delightful if shy lady and they were sure she could not have committed murder. Philip commented to Woodbridge on the way home that it was unfortunate friends only seemed to make themselves known when it was too late.

· · ·

It was Jake Brock's first day behind the counter of his bakery/convenience store since his son's funeral. Most of the day had been spent commiserating with customers over the travesty which had hit their small town like an unforeseen earthquake. However, he had had some time to go over accounts and supplier details. He was angry with his two clerks; they had done little or no inventory since he'd been absent. There seemed to be many things unaccounted for: several woolen goods were missing, two cartons of cigarettes could not be accounted for, the pantyhose rack was nearly empty, and they were low on various soup and stew cans. The suppliers hadn't been called to re-stock any of those items. Also, a good deal of imitation jewelry had not been put through on receipts, nor were several boxes of cartridges for various makes of hunting rifles. And deer season was still at least five weeks away! If they couldn't manage now, how would they manage at that busy time? He would really have to get on their case about it, threaten to fire them even. He couldn't afford to lose money like this.

He waited on two fellow members of the school board who came in to buy milk, bread and eggs, commenting on the utter stupidity of the police force for still questioning half the town when it was obvious Elizabeth Grimball was as guilty as hell and should be locked up in maximum security in the Dorchester Pen. for the rest of her life. She was a sleazy little number, one of them said—always smiling at his young son who had just turned thirteen, offering him extra help after school if he needed it. And it was so obvious she'd killed her aunt so she could sell the big house. Perhaps as soon as she was convicted, the money from that place could finally be handed over to the school trustees, as old man Sanderson had long ago promised.

Jake Brock nodded in assent, agreeing with everything that was said as he rang up their orders of groceries, cigarettes and pipe cleaners.

George Gibson said, "That Carol Caribou's installed in the post office now. Don't know what P.J. Whistler's thinkin', hiring a Maliseet that ain't never finished high school. But at least she's so quiet she won't be tellin' tales like that Henry woman done. I remember once I had a post card from my cousin Clare from California and Mary told everyone who'd listen that I had me a fancy piece from when we took that trip out west."

Jake Brock nodded again, but his eyes had strayed to his next customer. Damn! That Genevieve Stroud was a good-looking broad. About time she was back in town. He'd been wondering where she'd gone. He felt an itch that hadn't been satisfied in weeks. She had her short, thick cap of shiny hair pulled away from her face and she was bending over the bakery counter studying the pies and turnovers Rose had spent the morning concocting in a vain attempt to try to get her mind off the death of her only offspring. Mmm… look at how that young woman's blouse fell away when she twisted toward him. God Almighty!

When the trustees left, he offered her his assistance, all the while leering at her, wondering if he could ever get into her stylish pants. Her pin-striped polyester pants. They had such a sheen on them, why they almost looked like silk! Mmm… She was always so standoffish though. Like she hated men, or at least *him*! And she was at least fifteen years younger than he was. Still, there were other ways of convincing a beautiful woman what she really wanted. Jake was persuasive that way. Plus, he knew damn well that inside she wanted a lot more from him than the apple pastries, the milk, the screwdriver, the weed killer, and the three tins of soup which he rang up for her at the till. Oh, did he!

•   •   •

Genevieve still had her deep chest cold. It hadn't just been the remnants of her smoking habit or the damp night air after all, and it persisted in annoying her wherever she went. She would start rasping away in the middle of meetings, appointments, on the plane and in bed, adding to all the other tumultuous problems plaguing her. It made sleep next-to-impossible. The business trip to Halifax had not been as successful as she'd hoped. She'd come home early from it, feeling too restless, too worried about the events happening here in Victoria without her. Darn it! She should have picked up some cough syrup at the store, too. But that lecherous ass kept drooling over her; it made her want to vomit! One day he'd find out what she was made of! Ha! *He* should be the one behind bars, she decided—not Elizabeth. Besides, she was too caught up trying to decide between the Glendenning's Orchards apple turnovers and the Sea Buckthorn berry pie to remember medicine for herself. Maybe good ole Doc could give her something. Hmm. Definitely a better idea.

She changed from her business pantsuit into an old smock and comfortable moccasins, then went to the kitchen to heat up a tin of her soup—cream of broccoli today, she thought. And she'd use some of the fresh milk she'd just purchased, as the carton in her fridge smelled a bit off. Soup sounded cozy and she had the next twenty-four hours to relax. After all, no one was expecting her back until tomorrow. Just as that thought crossed her mind, however, the telephone rang. Vocally blaspheming it, she stumbled forward, burned her arm on the hot pot, caught her smock on the corner of the kitchen table and fell to the floor, coughing and swearing yet more vehemently. She held an ice cube from the freezer on her burn then, taking it as a sign she was not meant to answer the damn phone, went back to calmly stirring the soup. She thought she'd have a cup of hot lemon as well, to soothe her throat; the dish cupboard, however, revealed only one cup and saucer which were not still dirty in the dishwasher. *Hell*! She always forgot to turn on the damn machine before she left the house. The remaining cup was adorned with a long brown crack and was violently be-flowered. She looked at it with distaste but finally placed it on the table next to her soup. After lunch she would give herself the gratification of demolishing it.

After all these years, she still exulted in the pleasures which living alone warranted her. She loved to read at the table; they'd never allowed such a thing at the home! Her James novel had been finished on the plane; intriguing how the clue to the murderer had come from one of his cigarette butts. She coughed again, glad she'd quit but wishing she had a menthol now, just something on which to have a quick puff. Instead, she immersed herself in that new newspaper, the Moncton Monocle, which she'd picked up when she'd landed at the airport. She laughed until she nearly cried at the exaggerated Jenny Connelly story. What a silly twit! She hoped Elizabeth didn't get a chance to see it. Then, conversely, it might do some good. Who knew?

After lunch, she carried the remains of her lemon drink into her private living area. This was her retreat, her paradise, her hideaway. The cottage, when she bought it, had been overly decorated with a small front room stuck in 1950s chocolate brown and burgundy rosebuds, and a newly painted kitchen in too-bright yellows, with a bedroom in the latest wallpaper—turquoise and orange circles the size of dinner plates. *Ick*!

Genevieve had, with her usual efficiency, altered and renovated every room in sterile whites and creams—except for this 'back den', which she'd paneled in lightly stained oak. She'd given it a special flourish by having a stone fireplace added, flanked on both sides by untidily filled bookshelves. The final touch had been the addition of black leather wingback chairs to match the desk chair behind her enormous roll-top and she never cleaned or dusted this room. Because no one ever saw it. It was *her* living-space, shared with no one. Any guests were always invited to sit in the uncomfortable formal drawing room at the front of the cottage. However, many complaints had been pronounced on the decorating of that particular space. For as warm and agreeable as her den was, the drawing room was a cold icy-white box full of glass, marble, and a stiffly upholstered, square-edged sofa in pale eggshell. She despised it. But then, that's what she loved about it. She need never spend time there except when people intruded on her solitude. Then they would have to suffer alongside her in the starchy-clean sitting area.

The only person she'd ever felt compelled to invite into her private living domain had been Elizabeth, and that had been essential because she'd needed a huge effort to get close to her.

Now, curled up with her lemon drink and ensconced in her black leather, she thought of Beth Grimball, probably shaking with fright in a corner of her jail cell. Perhaps she'd better go down there this afternoon for a visit even though no one was expecting her back in town just yet.

Elizabeth's attitude to life had always been difficult for an energetic, independent woman like Genevieve to comprehend. She remembered the first time Bethie had finally accepted the offer to come in for a chat. Under the influence of Genevieve's cheerful babbling, Elizabeth's face had gradually lost some of its strained intensity, although she'd remained coolly polite and distant. However, with her instinct for striking the psychological moment, Genevieve had abruptly broken off the inconsequential triteness and demanded to know why her neighbor always carried such a vacant expression upon her face. Elizabeth had stared at her for a short eternity, then drily laughed.

"Vacant? Good word choice, there. See this body?" she asked, tapping her rounded shoulder. "No one lives inside anymore."

"What do you mean?"

And then Elizabeth had briefly described how she had finally, happily, decided to quit teaching in Victoria to move away from the 'family ties that bind—and *gag*'. She'd smiled with some bitterness at that. However, soon after, she had discovered her Aunt Esther had a serious heart ailment and couldn't be left alone. "So, I've now resolved that rather than having the life sucked out of me, I shall merely withdraw from it."

Genevieve had stood and walked toward the window facing the street. Then, with her unusual propensity for drama, she'd whirled around, inspired. "You know, Elizabeth, another name for this type of parlor is the drawing room. Short for 'withdrawing'. I've learned they generally had no 'life' to them and that's why 'living rooms' became the less formal versions for entertaining. My friend, look around you! You need to shake up your life a little, let in some clutter. Let me show you!"

Symbolically, Genevieve had then lifted a glass vase full of plastic flowers she'd just purchased from Woolworth's in Fredericton and had thrown it to the floor. Leaving fragments of the container and fake white carnations strewn everywhere, she had reached for Elizabeth's hand, had led her into her messy lived-in living area at the back of the house. Since then their friendship had grown over the last few years, despite Esther's intolerant disapproval and Bethie's own stiff-necked pride in refusing to accept more than she could give. Because of course, although Genevieve invited Elizabeth into the cottage for tea several times a week, Elizabeth could never ask her to return the visits. Genevieve had lived in Victoria long enough to have a fairly high insight into the idiosyncrasies of most of its inhabitants and although she was at first displeased by the omission, it soon became obvious that Esther was again at the root of the problem, not being noted for her hospitality or generosity. But Genevieve Stroud was nothing if not resourceful. There were always ways around an obstacle. Still, she knew Elizabeth would never understand what freedom of life meant now...

Deep in thought, she was almost at the bottom of her cup of hot lemon. Just as she was preparing to smash the cup into the fireplace with undisguised vigor, her doorbell rang. Now what, for God's sake? She considered not answering it, but on the second determined buzzing, she hurried to the front and swung the heavy medieval-style door wide.

"Good afternoon, Mrs. Stroud. I was afraid I might not find you in," said Inspector Steele. "I had heard you were back from your trip but when I tried to telephone a short while ago, there was no answer."

"Oh, hello Mr. Steele. I must've been—over at the store when you called. Want to come in?"

"I wonder if you could spare me a few minutes?"

"Certainly." Genevieve matched his polite formal tone perfectly. She ushered him into the drawing room, motioning for him to sit on the stiff white sofa. "Could I get you anything? Coffee? Tea?" She winced, realizing there wasn't a clean cup or mug to be had.

"No, thank you. I'm fine." Philip's eyes strayed about the large, sterile room. It jarred him. How could anyone have a room so stark and lifeless in their house?

Genevieve waited patiently while he struggled for a beginning. She had no idea what he wanted of her but decidedly she was in no mood to make things easier for him.

Phil cleared his throat. "I find myself in something of a dilemma." Even to him, the words came out sounding stilted and pedantic. He shot instead to forthright frankness. "It occurred to me you might be able to help me. It's about Elizabeth Grimball who is, I understand, a friend of yours."

"Yes she is. And for that very reason, I fail to see how I can help you. I am *still* a friend of hers!"

"Yes, well. I—*we*—need your help, regardless."

"Do you mean you yourself don't believe Elizabeth is guilty?"

"I'm not convinced she had anything to do with the murders, no."

Laughing, Genevieve clapped her hands together merrily. "Well then, it's all over but for the fat lady's encore, isn't it?"

"Hardly. It's not nearly as simple as that, I'm afraid."

"Why ever not? You put her in jail! Take her out!"

"You know all the circumstances we've made public, I assume?"

"I'm not sure. Oliver Brock was shot, wasn't he? And then Esther fell down the stairs and Mary Henry—what happened to her exactly?"

"She was strangled. It's been in the papers, but I understand you've been away working. The rifle with which Oliver was shot came from the Grimballs. It had only Esther's and Elizabeth's prints on it."

"Really? But surely you already had detectives around the house when Esther and Mary died?"

'*Died*'. Not '*were killed*', Phil noted. But he didn't respond. He simply waited.

"I heard, just before I left for Halifax, some conflicting reports on Elizabeth's state of mind. They range all the way from the supposition that she is a mentally insane maniac to a deliberate, cold-blooded killer."

"The problem is, we aren't sure any of the three murders was premeditated."

"Oh, I see. But how *is* Beth, really?"

"She's holding up quite well. The people who start these rumors do not have the rare advantage of knowing her past history and her character, as I gather you do. You know, of course, that she had reason to fear and dislike all three victims." It was a statement, not a question and when this time it was Genevieve who didn't respond, Philip said, "I feel I really only know her because I've been through her diary. Since then I've learned to read her face like an open book, as well."

"I see." Genevieve looked at him intently, intelligently absorbing all that his words might mean. "So you really don't need a character analysis from me then?"

"Not of Elizabeth, I think, no. But I understand from various sources that you could give me a great deal of information on some other personalities in this village. Your businesses must surely have given you a good background in this. Who else might wish those three people dead?"

This was *not* the direction in which Genevieve had assumed the conversation would travel. "Well, gosh! I don't know. You've come to the wrong person for that kind of information."

"Do you know the Brocks?"

"I've had no business dealings with them, if that's what you mean. They've never bought life insurance nor have they been interested in the real estate market since I've been here. Jake

Brock, of course, is often behind the counter of his store when I go in there but I've rarely seen Mrs. Brock and I didn't know young Oliver at all."

"What about Esther Grimball?"

"I–of course I knew Esther. I often bumped into her coming out of Beaufort Bromley's. His legal offices are in the same building as my insurance company. And I did once go to her house, to try to sell her some life insurance, but she claimed she was far too broke."

"Did you ever suspect that was not the case?"

"Well I couldn't say, really. I just always felt sorry for Beth, having to live like that."

Philip looked at her from under one eyebrow for a moment while appearing to be looking down scribbling in his note pad. She found that ploy inexplicably disconcerting—really, so clever.

"What about Mary Henry?"

"Not the most pleasant personality, I'm sure. I knew the Henrys a bit better as I sold their farmhouse several years ago and found them the place they're in now. Also, Mort took out a small policy for both himself and Mary last summer."

"Life insurance? How much is 'small'?"

"Oh, I'd have to check my records, but I believe it was under $20,000 for the two of them."

"I see. Still, I suppose $10,000 and the loss of a nagging wife could seem appealing at times."

"No doubt. May I ask *you* something this time?"

"You may ask. It doesn't mean—"

Genevieve jumped in. "Why do you doubt Elizabeth's guilt? I mean, I agree of course, but perhaps not because of the same line of thinking you've followed."

"There are several reasons I suppose I can share with you at this point. Never mind that she *appears* completely innocent and honest. In fact her apparent utter frankness extends to remarks which aren't going to act in her favor when this gets to court. Then there are the cartridges. She claims she has seen no ammo. for that rifle, yet the cartridge used to kill Oliver Brock is of recent manufacture, a much later date than the rifle itself or any .303 cartridges which her grandfather would have kept. But we've not been able to prove Elizabeth bought any. She hasn't been farther away than Fredericton for years and she certainly didn't buy them there or here in the village. Every merchant in both places has been thoroughly questioned until there seems no possibility of doubt. But that, unfortunately, is the only thing we've been able to prove conclusively. And it's purely a negative proof."

"No offense of course, but isn't your whole case circumstantial then?"

"Yes. Yet against anyone else there is no evidence at all. No fingerprints which can't be explained, no motives for all three murders. It's Mary Henry's death which is the real clincher, of course. Because the house was only unguarded for fifteen minutes. There was no one else about when Chet Anderson left for a pack of cigarettes and there was certainly no sign of anyone when he returned. The motive for murdering Oliver Brock and Esther Grimball is obvious for Elizabeth; yet it is pure opportunity in Mary Henry's death which points toward her. We just can't seem to get away from the fact."

"If Aunt 'Grim', as I liked to call her, had been *my* relative you wouldn't be having any 'whodunnit' doubts. But what if her death was purely accidental? Would Elizabeth still seem like a guilty party for killing just Oliver and Mary?" Genevieve queried, biting her index fingernail.

"I'm afraid she would." Philip responded by telling her of their recent suspicions into the death of Percy Collins. He'd already gone through these with Elizabeth and knew she'd tell her friend soon, anyway.

"Really! But then—why kill Mary?" Gen asked.

"Who knows? Why did anyone else kill her? She was annoying as hell, but harmless, really."

"Ahh, but 'the tongue no man can tame is an unruly evil'."

Philip chuckled. "You sound like my sergeant. He's always spouting off quotes, but in his case they're usually wrong. Or irrelevant. Yours is right on the money. So you think Mary was killed because of the things she was saying?"

Genevieve shrugged. "Or perhaps what she had the potential to say. Really, I blame a lot of this on Dr. Graham!"

"Wilf? How so?"

"Well, for ever telling Esther about her heart condition. He should have just let her go on gardening and running up and down stairs until she died of natural causes. And who knows? Maybe she did! You know, in many European countries the doctors are not required to be honest with their patients. If they're going to die, the doctors don't always broadcast it."

"You wouldn't have heard—Elizabeth found out Friday night that Esther had been lying all this time. She was not suffering from a weak heart!" Philip did not add she'd also been lying about their finances.

"Really! Now that *is* interesting. Typical of old Auntie Grim, I must say. Still, Wilf Graham is—well…," she broke off.

"What is it? You don't think he's a good doctor.?"

"Oh, it's not that. I'm sure he's excellent. It's just, well— he has the most effective technique of any doctor I've ever met. You know how everybody enjoys being fussed over—to the point of exaggeration? Well, Doc Graham is an artist. I remember once spending a perfectly delightful week agonizing over an incipient swelling of my skin all because Dr. Graham, while sewing stitches in my arm after I'd cut it, kept up a running accompaniment of: 'Fine, fine. This will be all right now. We just have to be cautious no infection gets in it. If I'm extremely careful, it won't leave a scar.' He does that sort of thing beautifully. And as there was no infection, no scar, naturally I had the feeling he was an especially clever doctor and it was only by his extra care and thoroughness that it healed so well."

"That's most perceptive of you, Mrs. Stroud."

"Oh, please call me Genevieve. It's been over a decade since I was married, so that 'Missus' is moot. Dr. Graham has another idiosyncrasy too. It doesn't matter what ailment you take to him—cuts, bruises, breaks, rheumatism, gallstones, *any*thing!—he immediately adopts an empathy as if he was the only one who could understand because he, too, has suffered from it: 'I know exactly how you feel. I've never suffered so much with anything. However, I think we'll be able to deal with it. By next week you'll feel on top of the world.' Which you probably would do anyway, regardless of his treatment. Oh, I don't mean to sound cynical. It's just—I've often wondered how he has ever found the time to practice medicine when he spends so much time *taking* it himself!"

"He's been rather ill for the last few days, in fact. Flu, he thinks."

"Really? Isn't that typical! Not serious, though, I imagine?"

"I don't believe so, although it certainly kept him off his feet during most of our initial investigations."

"Well, I'm perfectly convinced that while he was treating Esther for her arthritis or some such, he'd also be saying: 'Now, we must watch the blood pressure. Don't want it to affect the heart you know. I've had a tricky heart rate before'… And so on until she could actually believe she did have all those other things."

"I see what you mean. He tends to make hypochondriacs out of his patients. No wonder he's always so busy and worn out! That's quite amusing; I'm sure he doesn't even realize he does it."

"Perhaps not," Genevieve said noncommittally. "I suppose it would be too coincidental to imagine there are two separate murderers and that Esther did just fall accidentally?"

"That is rather stretching it too far, I'm afraid. And we haven't enough motive in either instance of the Brock boy or Mary—other than Elizabeth. I mean, mere dislike or disapproval are not usually sufficient reasons for killing someone. Just because Oliver Brock bullied some kids at school or shot a cow, or because Mary Henry likes to cart away more food from church suppers than she donated, is hardly reason to dispatch them to the hereafter."

Genevieve laughed. "You *have* been sleuthing!"

"Yes, we have. But only to arrive at the conclusion that there must be something major we've missed." Philip stood up to leave, looking behind him to make sure he'd left no dark lint on the snow-bright lounge. "Well, I do appreciate your help. If you think of any more of your intriguing little perceptions about anybody, I'd love to hear. In the meantime, Mrs. Quigley is happy to let visitors into the jailhouse. So please try to visit Elizabeth. Oh, and if she asks, it was you who sent her a bouquet of fall chrysanthemums today."

CHAPTER ELEVEN

Late that night, under the peach glow of a rich-burning full moon, Philip looked out of his bedroom window to the garden below and was instantly transported back to his childhood. There, in shimmering white cotton, in a film of transparent gauze-like material, danced his godmother, her private, secret dance dedicated to her fiancé—the soldier who'd taken her to Fredericton's Harvest Hunt Ball in 1941 and then promptly been killed overseas. Philip wondered that a love such as this could have survived so many years and so much heart-break. He had not witnessed this ritual since he was in his early twenties, right before he'd gone back to university and left Victoria for the last time. But it never failed to cause a lump to rise in his throat, which in turn made him catch his breath in a half sob. Despite her age, Polly Jane Whistler was still so agile, graceful and beautiful, skipping lightly along the meandering flagstone of her wild English garden, almost near the end of its season. He watched her for a few more moments, then gave her a silent applause and left her in peace.

The next morning however, he felt changed—hopeful, suddenly, and more determined than ever to prove that Elizabeth Grimball was not a murderer. He spent ninety minutes on the phone while Polly Jane hummed merrily in the post office as if nothing out of the ordinary had occurred last night.

At one point, he was amused to hear her tell Carol, the young Wolastoqiyik she'd hired as her assistant: "And Carol, dear.

People *will* try to engage you in gossip. But I know you; I know you'll just nod and continue on with your work. That's by far the best way in this job." Philip knew P.J. herself struggled with this aspect of her character versus her professionalism, and certainly if she'd managed to teach such a skill to Mary Henry the latter might still be alive.

By the time he finally put down the telephone receiver, he had settled an issue which until now he'd found most disturbing. Although Greg Armand was considered fair legal counsel, he knew Beth would need someone more adept and experienced in murder trials, should he and his detectives not find an alternate solution to the three deaths. Now, through his own arrangements with his new bank in Fredericton, he was secretly paying for Leonard Harmon, one of the best criminal lawyers in Atlantic Canada, to take on the case.

But still, he must find the real criminal. Beth deserved no less! Her name must be cleared and Philip wondered if he had relied too much on Woodbridge. In ordinary circumstances that wouldn't have been possible: Woody was thorough and diligent. But these were not ordinary circumstances and Philip suddenly thought he knew why Fate had compelled him to come back to New Brunswick—and even to Victoria—after all this time. And why he was assigned the case virtually against his will. He was *meant* to prove Elizabeth Grimball's innocence, even if everyone else thought her insane and guilty. But the only way to solve these murders now was to backtrack, more slowly if need be, covering all the ground himself which he had formerly relegated to his sergeant. There must be something; there *had* to be! A full moon always brought illumination to the darkness.

First, he would visit Jake Brock at the store. He knew Woodbridge had already covered this territory several times but Philip knew men like Brock could hide much beneath their gruffly abrupt answers. Especially when it was an obvious racist speaking to a person of color who was also in a position of authority.

A wind chime sounded as he entered the store and Oliver's mother lifted her head from the glass display case wherein she was placing several dozen doughnuts. The woman's thinly lined face looked worn and haggard. She nodded to him but did not attempt to speak.

"Good morning, Mrs. Brock. Is your husband in?"

"No. He's gone to pick up some supplies in 'Freddy'."

"I see. When do you expect him back?"

"Another half-hour."

"Would you mind answering a few more questions for me, regarding Oliver's activities on Friday?"

She looked helplessly at the door, expecting perhaps that a customer might come striding in, giving her an excuse to be too busy. She said, "Just let me turn down the oven in the back," disappeared for several seconds, then re-emerged minus her apron.

Philip made up his mind that he didn't have time anymore to skirt delicately around the issues. He opted for shock tactics. "Were you aware, Mrs. Brock, that your son was in love with Elizabeth Grimball?"

She raised her head sharply and stared.

"In fact, he was obsessed with her. He was going there to meet her Friday night."

Of course Philip was guessing at this, but it was often the best way to get a reaction.

"Wh–what do you mean? Oliver was just a kid!"

"A most physically mature kid, Mrs. Brock. With all the raging hormones of a normal fifteen-year-old."

"It's that—*woman*! She must've been leading him on! I heard she was always after the young boys."

"After them to get their homework finished on time—nothing more!"

There was a brief pause while she digested this. Then: "Well, maybe so. Who shot Oliver, then?"

"That's what I'm trying to find out, Mrs. Brock. Do you have any ideas?"

"No! Not–not if it wasn't her!"

"Do you know where Oliver spent most of Friday? Because it wasn't in school!"

"I–I don't—I wouldn't know. My husband and I weren't in the store. We had to go to a funeral down in Saint John. He has cousins there."

An inspiration suddenly hit Philip. "Ma'am, do you know if there's been anything missing from your store? Like maybe some perfume, or candles, or chocolates?"

She stared at him silently for a minute then rose to her feet. "I heard your Mr. Woodbridge ask my husband that yesterday. At least, he asked if there'd been anything at all missing since the last inventory. Jake told him 'no', but I saw he'd made a list and put it in the till. I think he thought our clerks were stealing from us and he was going to confront them himself." She went over to the cash register, punched in a few keys and grabbed a note from the drawer when it popped out.

"I can't let you keep this. He'll—Jakey—he'll be mad if he comes back and finds out I showed you. He thinks business is business, and nobody else has nevermind to poke around in it!" Nervously, Rose Brock glanced outside as she spoke, as if the shadow of her husband might be looming in the doorway at any moment. "Are those the kind of things you mean?"

Philip glanced quickly over the list and was surprised he'd actually hit on part of the solution already. Christ! He must be off form if he hadn't dug this up before; the list contained the following items: *cosmetic jewelry–gold plated pin with rhinestone, silver-plate locket, blue wire earrings, woman's watch, children's paint set*', as well as: '*nine pairs of pantyhose, three pairs of home-knitted gloves with polyester lining, several salami, assorted tins of soups and beans*'. He jotted the items down, then flipped the note over and drew in a sharp breath. Jake Brock had also written: '*cartridges–three boxes, varying makes*'.

"When I get this rusty…" he said, impatient with himself.

"I beg your pardon?"

"Why wasn't this reported to us?" Philip asked.

"What do you mean? It's just fake stuff, some cheap old things. We thought Sam, one of the fellows who works for us, was taking things home for his wife and kiddies, maybe."

"No, no! I mean these!" he showed her the back of the paper.

"Oh!" Startled, she looked up in amazement to meet his eyes.

"My sergeant came in here several days ago, specifically asking if anyone had bought .303 cartridges."

"Well, obviously, no one *had* bought them. And I didn't know there was any missing at all."

"*Dammit*," Phil swore between his teeth. "These could make a huge difference to the case! I've just got to get the right pieces put together. Could your son have come in here on Friday when you were in Saint John and helped himself?"

"I don't see how. One of the clerks would always have been on. My husband didn't think Oliver was responsible enough to mind the store." *Right you are, there,* thought Phil with repugnance.

"But mightn't Oliver have offered to watch the store for just a few minutes while they were baking in the back or something? Or maybe he grabbed some of these things while your clerks were waiting on customers?"

"But why? Why would Oliver take things like that? He's never stolen from us before!"

"Mrs. Brock, it is my belief Oliver had some definite plan in his mind which involved Elizabeth Grimball. Perhaps he expected to win her over with some gifts."

"Like father, like son." Rose murmured bitterly. "But winter gloves? Cheap nylons? What was he thinking?"

"No, ma'am. I think those things were for something else altogether, as were some of the missing foodstuffs." He handed her back the note paper and she hurried immediately to the till to replace it. "Please tell your husband I'll have some more questions for him later on today. In the meantime, you've been most helpful. I'll be back."

As soon as Philip left the store, the wheels started churning. He took a deep breath to try to keep up with the whirling. He must go back and question the hired help again at the farm of the bank teller's father. Turner had interviewed the mustachioed North Shoreman with little success but now that there was more to go on, perhaps...Also, he must check the gully again over a wider range to see if any of the missing items were scattered about down there. But first, he must go pick up Dr. Graham to take him to the promised visit with Elizabeth.

Upon arriving at the Grahams' however, he was stupefied to find an ambulance backed up in their laneway, its doors flung wide. With mounting horror, he watched as a stretcher and two attendants came hurrying out of the garage, Marcia close behind throwing a scarf about her head. Their small Boston terrier, tethered to a long leather strap, was yapping ferociously, adding to the intensity of the situation.

"Marcia! Marcia!" he called as he approached. "What's happened?"

She looked toward him, startled. "Oh, Philip! It's Wilf! He's taken a terrible turn through the night. Sick to his stomach every ten minutes and now he's so dehydrated and... Oh my God! I don't know what to do. I've never seen him this sick!"

The ambulance men were about to slam the doors with the stretcher loaded carefully on, but Marcia said, "Wait! I'll go with you!". She grabbed the terrier from his tie, thrust him inside and pulled the house door in the garage shut behind her.

Thinking fast, Philip called "What hospital?"

One of the attendants answered "Fredericton" and Philip glanced at Marcia's pale face as she climbed in beside the stretcher. As the back doors of the ambulance slammed, he met her frightened eyes to mouth the words "I'll meet you there." He pulled their garage door down; it then took him less than three minutes to run back to P.J.'s for his car.

·   ·   ·

Several hours later, with Wilfred Graham injected with Gravol and safely on an I.V. drip and with his wife breathing normally for the first time that morning, Phil showed the attending doctor his identification, asking if he could have a minute of his time for a few questions. The doctor agreed, nonetheless glancing at his watch.

"What could make a man that ill?"

"We suspect some type of poisoning, sir. They're still running tests."

"But he's a doctor! Wouldn't he recognize the signs?"

"Not necessarily. He'd have been too busy vomiting all night to notice."

Philip shook his head. "No. I mean, he's been feverish and thought he had the flu for days! Do you think they are not connected?" For once, Phil didn't mean the latter as sarcasm and hoped the doctor would sense its intended context.

"Oh, I see. Yes I suppose. Milder symptoms the first time, of course?"

Phil confirmed with a brief nod.

"And he was just starting to get better. But then it came on much more rapidly, his wife said. Hmm, yes. We'd better find out what he's been eating and if he's been self-medicating. You'll have to excuse me, sir."

Philip went back to sit beside a teary-eyed Marcia. "They won't let me see him yet," she said, dabbing her eyes with a ragged piece of tissue. Philip handed her a fresh one from his pocket. "Why, Phil? How can this have happened?"

"The doctor thinks it might be food poisoning."

"But he's hardly eaten anything but home-made chicken broth and dry toast for days."

A sudden thought struck Phil. "*Any*thing else? He hasn't had, say, a few slices of salami?"

"What? No! I wouldn't have that around! I've been on my diet and Wilf's been too sick for anything spicy. Although he did try a few sweets yesterday afternoon and last night. He had a sliver of P.J.'s cheesecake in the afternoon and adored it! Please thank—"

"Good Lord!" Phil stood up, his hands shaking. "The cheesecake? You didn't have any?"

"No, I can't. My diet—"

"Jesus!" Philip dashed to the phone, threw in a dime, and called P.J. at the post office number. Carol Caribou answered the phone. "Mrs. Whistler is lying down now, Mr. Steele. She said she was out late last night, needed rest. Should I get her?"

"No, don't disturb...*wait*! Was she feeling ill when she went to lie down?"

"I don't think so."

"Yes, Carol. Please do go get her after all. I have to talk to her!"

A few moments passed and then he heard scurrying feet. "Phil? What's wrong? You've scared this poor child half to death!"

"Sorry, P.J., but I was afraid you might *be* half-dead! Are you feeling all right?"

"I'm fine. Just a little tired. What's going on?"

"I'll fill you in later, P.J. You didn't make us any of that cheesecake you sent over to Wilf Graham, did you?"

"No. Do you want some tonight? It seems an odd thing to wake an old woman up for, but..."

Philip laughed, glad she sounded so natural. "No, no! It's just that Wilfred's very ill—in hospital, in fact—and we're trying to trace possible food poisoning. How long did you have your ingredients for the dessert you made for him?"

"Just a few days! Good Lord! Is he all right?"

"He'll be fine, I think. Did you buy those ingredients before or after Mary Henry died?"

"After. There's been no one in my kitchen except you and me, Phil."

"Not even Carol?"

"No. She doesn't gallivant around my house the way Mary used to."

Philip sighed, partly with relief, partly in frustration. He told his godmother he'd be home later that afternoon, apologized for disturbing her rest, then went back to Marcia.

"What's going on?" she asked as he joined her on the ghastly turquoise waiting-room sofa.

"Just another idea I had which didn't pan out. You can't remember Wilf eating anything else at all last night?"

"I've been racking my brain. Yes, about eight o'clock last night he felt well enough for a small helping of the noodle casserole Betsy Lawford had brought over. She'd made some for supper for her family and brought us the last of it. He only had a few spoonfuls! So, unless they're all sick too, it couldn't have been that. Oh, yes, then at 10:00, right before bed, he had a glass of milk and half a pastry. I *told* you he had a terrible sweet tooth."

"Was the milk fresh?"

"Yes, I had a glass at lunchtime."

"And the pastry? Did you bake it?"

"No, Genevieve Stroud has had a terrible cough and she came over wondering if Wilf felt well enough to see her for a minute. She said *you'd* told her he was sick and after he examined her throat then wrote her out a prescription, she kindly gave us two apple turnovers from the bakery."

"You didn't have any?"

Marcia looked at him crossly then repeated with the exaggerated patience one uses for a child: "No, Philip. My DIET!!!"

"O.K., so… Wilf had a nibble of turnover and you didn't. They were from the bakery in Victoria?"

"Yes. At least, that's what the brown paper bag was stamped. And they look just like Rose's turnovers."

"Stamped 'Brock's Bakery and Convenience'?"

Philip barely waited for Marcia to nod before he was heading back to the phone.

"Woody? Phil. Go pick up Jake Brock for questioning, please. Take him to the station. Also, send someone to Wilf Graham's house. Go through the garage; it's not locked. Have them collect an apple turnover left in their kitchen. And the paper bag it came in, stamped 'Brock's'. Take it to the lab and tell them we need the results immediately. I'm in the city now and I'll be over at headquarters in an hour."

• • •

Philip had hoped to have more answers by that afternoon when he went to see Elizabeth. But Jake Brock had not been cooperative. He'd answered questions with short 'yesses' and 'no's', snarled barbs of bigotry directed at Woody, calling him 'nigger cop' and 'darkie'. He'd scowled continually at Philip and, when confronted about the missing items from his store, had become belligerent, started yelling that it was none of their business. Woody remained steadfast and calm throughout, having dealt with racism his entire life while Philip, showing a great deal more patience than he felt, managed to cajole Brock enough to discover that his father had, in fact, suspected Oliver of stealing the miscellaneous objects. He refused to believe his son had had any intentions toward his teacher, however. He'd then contradicted himself by saying that if he had, surely it made it even more obvious that the bitch had killed his son in cold-blood. As to the possibility of having poison found in the remaining turnover, he swore he knew nothing, and that it was ridiculous; there was nothing poisonous in their bakery that could, even by accident, have been put into the pastries. The lab had sent the test results back as 'negative', indicating there had been nothing suspicious found in the turnover left in the Grahams' orderly kitchen. Philip felt that every time he moved a step ahead, he was abruptly yanked back two more.

Just as he was preparing to head back to Victoria in the wake of Jake Brock's furious departure, Woody called him aside with a sly look.

"We might be on to something else, sir. Like you suggested, I had some of the boys take another look around the gully this morning and told them to go back also into the basement for a good once-over. MacCarrey just called in to say they didn't find any jewelry in the woods like you were hoping for, but they did find three cartridges that looked as if they'd been exploded 'like wee firecrackers', he said. Also, they did open the wood furnace in the cellar of the Grimball house. Since it's been empty for days there's been no fires, of course. The last one burning was on Saturday. Chet Anderson and Mary Henry took turns keeping it stoked up all day, Anderson said. Anyway, Mac found the remains of some old blanket or other tossed in there—just a few ragged pieces which hadn't burned because the fire had died down. In fact, they think Mrs. Henry might have gone down there to put in another log, but before she had the chance someone came up behind her and—whammy! And get this! You know how there were no prints or even indentations found around her throat? MacCarrey's thinking someone threw this bedspread or whatever it was over her head first *then* strangled her. They wanted you to stop by there to take a look."

Philip nodded. "Good work. I'm on my way. Call the hospital for me, will you? See what the status is on Dr. Graham. I'll be at the Victoria jailhouse in, say, an hour and a half. You can reach me there."

•   •   •

It was Mrs. Quigley who took him back to the little cell where Elizabeth, reading a magazine, looked up with pleasure as he unlocked the door and entered.

"I'd hoped to be here before now," Philip said, wondering why he found it necessary to assure Beth that he hadn't forgotten her. "But it's been a busy morning."

"Has it? For me too! As soon as I woke up, Mrs. Quigley washed and cut my hair."

"Very nice." Philip grinned approvingly.

"Thanks. And then Genevieve came for a visit, and your dear godmother popped by. Goodness, she's so thoughtful! She brought me all these magazines. Then, the principal from the school came by with a card from some of the teachers saying they supported me, believed in me. Wasn't that lovely? What have you been up to?" Philip marveled at the lilt in her voice, the light in her eyes—so different from the woman he'd met only a week ago when he asked if he could jump over the fence in her backyard.

"Well, let's see. I'm not sure I can top you for activity level, but I did manage to get you a better lawyer, one from Saint John. His name is Leonard Harmon; he's brilliant. He'll be up here in a few days." Phil purposely glossed over this, hoping Beth would just assume the province would cover these costs as for Greg Armand. "Then, I spent some time questioning the Brocks—both Rose and Jake. And poor Wilf Graham has been taken to the hospital—some type of poisoning. So I've been there for a while with Marcia."

"Oh, no! How awful! Is he okay?"

"I think he'll pull through. Mostly dehydration at this point."

"Was it on purpose? Someone poisoned him, do you think? Why?"

"We're certainly looking into all the details. I was also at your house. My men found this. Do you recognize it?" From his pocket, Philip took out a transparent plastic bag with several charred pieces of what appeared to be a thick multicolored rag. He handed Elizabeth the packet. She stared in disbelief.

"What happened to it? It's my old quilt! I've had it since I was a baby. My mother made it for me." Tears rushed to her eyes and Philip knew that no one could act that well on the spur of the moment. Her honest shock and despondency at seeing the blackened bits of cloth were the last confirmation he needed of her innocence.

He put a hand softly over hers as he took the plastic bag back. "I'm sorry, Beth. It had been burned up in the furnace."

"But how crazy! Why? Who?"

Philip shook his head. "We're not sure. They'll run a test for some hair fibers. But it might have been used to help strangle Mary."

"Oh, God! My poor old 'Threads'! It's comforted me through so much."

"But you've been here all these days without it."

She smiled sadly. "You're right. I guess it's symbolic somehow. I suppose this being mine proves yet again I had something to do with the killings?"

"Not really. It doesn't prove anything—yet. But it does lead one to believe that it must have been someone who was in the house or at least knew it well. I mean, it hardly seems likely a stranger would go in off the street, head straight for your old room, grab the quilt and then go into the cellar to strangle a woman who was just down there for a few minutes, as supper was baking in the oven. But I'm determined to find out the truth behind all of this."

There was a pause as Elizabeth looked down at her feet. "Inspector Steele. I hope—that is, I hope you don't think I'm innocent purely for, er—personal reasons."

A cranberry-rose flush filled his cheeks and he knew his freckles were popping off his face. Good grief, at the ripe old age of forty-three. Well, wasn't *this* professional? *Oh, who cared?* "Personal? What do you mean?"

"When Genevieve was here...she seems to think you are—well, that is, that you and I might have become..." Elizabeth paused to draw in a breath and looked up at him from under her new bangs. "She thinks you are 'enamored' of me! Her archaic word, not mine."

Philip smiled. "That friend of yours certainly is astute."

"You mean...but you don't just *hope* I'm innocent, do you? You really do believe me?"

Deliberately, he looked deep into her huge, fragile eyes—like those of the antique china doll P.J. kept in a glass cabinet at home. "I believe you," he said.

"But you don't know me well. I could be lying," she protested.

"I think I know you quite well by now."

It was Elizabeth's turn to blush. "Yes, Genevieve said you'd read my diary. And I *know* she didn't send these flowers; she tried to fib to me about them but really, she's no good at lying. And—thank you." Elizabeth's beautiful dark lashes fluttered as her eyes focused on his amused face. They were like the wings of a butterfly coming to light. "Wait! My diary! You sent me the suit too, didn't you? I thought it was the Grahams, but they wouldn't have known...Oh, it was *you*!"

"I'm sorry. Don't ever let anyone from my precinct know or I'll never be able to live it down. It's just that I couldn't bear to think of you here alone, scared. It's so dull and dark back here. And you seem to enjoy yellow. I just trotted into the Simpson's-Sears store first thing Monday morning and there it was, same as the catalogue. I hope I guessed the size all right?"

"I tried it on right away. It's a bit big in spots, but Mrs. Quigley offered to take it in here and there before my next court appearance. Oh, I love it!"

"Anyway, you've made it somehow, I don't know…Almost *cozy* back here now. At least a lot more cozy than your friend's front room!" (Or the so-called 'living' room at the Sanderson/Grimball house, Phil thought but didn't add.)

"Ahh. Genevieve made you experience her taste of 'withdrawal,' did she? Actually, she has a wonderfully snug living room or den area in the back of her house. But she never takes anyone in there. Once I told her I was going to withdraw from life, simplify everything into blacks and whites. Yet now I've done that, my life is suddenly full of color and design and activity! I didn't even know I had so many friends! Isn't it funny? I wasn't allowed to have visitors at home! Now, I'm locked up in prison as a murderer and everyone acts like I'm hosting the social event of the year!"

"Well, not *every*one," Philip remind her. "There are still some crazies out there on the rampage, so I think you're much safer in here under Mrs. Quigley's care. Besides, you've needed a rest like this most of your life, I'm guessing. I'm just sorry you can't go out for walks or have a bath—take some other little pleasures too. How's Rod Hansen treating you at night?"

"Oh, I just stay out of his way," she said. "Not that I have a choice! But by the time he comes on duty I'm usually asleep, anyway. Also, I think Chet Anderson must have had some words with him about spitting at me. I heard them shouting out there the night after it happened and he's never bothered me since."

"Good. Your discerning Mrs. Stroud had a few ideas about your aunt as well. She thinks Dr. Graham may have made some innocent comments about heart and blood pressure, that Esther picked up on those. It *is* possible, you know Beth, that she wasn't being entirely untruthful. She may have actually needed you—in her own strange, possessive way."

But Elizabeth shook her head. "No. She's never needed anyone or anything. I've never known her to be sentimental or sympathetic to a soul. How could she be? She'd lived a bitter life shut up in Victoria. And tiny villages like this may be quaint, but they don't encourage open-mindedness. Also, with no telephone, radio or television, Aunt Esther could never see how the world around her had changed. She never met or spoke to new people. She had this tiny tunnel vision. Everything had to be her way or no way."

"Esther Grimball never left this village?"

Elizabeth shook her head. "Not even for a trip. Oh, wait. I'm wrong. I think Grandpa did tell me once that they'd sent Esther away to some relatives in the States for a while to get her to take a different outlook on life. She'd been so upset that my dad had gone off to university. But Grandpa said, if anything, she only came home worse than before. Angry, frustrated and afraid to spend money on anything pleasurable. Of course, that was long before I ever came to live with them."

"You don't think your aunt was being stingy so she'd have more to leave you when she died?"

Elizabeth laughed. "Wow, you really know how to play Devil's Advocate, don't you? I don't even know if she's left me a cent! After all, if Dr. Graham says there's a new will, for all I know Aunt Esther left any money she had to the local cemetery. Or something equally morbid."

Philip stood up to leave. "Beth, I promise to get you out of here. I hope by the time your aunt's will is read next week. Because I believe there has to be some good in most people—not all, mind you, but most. My father stoutly believed in Plato's 'Just State'. And in a way, that's part of the philosophy. I think you're going to find your relative did, in the end, have your best interests at heart." He reached out to touch her arm as she stood also, like any good hostess about to usher a visitor to the front door. He didn't really believe this about finding good in most people, of course. Nor did his father; he had slightly skewed Plato's theory. No hardened police detective could believe this, not after experiencing the blatant evil witnessed across a nation of supposedly impeccably-mannered civilians. But he wanted to give Elizabeth that hope, that comfort. "I'll see you later. Enjoy your reading."

And with that, he smiled warmly and took his leave.

• • •

"Turner's not real thrilled you're stepping in on his case," Woody said as he met Philip outside the jailhouse.

Phil folded himself into the driver's seat. "I wouldn't have expected him to be."

"And he wouldn't let me see the notes his men took on the questioning of the hired hand out at Bergers' farm. I had to go over his head, got Stafford to OK it." Woody slid into the passenger seat and Phil started the engine. "And of course that pissed Turner off even more."

"But you did see the notes?"

"Oh yeah. Flimsy work, if you ask me. Turner obviously has his mind set that all the bank thieves took off way out of town. That when they deserted the stolen car, they were all together and hours south of here. They were just more or less doing a routine check when they questioned this Gaston Hauche guy."

"But what about after they discovered the package from Brock's store?"

"Oh, they just figured the thieves stopped off to buy pantyhose there before the robbery. The Brocks were away that day, so Turner questioned the clerks but they don't remember *any*one buying stockings, never mind men!"

"Don't think they were purchased at all."

"So you mentioned. Could be. I thought we were going to Jeremy Berger's farm?"

"We are. Why?"

"Well, according to Turner's directions, we just passed the turnoff."

"What? I thought they lived three miles on the *other* side of Victoria. The teller told me that day at the bank: they lived 'down' the road." Philip slammed on the brakes and clutch simultaneously, then ninety-degree-cornered sharply to the right. "We always used to call this 'up' the road!"

They continued to drive for several minutes in the opposite direction, skirting the village environs. As Philip drove along the curving, twisty back route, he felt rising excitement. "Woody! How is the house described in Turner's directions?"

"He said, let's see—a large frame house, cream with green shutters."

"Does he mention a cupola on top?"

"Cupola?"

"A little tower thing? On the roof?"

"Nope. But I heard Armstrong mention the place looked like some squire's castle."

"Damn! Things are starting to come together!" Philip spun the wheel as he pulled into a driveway. "This is it! The house used to be white with black shutters, I think. Woody, this place used to belong to some people called McKinley. They had two sons who were pals of mine when I spent my summers here. I used to spend the day helping them on the farm, then I'd hike home when it started to get dark."

"Good Lord! Quite a hike!"

"No, it used to take me just under six minutes."

Philip pulled to a halt in front of the hedge, aware that Woodbridge was staring at him, awaiting an explanation. Phil gestured toward the back of the huge house. "See that ravine behind there?"

"Yeah. So?"

"So, do you know what lies just on the other side of that ravine?"

"Nope. Trees? More orchards? Potato fields? More mud and dog doo for me to trudge through?"

"Nooo—a certain small village called Victoria. And if you follow the old abandoned path we used to use, you come out of the gully right beside the fairgrounds where a certain soccer match was played last Friday."

CHAPTER TWELVE

"Gaston Hauche? Inspector Steele and Detective Sergeant Woodbridge. I believe you were expecting us?" Philip inquired politely as they walked up to the door of the bunkhouse beside the great barn.

"Oui, c'est vrai. Monsieur Berger, he say I take afternoon off. How I get paid though, eh? If I need keeping talk avec yous guys? Parler au flics, uh?"

"Oh, now Monsieur Hauche. I don't think you really need much more money, do you? After all, that bank job should just put you happily into retirement. And with a split of Oliver Brock's share of the deal... Hell! You're set for life!"

"Eh? *Pardon*? Je suis—" Hauche's eyes widened, then glanced furtively to a side door of the bunkhouse.

"Don't bother, Hauche," said Woody in his best menacing tone. "I've got legs twice as long as yours and a little assist besides." He patted the pistol strapped to his belt for this occasion.

"Do sit down, Monsieur Hauche," Philip continued. "We just want to confirm a few facts with you. Now—last Friday, I believe you wolfed down a whole passel of salami for lunch?

"Merde! Etes-vous fou?"

"Not crazy at all. Answer the question, please."

"Bâtard! How do I know what I eat a week past?"

"Well, I believe you do know because you and one or two of your North Shore cronies were sitting here in this bunkhouse counting bills while you ate. Large bills. Now this is how we see it: you and your buddies came south to work in harvest, earn some big bucks fast. But then you figured out an even quicker way. Your boss's daughter worked at the bank in the village so you heard her talking somewhere about all the extra money they were doling out every Friday for farm workers' pay. You've likely heard quite a lot over the last few weeks, keeping your ears open, haven't you?"

"Bâtard!" Hauche spat on the bunkhouse floor, aiming for Philip's shoes.

"So you told your pals, got them involved too. One of them stole the get-away car, am I right?"

Philip received only a glare for his civility while Woodbridge stood feigning boredom, as if he'd heard this story unfolded previously several times. He hadn't.

"Problem was, you needed some guns if you were going to rob a bank. Your pals 'borrowed' a couple of revolvers, probably from the farmers they work for. It's just you on Berger's farm, right? And *you*—you found a treasure in a lad called Oliver Brock. Perhaps you met him down in the gully taking pot-shots at squirrels and chipmunks? Blowing up cartridges from his father's store, just for the pure joy of hearing the bang? Anyway, you said you'd split the money with Oliver if he could manage to get you a gun or two plus some of the supplies you'd need. That way you would never seem suspicious yourselves; you had the kid do all the dirty work for you! Now Oliver, he couldn't get his hands on his father's rifle, but he'd done some yard work this past summer for the Grimballs. He remembered seeing a hunting rifle down in their cellar. He broke in there one night, didn't he? A cellar door latch is easy to jimmy, really. And he stole the rifle. The only problem is, someone saw him coming out with it. What we want to know, Hauche, is *who that person was.*"

Bulging eyes stared at them through greasy blond strands of hair. "Eh! I need un avocat 'ere, n'est-ce pas?"

"Certainly you can contact a lawyer. We can even help you with that. You can consult with him before we have our next few chats, but he won't be in the room with you when we are. It's not how things work in this country, so you'll be on your own with us, regardless. And if we have to wait for a French lawyer from Moncton or somewhere up north for you, that's going to take a while, isn't it, Sergeant?

"Yup. Maybe not even tomorrow."

"And in the interim, we go to a judge to get a search warrant for these premises. But these matters all take time. And time is what you don't have, my dear sir. Because you see, after this you're going into the city to be fingerprinted, searched to within an inch of your life, to get a haircut, get your mustache shaved, have a lovely photography session, meet some really pleasant room-mates. It could be days before a lawyer of *your* choosing can get to you! But you see, if you tell us here and now, what we need to know—well, I can promise a deal for you. Can't I, Sergeant Woodbridge?

Woody shrugged. "I s'pose."

"Sure we can. A deal, see? Starting with this: I'll let you phone a lawyer before we even leave this farm today. And my friend Woodbridge will testify that I am a man of my word."

This time Woody nodded and said, "Thou'll get thee fairin'…"

"Eh?" Philip was grateful Hauche would have no idea that Robbie Burns concluded his sentence by threatening a good roasting in hell. "He means: 'yeah, you can trust me'. Now, did Oliver Brock tell you he was being blackmailed? Exploited?"

"Je ne comprehend pas."

"Oh, you understand completely. Answer!"

"I never kill dat boy!"

"Then tell us what happened or you could be charged with murder as well! Start when your driver dropped you off at the end of this road and led the local cops on a merry chase that afternoon."

"How you—dat Duguay, he squeal? Bâtard!"

"Let's just say 'Duguay'"—Phil noted with satisfaction that Woody, standing behind Hauche's chair, was jotting the name in his notepad—"your good buddy Duguay, is only a heartbeat from a locked cell as we speak. Now, let's have it."

"I do not know what happen to dat kid. Non, je ne sais pas! We divide money in car, then Duguay, he drop us off. Me and Edwards," (Phil glanced sideways again at Woody), "we head back here to bunkhouse. Everyone else having le barbeque dejeuner in orchard dat day, uh? An de kid, he give us some salami he'd grabbed, then he away off home through woods. He say he have a date, now he so rich."

"How much did you give him?"

"We very fair. We give him one t'ousand!"

"And the guns? What happened to them?"

"Duguay, he take back de revolvers to his boss's case. And de kid, he take back his rifle. C'est tout. Dat is all. Duguay keep rifle in car with him while we in de bank. Edwards and me, we burn gloves and lady-socks behind barn here. We do whole job in lunch hour. No one even know we gone from here, uh?" Hauche boasted.

"And where's the share you and Edwards got?"

"Hmph, you need, what-you-call-it—*warrant,* mais non?"

"Not if we're just helping you pack before you leave for your extended vacation. Woody, maybe you want to help this fellow with folding clothes for his trip?" Woody wandered to a crate with "Hauche" labeled in black marker. He made quick work of emptying the crate, then lifted the oval braided rug on the rough plank floor. Next, he moved toward the six bunks, reached under two mattresses, then another—and his hand came out with a pantyhose package, bulging with brand new bills.

"Well, lookee here!"

"Where's Edwards' share?" Philip demanded.

Hauche had given up any pretense now. "'e don't work here. He next door at Doblin's"

"I'm curious, Hauche. Why'd you need a fifteen-year-old to help you rob a bank?"

The man's shoulders hunched and he kicked the table leg. "We not need kid. He just got us de stuff from his store. Mais, big bully, dat. 'e say he wouldn't do it 'cept he go into bank with us, aussi."

"Who shot Ouellette, the manager? Was it the kid?"

Hauche nodded, not meeting Philip's eyes. "No brain, dat one. Epais!"

"And you knew he was just thick enough he'd be tickled with whatever cut you chose to give him? He thought a cool thousand was your four-way split, did he?"

Gaston Hauche sourly eyeballed them, repeating, "I not kill dat kid. None of us do."

"And he never told you someone had seen him stealing the rifle? And no one recognized him in the bank?"

As Philip said the words, an idea struck him hard, like he'd been gut-punched.

"'e never say nothin' bout dat. But I guess someone know'd us, eh?"

"Actually, it was your own mustache, Monsieur Hauche. Showed up through the stocking. Too bad you'll be in prison for a good many years to come, because I think the boss's daughter might have had a thing for you." With that parting shot, Phil nodded to Woody, who then made the formal arrest, bringing out his shiniest handcuffs. Phil told him to take Hauche up to the house to make a phone call to legal aid in Fredericton and that he'd meet them in his car. He sat in the front seat for a few moments, his head on the steering wheel, eyes closed, trying to put more pieces together, to let the adrenalin from his 'performance' ebb. Then, he radioed an antagonistic Turner at headquarters, requesting he send his men out to pick up Edwards and Duguay and to search for the remains of the bank's finances, which Philip reported they would likely find in pantyhose packets under the mens' mattresses.

• • •

Fatigue hung like a shroud around her ankles, hampering her as she tried to run. Only a few more yards to go before she could hide herself in her room and shut the door, cover her head with her old quilt. Yes, tonight she would shut the door and lock it too. She wouldn't pull the blinds down, either. In fact, she might even undress right in front of the window! There was no one down in that gully.

But wait! *He* was there watching her, licking his lips... He snuck in through the cellar door and came tip-toeing up to her room. Cell. Cellar. Locket. Locked. *Was* the door locked? Yes. More tip-toeing up and down stairs. *This* again. She must get out! Quietly, she slipped out the window, running, staggering, falling. Falling down, down, down to the bottom of the ravine. Oliver Brock followed her, his menacing bulk making her cringe. He was carrying a rifle. He told her he was hunting—*her*!

She must be brave. He was, after all, only a child. But the child was on top of her, heavy, weighing her down, struggling.

She must have courage. She must find strength! She grabbed the rifle, tried to push him off. His pants were unzipped. He was leering at her. Nerves. She had nerves. Of Steele. Oh, where was Philip Steele? *Help*!

She grabbed the rifle again, more firmly this time, and the night shook with explosive sound.

Dizzy with terror, she felt the heavy, lifeless body roll off her. The shadowy figure, a gleam of white eyeballs, crumpling beside her in the dead leaves of autumn.

She screamed. She screamed and screamed and ... Lights blazed suddenly about her; voices raised in anger, another shot rang out—

Then gentle, quiet hands were lifting her. The screaming stopped. She opened her eyes, looking directly into those of Chet Anderson.

"It's all right. I'm here. You O.K.?" the local constable said soothingly, but awkwardly. "I'm here. He's gone, the *creep*! Did he hurt you? Or just scare you?"

Confused and shaking, Elizabeth sat up. She looked around. Why, she wasn't in the woods at all. Oliver Brock's body was not beside her! She was in her prison cell. But—safe?

"Wha–what happened?"

"You O.K.?" Chet asked again. "I think I got here just in time. I've had my eye on him for a while. Think I shot him in the groin, the good-for-nothin'. Or at least the thigh." A hollow laugh trickled from his chest as he helped her to her feet. "That should put him out of action for a hell of a long time. If I can prevent it, he'll never work again either. Not in this province."

"I don't understand. I was asleep, but…"

"Rod Hansen, the bastard! He was in here on top of you! Dammit, if I'd been five more minutes…But—hey, you're sure you're all right? You're real white. I'll call Mrs. Quigley in. Christ! I should have known better than to trust a piece of shit like that. In fact, *any*one related to a Brock." Leaving the cell door wide open, Chet Anderson stomped furiously into the front room and dialed Trudy Quigley, explaining briefly and asking for her immediate assistance. Then, still swearing lightly under his breath because he felt yet again that Phil Steele would secretly blame him, he rang Polly Jane's number.

Philip arrived in less than five minutes and was in the cell holding a sobbing Elizabeth in his arms. He stroked her thick hair softly, breathing harder than she, his heart pounding louder than her own. If they fired him for inappropriate behavior with a murder suspect, it was essentially only what he'd requested before he'd come back to New Brunswick, anyway. So he just didn't care.

"I'm sorry. So sorry. I really thought you'd be safer here."

"Oh! I dreamed that it was Oliver. I thought I shot him! Maybe it *was* me?!"

Mrs. Quigley arrived with an overcoat hastily thrown over her extra-large flannel nightgown. As it turned out, she had harsher words for Chet than Philip did.

"I told you that lecher couldn't be trusted! Why didn't you listen? Where'd he go? I'll shoot him myself!" she said, her anger growing, her voice rising as she heard Elizabeth's weeping. After speedily arranging for a patrol car from Fredericton to assist, Chet left on his motorbike in something of a blind pursuit of the injured man. Trudy calmed down and put on her requisite pot of tea, just as Polly Jane Whistler threw open the door to the old-fashioned jailhouse.

"She all right?" she asked the other woman breathlessly. Dancing barefoot in the garden under a full moon was one thing; running down six blocks of concrete sidewalk in fluffy, non-arch-supporting slippers was quite another.

Trudy Quigley nodded, then motioned to the back, putting a finger to her lips. Polly Jane peeked around the corner to see the cell door still open wide, Philip sitting on the cot with Beth curled up on his lap like a small child at bed-time. He was crooning soft words, rubbing her fragile hands between his own and gently leaning to kiss her forehead. P.J. flicked a tear from her cheek and joined Trudy out front for tea. The two in the cell were not offered their hot drink until more than ten minutes had passed.

•   •   •

As daylight dawned, the horrors of the past night seemed surreal. Trudy Quigley had slept in the cell adjoining Beth's while Philip Steele had sat up all night at the front desk thinking and jotting down notes—snatches of conversations, ideas which had struck him oddly—on recipe cards which he could arrange and rearrange, as he organized his thoughts. Two hours after Chet

Anderson had zoomed off, he called from Fredericton to say that Rod Hansen was in the prison hospital there. Philip, instead of berating him for having hired such a reprehensible no-good, praised his boyhood chum for his quick actions. He realized Elizabeth perhaps even owed her life to Chet's suspicious nature and Victoria's sheriff was told that if he ever wanted a job in a city department, Philip would most highly recommend him.

There Phil continued to sit, sipping brutally strong black tea through the early hours of the morning, desperately trying to connect pieces together so he could get Beth out of here *today!* Had he ever felt so helpless? He knew he was a good detective; his success rate proved that, perhaps better than many, and he had a number of citations and awards stuffed into cardboard boxes in his new apartment in his new city. But he was not that commendable detective from some highly-developed sense of loyalty to any policing organizations. He had only chosen this career because he wanted to follow in his father's footsteps, to prove to him he could be proud of his only son. And Philip Steele couldn't endure doing any job other than well. But now? He'd made a hash of this whole business from the beginning, all because he was allowing sentiment to interfere with lucidity. Dad had warned him long ago—*let your emotions get in the way, and your judgment will always be clouded.* He'd been stupid. Phrases from the past week swirled in his head, but he still couldn't thread them together properly: 'Like father, like son' Rose Brock had muttered. And Genevieve Stroud: 'if Aunt Grim had been a relative of *mine*'…She'd told Beth 'Esther was likely just jealous because *she* was still a virgin!" Which of them had she meant? And just yesterday he'd heard that Esther had once been sent away but had come back more bitter than before… Plus, Oliver had stolen not just supplies for bank thieves, not just costume jewelry, but *watercolor paints* from his father's store. Why hadn't he drawn conclusions sooner?

What was it about Esther Grimball's will? Mary Henry had witnessed the codicil and she was dead. Dr. Wilf Graham had also signed it and he had been ill almost since doing so. But then Genevieve Stroud had told him Wilf always seemed sick with some ailment or other. Also, both Genevieve and Elizabeth had mentioned Esther going off to her lawyer's office from time to time. If only that will could be unsealed *now*! And life insurance. Had Esther bought any? If so, with whom, and who knew about it?

So many questions. The fact of the matter was that he'd had so many answers gifted to him already. He'd just been too obtuse to realize it, too caught up in admiration for a woman he'd barely known for a week. Yes, and there was Shakespeare's infernal rub, dammit! He'd never felt so out of control. He'd only ever been in love once before and when Rainey was murdered, Philip Steele—playing at being as strong and cool as his name suggested—had sworn he'd never fall again. And now here he was...He'd made a mistake, developed a blind spot. Last week, before all this activity, he couldn't make a decision about his future to save his life. Now, to save someone *else's* as well as his own, he was prepared to act more irrationally than he'd believed possible.

Last night when he'd held Beth close, he knew his ideas were a *little* crazy. He'd loved Lorraine Arnatsiaq and it was his fault she'd been killed—out of revenge for his arrests. He was not going to be responsible for putting another young woman he'd grown close to, at risk. Yet, hadn't he already?

Today, of course, as sunlight began to stream through the windows, he knew his fantasies were preposterous, impossible. But he had been prepared to help her escape from jail, from the country, from the continent, if need be! A fugitive from the law but not *pursued* by it. *And* accompanied by one of its former representatives. He knew it was insane. What sort of life could that be for either of them? Yet if they could be together, anywhere, with Elizabeth free to paint and Philip never having to deal with another abused child, or see another mutilated murder victim...

No. What he had to do was find the person responsible for putting so many people, including himself, in such an equivocal position. That was the only satisfactory end to the matter—for him, for Elizabeth, for the entire community in which a murderer was still at large.

He would find this killer. He would find him today. And then he would ask Elizabeth to spend the rest of her life with him.

Then neither of them would ever use the word 'loneliness' or 'murder' again.

After today, he was finished. Because he was just beginning.

CHAPTER THIRTEEN

When Mrs. Quigley was up, Philip sent her home to shower and change into day clothes while he went to the back of the building to see how Elizabeth had fared through the rest of the night. As he entered the cell and looked at her, still crouched on her cot but staring straight ahead, a fist tightened around his heart and squeezed. Oh God! Her face had lost all color again! Her eyes were as he first remembered: hugely hollow and black-shadowed. She could not bring herself to look at him as he spoke softly to her.

"Elizabeth? Beth?" He kneeled beside her cot, taking her shaking hand in his. "I know it was a terrible night for you and I'm so sorry. Rod Hansen is behind bars now, where he belongs."

"I'm behind bars too, Inspector Steele. Philip. What makes you so sure I don't belong here?"

"What do you mean? What's happened to—"

"Oh, Philip! Maybe I did kill them! Maybe I just can't remember! You know what they say about psychologically blocking anything too traumatic. Plus, with the sleeping pills I'd had... I think I might have killed Oliver Brock because he tried to rape me!"

"*What?* When?"

But she shook her head. "I'm not sure. I don't know if it happened that night or if I was just remembering something that happened before. Or if it was just a nightmare blended with what was happening in reality. Oliver *did* like to touch me a lot. You know, just nudging up to me or touching my arm. Of course, I always tried hard to discourage him but maybe there was more. Something else I just can't remember?"

"Did last night bring all this back? You remember something now?" Fear gripped him; he knew if he moved, breathed, looked away, he would choke.

"It's not that I remember anything, really. It's just—I told you I was dreaming that he was on top of me, that I was wrestling to get the gun away from him. It went off, Philip. It was so loud. I–I shot him. I shot Oliver!"

His breath went out with a whoosh and he pulled her to him. "No, Beth. No! It was just a dream. It was because of Hansen, that's all. Nightmares are only interpretations of our real fears, not necessarily a news broadcast with live footage!" He held her tightly. "You know our dreams and reality can become confused simultaneously."

"Yes, but if it could happen like that then, why not in some crazy sleeping trance when I shot Oliver, or strangled Mary?" She tried to pull away from him, to wipe a tear as it rolled from her dark eyes. Philip reached up to detour its path but she turned her face from him. "It was an accident, really it was! I didn't mean to…"

She proceeded to tell him from beginning to end about dreaming she was running, dreaming she had heard footsteps up and down the stairs, dreaming about the fall into the ravine. She didn't pause for suitable adjectives in her narrative. Every feeling, every action, every look was described as if it had really happened—and only moments ago.

When she had finished, she finally turned back to Philip and met his eyes with a muted plea for forgiveness. The look she gave him caused him to shudder inwardly. And with such force that the last of his barriers of cynicism and detachment melted away. Tenderness overwhelmed him as he pulled her back into his arms.

"Beth. Aw, Beth, please! Don't do this yourself! I can't stand to see you looking so haunted, like you did the first day I met you. I haven't been able to get you out of my mind since then, you know."

"I can't take your pity," she said as she blew her nose. "I can't bear to have you feeling sorry for a—a murderer!"

"You've not been convicted of any such thing, my dear!" Philip said staunchly. He stuck an index finger under her chin then tilted her head, forcing her to look at him again. "And you won't be! *Today*, I'm going to find the real killer! I promise you, I will not rest until I have!"

"But what about...How could I have just dreamed something so vividly? Unless it really happened?"

"Beth, listen to me. I don't really believe you've ever done or said an unkind thing in your life, never mind hurt someone, kill someone. But if you did—*oh, don't look that way!*" Philip reached this time for both of her cold, blue-veined hands and rubbed them tenderly between his own. "But even if you had committed a hundred crimes, I would—I would *still* feel this way about you. Now, I can make an appointment with Dr. Haldrick for you for later this morning, if you like. I know he's still in Fredericton and I'll tell him it's an emergency. Perhaps he can even do some regressive hypnosis if you think you're up to it. But I guarantee you, that *was* a dream last night. At least the part about you shooting Oliver! And if the only thing that will prove it once and for all is for me to 'get my man'—well, just you wait and see what the end of this day brings!"

Elizabeth faced him squarely then for the first time. Her shoulders pulled back, her head raised, and a faint hue of rose pricked the highest point of her cheek bones. "You don't just feel sorry for me? You're sure?" Her hands clenched with anxiety.

But Philip deliberately took her fingers, uncurling them one at a time from the little balls into which they'd contracted. "Beth, I don't feel sorry for you! You're a strong, generous, intelligent lady. Why would anyone feel sorry for you? Please, Beth, believe me. It was just a terrible dream, happening at the same time as a nasty incident that could have been prevented, if we'd all been less obtuse."

"I feel as though I've just found myself in these last few days, and now, in one swoop, I'm lost again."

"You're not lost! You hold tightly on to my hand, O.K.? I'll lead the way!" His voice mellowed to a whisper. "You're beautiful, Beth. You've given me no peace for days, woman!" Laughing softly, he touched her hair, her neck, her cheek. "If anyone's lost, it's me—lost in love!"

Tentatively his lips moved toward hers and she felt a tingling light-headedness as their eyes evaporated one into the other. Their kiss was a connection of far more than soft flesh, Philip thought to himself. It was a fusion of souls, a welding of two 'steele' hearts, now melted with flame.

He grinned at his wit as they pulled slowly away. "If you are a criminal at all, you are only a thief." He thrust a pointed finger at her, speaking lightly. "You're a Steele-r!" He tapped the left side of his chest, feigning a heart attack.

It worked. She laughed then, and the sound was like the lilting joy of spring's first song-bird. Her eyes looked less vacant now. And this time she took *his* hands and stroked them: those hard-knuckled appendages which for years had grasped at nothing other than metal triggers and clasps on cold handcuffs.

• • •

No one would have ever believed that Philip had been up all night if they could have seen him five minutes later jogging down the sidewalk on his way to P.J.'s to grab a quick bite of breakfast. The cement felt like clouds under his feet, his arms swung at his sides like willow branches on a breeze.

But as soon as he opened the door, his godmother flew out of the post office with her hand over her mouth. "I was just about to call you at the jail! You'd better get over to the Grahams' right away!"

"Why? What the hell's going on *now*?"

"I'm not sure, but there's something weird. Betsy Lawford just called. She occasionally does some housecleaning for Wilf and Marcia. Well, apparently Marcia stayed in at the hospital last night because Wilf is still in intensive care. So she called Betsy first thing this morning to ask her to go over to feed Pecan, their small dog, and to let him out on his tether for a while. Betsy went to the garage, got the key out of the tennis ball can where they keep it, unlocked the door and went in. Pecan was dead on the floor in the hallway.

"Good Lord! Was he old?"

Polly Jane shook her head. "No, Phil. That's just it! He was only three! There's something going on. But no one had broken in! Betsy checked. And both doors were definitely locked!"

"Marcia left that interior garage door unlocked when she left, because I watched her just pull it closed. But two of my men were there not long after picking up some evidence, and they locked everything up after themselves."

"Why would a young pup just die like that? He's not often left alone, but he has his own news-papered corner as an indoor lav if he chooses. On top of which, they have water out for him in nearly every room of that house."

"Yeah, now that I think about it the dog was feeling fine yesterday, practically turning somersaults. Let me just grab a muffin and I'll go right over."

As Philip munched a whole wheat English muffin with a quick slathering of butter, he called Fredericton and directed Woody to meet him at the Grahams' as soon as possible with a squad car. Then, he kissed P.J. lightly on the cheek, ran out the back door, crossed the garden diagonally and arrived at Betsy's house to retrieve the key.

"Oh, my word! That gave me half a fright, that did!" she exclaimed. "I didn't touch a thing, Inspector! Not with all that's goin' on in this village. But there's something awful wrong there. Poor wee creature had been throwing up, too. I'll clean it up later, if you like, but I thought you might need it left as is!"

Another senior citizen who enjoyed watching her television murder-mysteries, Phil thought, amused, as he reassured her. "You did just right, Betsy. My sergeant is meeting me over at the Grahams', shortly. We'll take the dog's body into the lab in Fredericton." He thanked her and wound his way around the front heading to the doctor's house once more.

By the time Woody arrived, Philip had done a thorough investigation and had scraped samples of the dog's vomit from the carpet and the kitchen floor as well as placing its body in a plastic bag.

"Are we vets now, or what?" Woody asked as he entered from the garage.

"Come in. This all fits somehow, I'm sure of it!"

"Fits what?"

"Listen, Woody. The dog is connected to the Doc being poisoned which is connected to the three murders which, we now know, was somehow connected to the robbery. You and I have to make all the pieces fit! And we have to do it today!"

Woody looked at him intently for a moment, summing up the complete situation for the first time. Then he said, "Yeah. I heard about the Hansen thing last night. Is Miss Grimball all right?"

"She is now," Philip said. "But I think we can save Len Harmon a trip out here. Elizabeth Grimball is *not* going to need a trial lawyer because she is *not* going to trial. She doesn't need a defense because you and I are close to finding the truth. Really close, Woody. If I could just—oh! Hold on!"

"Ah, a 'flash upon that inward eye'. I saw you do that same thing in the Caswell case too. What'cha got?"

"Yesterday, I thought maybe the turnovers had been poisoned. That's why I had you bring Brock in for questioning, because they came from his bakery. But when the lab tests came up negative... I've been a dolt! Marcia said Wilf Graham only had *half* of one the night he got so ill. And there was only one tested, so half a pastry is missing somewhere. I'm betting we're going to find the remains of it in our little terrier, here. In fact, this dog is going to tell us who the murderer is. Then, we just need to know *why*! And then we need proof. Come on, Wordsworth! We have to get to the lab!"

•   •   •

Genevieve was getting annoyed. Really, one minute they were certain Elizabeth was insane, then guilty, then innocent—and now this! How much more could a girl take?

As she sat at her scrambled eggs, she unfolded the newspaper and was greeted with the bold headline: ATTEMPTED PRISON ESCAPE THWARTED BY LOCAL CONSTABLE. She went on to read with disgust the media's fairy-tale version of what had happened in the early hours at Victoria's jailhouse. The Moncton Monocle reporter had again managed to get her facts twisted to describe events as she and her editor wanted to see them. Elizabeth Grimball was illustrated as an 'unfortunately incarcerated' accused murderess who had attempted escape when her cell door had been left open during an argument between herself and the night guard, one 'Ron Jensen' (they hadn't even gotten his name correct!) The local sheriff, Constable 'Chad' *(sic)* Anderson, had arrived on the scene, it said, firing a shot to prevent Grimball's flight, but injuring 'Jensen' instead. This was nothing like the story she'd heard this morning from Trudy Quigley.

However, both the Brunswick Banner and The Daily Gleaner described the capture of the three Victoria bank thieves, then quoted Inspector Philip Steele as remarking that they were 'closing in on the real killer of the homicide victims' in the little village, despite Crown Attorney Sasback insisting they had the murderer already behind bars.

Genevieve decided she would cancel her appointments for the morning. Other matters were more urgently in need of her attention.

• • •

Jake Brock threw down the Banner with distaste. What crap! Who did that Steele guy think he was? A transplant from another province, and he had those foreigners working for him too. Some Spanish guy with greasy hair, and that blackie who kept staring at him with those devilish-white eyeballs. What made them think they could take over this village? Threatening his wife, insinuating that his son had been at fault for his own death. Those Grimball women had always been tight snobs. He was proud of his cousin Rod for trying to take Elizabeth down a peg. Esther'd been the exact same. And the whole Sanderson clan before her, too! The "real killer" indeed! Who did Steele think he was kidding?

• • •

Polly Jane Whistler sorted the last bag of mail then turned over the counter to Carol. The Wolastoqiyik girl was a good worker and because she didn't stop to chat with every customer, she steadily got things done a lot faster. And *because* she was zip-lipped, P.J. felt she could indirectly help with detective work. She frequently questioned her about anything Carol might have overheard whilst people stood in line chatting. Though Carol had been uncomfortable with this situation at first, her employer assured her that she was genuinely assisting the investigation.

So now she reminded the girl to keep her ears open, then headed to her stove and her cushioned captain's chair. P.J. was exhausted. She'd been awake most of the night, worrying about Elizabeth, fretting about Philip, praying they might now have a happy life together but feeling impending doom...

Just as she was about to sit down to a cup of tea, someone rapped on her kitchen door.

"Genevieve! How have you been?"

"Fine thanks, P.J. Just getting over a chest cold, but fine now. I was on my way home from a visit with Elizabeth and thought I'd drop in to say hello."

"How is Beth this morning? She had a dreadful experience last night."

"I know. Poor thing. She does seem to be gaining strength within her own skin, though. I understand Philip thinks he's close to finding the real killer? Bethie is quite excited."

"Is he? Did he say that?" The older woman put another cup of tea in front of her guest.

"Oh, come on, P.J. You know me better than that. I'm not a gossip. What do you know?"

"Really nothing at all. If Mary Henry were alive, I'm sure all kinds of theories and suppositions would be flying through the air, but actually it's been rather quiet around here. Phil's gone most of the time."

"I suppose Mary used to make up her stories, mostly?"

"Well, she did exaggerate! It was she who first started saying Elizabeth was the murderer, I believe. Certainly didn't help the lynch-mob mentality around here."

"Indeed. Hmph—Victoria—all those white picket fences are just designed to remind us of white pointy Klansmen hats."

Polly Jane was silent. Genevieve was too young to remember the ominous KKK presence in the Upper River Valley, but it wasn't something P.J. would ever forget.

"Did Mary seem—I don't know—*strange* at all, in the last few weeks she worked with you?"

"Not really." P.J. could not figure out where this was going. "Why?"

Genevieve shrugged. "Oh, I don't know, really. Just a theory I'm developing myself, I guess. Maybe I'm wrong. Mary and Esther were close, weren't they?"

"Oh yes. As close as you could be, I suppose, two women like that. I'm not sure they would have truly listened to each other, but they did seem to be in good company together."

"Did Mary ever mention to you that she and Mort had recently bought life insurance from me? I don't mean to pry. It's just—well, I think I might be on to something that maybe Philip should know about."

"Well, yes. She did say so. She mentioned what an excellent agent you are, Genevieve."

"Oh, thanks. That's kind. I was also wondering: did Mary ever mention any life insurance policies of Esther's? Or talk about her will? Anything like that?"

Polly Jane stared at the well-dressed woman across from her. "Esther's will? Do you really know something about this? Or are you just guessing?"

"Well, I'm almost sure from something Esther told me once when I went over there to try to sell her a policy, that she had just made a codicil to her will. I was just wondering if Mary had ever mentioned such a thing in your hearing? She'd have been sure to know, don't you suppose?"

P.J. smiled. "Yes, Mary probably did know. I think she may have said something one day about witnessing an important document for Esther but frankly, I didn't always pay attention to what Mary was nattering about. It was hard to sort mail and still concentrate on her every breath."

Genevieve nodded understandingly. "I thought as much. Oh, by the way— Beaufort Bromley's out of town so he asked me to collect his mail for the next few days."

"Oh, dear. Stu's just left to deliver for your side of town. I imagine he'll have dropped both yours and Beau's at your offices by the time you get there."

"That's O.K., then. I wasn't going in to the office today. But now, I suppose I'd better just pop by to pick up the mail. Thanks for the cup of tea! See you later!"

With that, Genevieve sailed merrily out of the kitchen door again, leaving Polly Jane staring at the patterns the tea leaves had made in the bottom of her cup and thinking very, very hard.

CHAPTER FOURTEEN

"I'm afraid there's no doubt about it, Inspector," said the lab technician, stripping off his rubber gloves after examining the body of the Grahams' Boston terrier as well as samples of its vomit. "That dog was poisoned. Ate some bits of apple, looks like. We'll keep running tests till we come up with the components and ratios, but my first guess is there's no way it's natural food decay. Whatever it was, it was quick-acting and potent."

Philip discussed the details, then went back to Woodbridge who was waiting in the hall, diligently going over some of the notes he'd taken from the previous Saturday. "Woody, we have to go through the dumpster out back. I'll flip you for the top of the heap."

Woody looked at him disparagingly. "I could have sworn it was your turn to be below. Sir," he added as an afterthought.

"Call it!" Philip ordered, taking a dime from his pocket.

"Heads!"

"It's tails. I'm up. Here ya go," Phil said as he handed his sergeant a pair of gloves and led the way out the back door of the lab.

"What are we looking for?"

"Mick told me they tossed the bag the turnovers came in. Ridiculous. Should have been entered as evidence. This province needs some professional development seminars!"

"Yes, but if it was just the half turnover which had poison in it..."

"I just want that bag. I've got a feeling."

Ten minutes later with a cry of victory, Philip pulled a greasy paper bag stamped with Brock's store's stamp from the pile of plastic and glass vials, rubber gloves and old sterilizing equipment. He gave Woody a boost out, then handed the bag down to his sergeant and climbed from the dumpster himself.

"Look inside. Is there a receipt? Anything?"

"No. A few morsels of icing and crumbs."

"O.K., we're going to see if there're fingerprints left on it, though I doubt there's anything useable by now."

"Why just poison the one turnover? Not both?"

"Twice the evidence left, plus Dr. Graham famously had the sweet tooth. Mrs. Graham is apparently on a perpetual diet and makes sure everyone knows it. Even as ill as he's been, the Doc insisted on eating half of it. Thank God he *had* been sick prior to tasting it or he wouldn't still be with us."

"And, assuming he'd eat the whole thing and it did kill him, there'd be no reason to suspect anything but a bad relapse of his flu. So, no autopsy, probably."

"It's sad for little Pecan, but it's worked well for us that he decided to snoop around for human food. Doc left that half by his bed, I imagine." Phil said.

"And if the Grahams hadn't both left the house for so many hours, the dog would never have eaten it."

"Right. Now—those two cohorts of our Mr. Hauche. They were thoroughly questioned?"

"Last night. Seemed to know less than Hauche did, though."

"Or so they'd like us to believe. All right. We know Genevieve Stroud bought these pastries, then took them over to Wilf. I've got some calls to make—some background checks. I'd like you to go back to Brocks', find out what else she's bought in the last few visits to their store. I can't think how all this ties in, but it must!

If we need to, we'll get a search warrant before the morning's over. I'll meet you for lunch at my godmother's house. 12:30."

"See you there."

• • •

Behind his desk at the Fredericton station house, Philip kept himself and MacCarrey busy on the phone for the remainder of the morning. He talked to the Insurance Certification Bureau, the New Brunswick Real Estate Association and several retired lawyers who had lived in the Victoria/Nackawic area between thirty and forty years ago. When he tried to contact Beaufort Bromley's office, there was no answer. MacCarrey spoke to three American adoption agencies in Maine and Massachusetts, several hospitals in those states as well as Vermont. Philip waited on hold for nearly thirty minutes with the F.B.I. until finally speaking to a Special Agent Lipsit, while MacCarrey contacted administrators at twelve orphanages which had still been functioning in the 1930s and 1940s, on both sides of the border. Philip had MacCarrey check for previous criminal records of Jake Brock, Morton Henry and one Jennifer Brown while he spoke to a social worker named Peter La Fontaine. By noon, they had nearly all the answers for which Philip had been looking. He headed back to Victoria to meet Woodbridge.

In the meantime, Woody had enlisted the help of Chet Anderson and had been to the Brocks' general store as well as their home. Rose Brock had not been in to bake that morning and her husband was furious, assuming she'd slept in, he said.

Anderson and Woodbridge went to check but found no one at home. Her car was gone.

Next, Woodbridge called the lab, asked several questions of the technician Mick, spoke briefly to Philip at headquarters and per his instructions, dispatched Anderson to Judge Stone's offices to collect a search warrant. Woody arrived outside the cottage with the medieval arched door but found no one answering his persistent knocking. Far from inspired by the early morning rummage through the dumpster but knowing it was only a part of good detective work, he went to the back of the house and began digging through the garbage cans feeling like the prying paparazzi he'd once aspired to become. Initially he took note, with little surprise, that there were absolutely no gardens or flagstone walks on the premises. Exactly six minutes later, he noticed something even more interesting.

•   •   •

Jake Brock left the store in the hands of Sammy, his clerk. He was determined to find his wife to try to settle things between them once and for all. At first, he'd been angry that Rose hadn't shown up. Last night they'd had a fight about Rod and his roving eye. Rose had said they were made from the same mold, that all his family had a penchant for women who didn't belong to them. It had pissed him off. He'd had enough problems in the past seven days without her running off at the mouth at him. She was either bawling or pouting. He'd told her to shut her trap and had gone out to his shed to have a few beers. He figured she just wasn't coming into the store because she was angry at him.

Of course, he didn't tell those pigs any of this. They'd try to blame him for that too.

•   •   •

Philip drove straight back to P.J.'s and helped her make sandwiches while Carol tended the post office.

"This food's fresh from the supermarket?" he asked his godmother as he diced cucumbers.

"Of course. I never buy anything at Brock's, anyway. How's Wilf doing?"

Philip described a little of the doctor's condition, of what they had found out about the dog and the poison in the one apple turnover. When he told her that Genevieve Stroud had been the one to give him the baked goods, she squinted her eyes at him over the rims of her glasses.

"Phil—that's very odd, you know. Genevieve was here this morning for a visit. She was just getting over a bad cough, so I suppose she was telling the truth about going to Wilf for medication. But she was asking the most peculiar questions."

"How so?"

"Oh I don't know, really. My imagination's been getting the best of me lately. She wanted to know a lot of things Mary had told me about Esther. She said she thought she was on to something, some theory or other. She kept mentioning a will—had Mary ever mentioned a will? And then, just before she left, she wanted to collect Beaufort Bromley's mail, along with her own. Said he was out of town for a while. Of course, she has collected it for him before. It's probably nothing."

"I tried to reach Bromley this morning from Fredericton. I've been trying him on and off for several days. I guess he *is* gone. Say, hold on a minute!" Phil went to the front room doorway.

"Carol? Do you know who Mr. Bromley is? The lawyer?"

"Yes, sir."

"Have you seen him in here since you started your job?"

The native girl's beautiful coffee-brown eyes widened. "Did I miss giving him a letter or something?"

"No, no—not at all. You're doing a terrific job in here from what I've heard, Carol. I just wondered if you'd seen him. Or heard anything about him?"

"I haven't seen him, Mr. Steele. But I did hear Mrs. Jackson say to Mr. Lupeau that he'd not shown up at her house the other day for an appointment."

"Great job, Carol! Thanks!" Phil returned to his godmother. "Seems it's true Bromley's not been in for a while, then. But if he'd gone away, wouldn't he have canceled any appointments? And doesn't he even have a secretary?"

"Just part time. Her name's Melissa Townsend but she only goes in three days a week, I believe."

Woodbridge appeared at the kitchen door. He nodded politely to Polly Jane, then holding up a wrinkled scrap of paper, announced "To live and act and serve the future hour."

Philip sat down, staring. "What's that?"

"Wordsworth again. You didn't know it?" Woody asked, not trying to hide his smugness.

"No, I meant what's the paper?"

"That's what I'm telling you: 'If something from our hands has power, to live and act and serve the future hour'..."

"Sounds ominous, Mr. Woodbridge," said P.J., motioning him to sit as she placed sandwiches in front of them.

"Woody—enough." Philip held out his hand excitedly and received the crumpled paper.

He read the typed words:

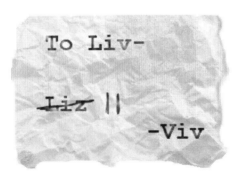

"Whose garbage were you poking about in now?"

"Stroud's. She wasn't home and Anderson's not back yet with the warrant."

Philip's face was grim. "I'm not sure it will be admissible."

"I'm not sure it even *means* anything!" Woody said. "But it's damned interesting! You don't think it will 'serve the future hour'?"

Philip and Woody peered at the small, stained scrap as they ate.

"All I can get from it is that 'Liz' *could* mean Beth—'Elizabeth', I suppose. I don't much care for her name being crossed out, esp. if the heading is 'To Live:'" Philip frowned. "Do we know other Elizabeths in the village?"

"Betsy Lawford," said P.J. promptly. "And Elizabeth Jackson, but she's closer to Nackawic."

"Hmm," said Philip.

P.J. extended her hand. "May I?"

They handed it to her and she studied it for several moments. "I don't think there's an 'e' missing on the first word. It's not 'To Live'. It's a note to 'Liv'—Livvy Brock. Everyone called Oliver 'Liverwurst.'"

"Well, damn if you didn't get in before me for once, P.J., you wily old thing!"

"So who's 'Viv'? Vivien?" Woody asked. "Do we know a Vivien? Or is it like 'vivre', 'to live', in French?"

"Vivian is a man's name as well as a woman's," commented Polly Jane.

"Vivian Mercier!" Woody said. "I studied him at uni!"

"But I can't think of any Vivian, man *or* woman around here."

Philip thought it was time to end the speculation before his sergeant began quoting from reviews on Waiting for Godot. "Or it could be 'Genevieve' itself, which would be my guess. And 'Genevieve', as I found out this morning, is French for 'Jennifer'," Philip said. "P.J., who calls Mrs. Stroud 'Gen', or 'Viv'?

"No one as far as I know. She's always been insistent on the full 'Genevieve'. Said it made her feel the height of 'haute couture'.

"And what about those parallel vertical lines? Any ideas there?"

Mystified, P.J. could only shrug and shake her head.

Woody said, "I forgot. Stroud also had the newspaper with that Connelly article in her garbage, plus two Halifax papers covering the murders. Didn't you tell me when she returned from her work trip, she didn't seem to know all the details?"

"Hmm. I did."

"Well, I'd say *that* was a pretense!" Woodbridge ran a hand through his tight-knit afro and furrowed his brow. "Because Connelly had been snooping around inside for at least an hour that day, she must have overheard from one of our team that Miss Grimball had died of a broken neck. We weren't going to release that to the media at that point, but the Monocle published it. Did Stroud know that?"

Philip thought back hard. "No, I think she just offered: 'Esther fell down the stairs' and then didn't know how Mary had died."

"Well, that's either amazingly good acting, or—"

"Woody, did you write down what Mick told you at the lab when you called?"

Taking his carefully scribed notepad from his pocket, Woodbridge leafed quickly to the last page. "The dog had diluted doses of sulphuric acid in his gut as well as something Mick called M.C.P.A.—methyl-chlorophenoxyacetic— he said you find both components in commercially mixed types of weed-killers."

"And?"

"And Genevieve Stroud does not have any gardens or pathways, front or back. Plus, her driveway is paved. But Brock said she definitely bought weed-killer that day. Even though he refused to speak directly to me and probably only coughed that up because Anderson was with me."

Polly Jane clicked her tongue disapprovingly and put the kettle on to boil.

"It was wise of you to take him along, then." Philip said. "All right, so we need more proof still—but here's what I found out." Philip took a final bite of his sandwich, then laid the crust to rest. "Thirty-four years ago, Esther Grimball got pregnant and was sent to a small 'retreat' for unwed mothers outside Stroudsville, Vermont. Her parents, needless to say, must have been furious. She would have been nearly thirty at the time. She was gone for close to a year and other than that, it is apparently the only time she has ever been away from Victoria. Whether or not it was her choice is unknown, but the baby—a girl—was given up for adoption. However, the girl remained in an orphanage and a few foster homes for the rest of her childhood years, in the system as a 'Jennifer Brown'. When she was nineteen, she married a man ten years her senior, who'd been acting as her social worker since she was fourteen because she kept running away. His name was Peter La Fontaine. She took on a French persona then 'Genevieve and Pierre' moved back to Montreal, where he was from. The marriage only lasted two years. I spoke to Mr. La Fontaine this morning. Apparently Genevieve was always obsessed with finding her roots; she was always striving for success and, according to her ex, would quote: 'stop at nothing in order to gain money and power.' He said, in French, that she was chasing the 'noblesse' without the 'oblige'. "

"And insurance agents, realtors—you don't even need college for those. But they sure can make people a bucket-load if they're good," Woody said, while P.J. listened, astounded.

"I've lived here my whole life and never heard a peep about any of this! How on earth did you ever find out?"

"Oh, I've been slow, really," admitted Philip. "But little bits and pieces of what people have said... The Real Estate Association passed a Jennifer Brown many years ago, but has no record of a Genevieve Stroud. She's been using both names, off and on. I presume she took 'Stroud' because of the town in which she was born. There's more, too. Although a lot of it is circumstantial at this point. That's what Woody and I have to get to work on this afternoon. I believe Esther Grimball grew bitter for many reasons.

She despised men because someone had left her with child. She despised her parents for taking in Elizabeth, also an orphan, when they wouldn't accept her own child. Also, it would seem her father cared about Elizabeth more than he did his own daughter. But I'm just guessing. Regardless, she felt compelled to hoard her money all these years and essentially to hide herself away as well, as a recluse. Now I'm more curious than ever to find out from Bromley about the new codicil. Because I believe it must have a great deal to do with why three people were murdered and Dr. Graham nearly so!"

"So—Genevieve was right, then—you did know something about a new will of Esther's?" P.J. interjected.

Philip glanced at her sharply. "She asked you that specifically?"

"Yes, but I told her, quite honestly, that I didn't know. At least I think maybe Mary mentioned it once, but I can't be sure."

"Good God, P.J.! You've got to be so careful what you say!" Philip explained to her about Wilf Graham having admitted to signing a codicil to the will and declaring that Mary Henry had been the other witness. "*Was* there any mail for Beaufort Bromley this morning?"

"Of course. There always is."

"Well, from what I can gather from other lawyers in these parts, Bromley knows a good deal more about this case and the conditions surrounding Esther's rather large estate. He's been sitting on the resolution to this whole thing, I think."

Chet Anderson hollered 'hello!' from the front of the post office, then came hurrying into the kitchen before any of them could rise. "I've got the search warrant!"

"Great work, Chet. Let's get going. I'm getting nervous, I don't mind admitting. Knowing too much isn't always a great thing. P.J.—I want you to stay in the front all afternoon, please. *With*

Carol. And make sure neither of you are alone for any reason until I get back."

·   ·   ·

Chet and Woody started walking down the street toward Genevieve Stroud's cottage, but Philip stopped them with a sharp 'Wait!' He ran back into the post office, spoke briefly to his godmother, hurriedly dialed a number on the phone. Four minutes later, when he returned to them, his face was ash-gray.

"What the hell is it now?" asked Woody.

"We'd better go to Beaufort Bromley's office before we do anything else. I just spoke to Miss Townsend, his part-time secretary. I haven't been using my head! She says he fired her two weeks ago because a lot of papers kept getting misfiled, or were going missing altogether. She *swears* she wasn't careless and she's also pretty sure that Bromley had no intention of going on a business trip any time in the near future," Philip said. "Also, I need one of you to volunteer to stand guard with Mrs. Quigley at the jail for the rest of the afternoon. I'm getting a really sick feeling in my gut…"

Chet spoke up quietly. "I'll do it, Phil. If you think you can trust me after all my screw-ups."

Philip held his breath a split second then laid a hand on Chet's shoulder. "After seeing how you followed your instincts last night, my friend, I would trust that you could straddle Jupiter if you said so. Listen, remember when we used to play Holmes and Watson? Remember the Sherlock violin wail we used as an S.O.S.?"

Chet grinned then puckered his lips, letting out a high-pitched open E-string whine, complete with vibrato. Philip imitated him and Woody rolled his eyes and put his hands to his ears.

"*Must* we?" he whined.

"Just keep that in mind in case we need it. And Chet—Elizabeth is not to be left alone at any point. I don't care if someone says a tornado is coming through town or that the jailhouse is on fire."

"Or else," added Woody for good measure.

"Or else what?" Chet asked.

"Or else you don't get to stand up as a groomsman in their wedding party."

Philip pretended to cuff his sergeant along the side of his face then said seriously to Chet: "Just watch your step."

"Roger." Chet Anderson scooted off in the direction of the tiny historic prison as Woodbridge and Philip climbed in the latter's car and drove to the other side of the village to the clapboard-sided office building which held both of Genevieve Stroud's businesses, in addition to the law practice of Beaufort Bromley.

The first floor housed a small but busy village tea-room, YorKups. There were no lights on in any of the offices on the second story. Tentatively, Woody tried the door of the lawyer's office where a 'closed' sign hung in the window. After several unsuccessful jiggles of the handle, the latch loosened of its own accord; the barrier swung wide. Philip was used to the informal security of this village and its citizens, but Woody shook his head in disbelief. The detectives found themselves in a ten-foot cube of a waiting room with a suede loveseat, two ferns and an over-powering odor of decay.

Swearing fiercely, Philip led the way into the adjoining room. There on the floor behind a solid cherry desk, lay the long-dead body of what had been Beaufort Bromley, LLB.

CHAPTER FIFTEEN

It was at least another hour before Inspector Steele and Sergeant Woodbridge were able to arrive at their suspect's cottage. First, from the tea-room's phone below, Woody had called Fredericton to report this fourth homicide, a stabbing. (Bromley was lying on his side with an apparent letter opener sticking out of the middle of his back). Phil had told his sergeant to order an unmarked car to come immediately to investigate and to request that they bring a search warrant for the insurance and realty offices next door. While waiting, he himself donned gloves from his pocket, then called both the jail and the post office from Bromley's secretary's desk phone, reiterating the vital importance of keeping Elizabeth and his godmother in the company of others at all times. Since, as Phil had expected, there was no recent mail delivered through the slot of the lawyer's doorway, the detectives spent the next hour searching through paperwork or files which may have been relevant—to no avail. In fact, what was conspicuously absent were any documents pertaining to his late client, Esther Grimball.

When the plain beige police car arrived, it was parked three doors down from the office building and Santana, MacCarrey and Burns exited from its doors as unobtrusively as possible, then walked almost casually up the street. As Woody had requested, none were in full uniform. After renewing his knowledge of Victoria again these last two weeks, Philip well knew that the news of more police in the village would spread within minutes. Especially when entering above a bustling tea-room.

After quick instructions on what they should be searching for in Genevieve Stroud's offices followed by an even briefer report on the condition of the body, Philip and Woody hurried to the cottage which had been their original destination following lunch. Luck was with them; Woody heaved an audible sigh of relief when they discovered Genevieve was still not at home. In contrast, Philip was not certain it was something about which they *should* be relieved. He said nothing, however, and as they burst through the screen door at the back of the house, he felt a surge of excitement, feeling they were close to answers which had plagued him, it seemed, for countless, sleepless nights.

They searched the cozy wood-paneled living room with its stone fireplace, causing an even greater mess over the space of the desk and shelves than the one which already existed. They tried to remember, however, how the disarray had been positioned, and to leave it much the same. They searched the kitchen cupboards, the basement work-bench, looked for loose floorboards, scoured the medicine cabinet and a humped-back trunk in the woman's bedroom. Even the uncluttered drawing room fell to their upheaval. However, after two hours of exhaustive work, they had still found nothing to label as evidence: no weed killer, no extra boxes containing cartridges for a .303, no documents which did not belong to Stroud herself. Just before leaving, however, Philip decided to glance through her unopened mail, still lying on the floor where it had fallen inside the front door when delivered by Stuart, the postman. He was startled to see Polly Jane's much-slanted handwriting adorning one of the envelopes. It read: "G. S.—This is your address, but...?? Please return if person unknown." The envelope was addressed to a Susan Margaret Smith.

Upon returning to the office buildings, Philip and Woodbridge were surprised to see fewer cars in the street than when they'd left.

The village residents, having watched the morgue van arrive and depart, had naturally now spread the shocking word of this fourth killing. MacCarrey had asked the YorKups owners to close for the rest of the afternoon. From a cigar-puffing Santana who was sitting with his feet up in the alcove outside the solicitor's office, Philip learned that there were no prints on the handle of the letter opener which still remained in the victim's back, even as the morgue van had rolled away with him inside, and that there were so many other prints throughout the rest of the small law office, it would be impossible to trace them all.

Nonetheless, Santana was dispatched to take Melissa Townsend's prints for elimination purposes. Next door, MacCarrey and Burns had just completed their work as well, leaving the sparsely furnished rooms in a cacophony of disarray. They had, as directed, put aside any files and notes which they had considered relevant. Philip picked them up hopefully. Upon perusal of one manila file labeled: HENRY,MORTON/MARY, he discovered only copies of their life insurance policies which Genevieve had, apparently truthfully, already described. A second file contained another policy, bought by his godmother in which he was surprised to note that he and P.J.'s sister in Ireland were co-benefactors. Next, a maroon-colored file, apparently from a different section set aside for real estate dealings, was unlabeled. Inside, Philip found lists of addresses in the village of Victoria which were considered of high market value. Of these, one was the old Sanderson house, one—remarkably, Phil thought—the fairgrounds and playing fields, and another on the main street, which Philip recognized as the location of Brock's Bakery and Convenience. He considered these. They were either historic, roomy buildings, had great views across the ravine, or—in the case of the Sanderson house—both. In addition to this, MacCarrey had set aside a note from the telephone pad on which were scrawled two brief messages: 'call J.C.' and the other, in French, read 'Tout le monde est faux'. *Everyone is False*. This was heavily underlined several times.

"Damn," Philip said. "Is this *it*? It's all interesting, granted, but there's still no evidence to arrest her!"

"Too bad we couldnae catch her in the act!" said MacCarrey.

"This was the *last* act!" Grimly, Philip turned away from the papers. "We've seen the final act, the encore, and the curtain call."

"And so the velvet curtain falls, o'er the fiery moon," quoted Woody, taking off his rubber gloves with a snap.

Philip stared at him. His eyes widened as the wheels churned. He then barked out orders in a manner never before witnessed by the officers in their short time working with Inspector Steele. All five left the building together: three escaping in the beige Chrysler toward Fredericton, Philip and Woody driving quickly into Victoria and the setting September sun.

•   •   •

Rose Brock was furious. She could never remember having been this angry and it almost felt marvelous. Her hands gripped the steering wheel with determination as she passed the road sign reading 'Moncton—8'. Last night had been more than she could take—the screaming, the abuse. After a week in which grief had ripped into her, weakened her, folded her in half, she suddenly felt stronger and taller than ever. She had found things out in these past days which she'd never thought she could bear to hear. No one could ever convince her that her son was a killer; he had been, however, as much a dishonest philanderer as his father. Even at such a young age. In the past, of course, there had been many instances where she'd caught Jake out in his lies—found a lipstick which wasn't hers in the back of the pickup, or discovered receipts for perfume which she hadn't bought (or which certainly hadn't been gifted to her!) or found his pornographic magazines in his shed. She had even suspected from some of the stories she'd heard others telling, that Jake, like his cousin Rod, had taken women against their will. But she'd always partly believed him, each time, when he said it hadn't happened, it was her imagination. Or sometimes that it 'hadn't meant anything', he'd been too drunk to know what he was doing. She had also, of course, believed him when he said he'd never hit her again.

But those days were over. She would never in future be so gullible. Naivety had been bred into her by a Southern belle Acadian mama from Louisiana and a father who'd believed until the day he died that soon someone would come along and offer him millions for his invention of a reversible metal lamp shade. It was more than time to break that pattern of blind gullibility and pure denial.

She picked up the newspaper and, keeping one eye on the road, glanced again at the headline: ATTEMPTED PRISON ESCAPE THWARTED BY LOCAL CONSTABLE. Ridiculous! She would *give* them the proof, she would tell them now: everything they needed to know to print the truth, or what she knew of it. Rod was not in the Fredericton prison hospital because he'd been a hero in some prison escape and Jake Brock was not the upstanding citizen he pretended to be as shop owner and trustee for the school board. If it took a media scandal to right all the injustices, so be it! If it meant she would have to suffer embarrassment and humiliation—well, she was going to be moving far away, anyway. Perhaps follow the Acadian trail of her ancestors right back to Louisiana. Why not? After all, she knew what their store and attached home was worth. Genevieve Stroud had told her so. She would give Jake no option but to agree to sell it.

She pulled up in front of the brick building where a huge banner announced "1971—Year of Integrity and Change in Journalism—Read the NEW Moncton Monocle!" Despite her angst, Rose laughed out loud. Or rather, she snorted. A glass door swung open for her as she entered the reception area. On the front counter she flung the paper, pointing to the article, saying "I need to see the reporter who wrote this—immediately. I have much to add, and much to correct."

Her self-assured demand came out sounding steady and unequivocal. Even she was surprised at her fortitude.

• • •

No one knew where Genevieve Stroud was and this was as disturbing to Philip as that stillness on a humid summer night when the sky gradually becomes streaked with forbidding clouds and the scent of storm in the air is almost tangible. Tonight though, the forecast was clear and—because of the idea he would afterwards credit to Woody and his misquotes—their suspect would be found one way or the other. MacCarrey was right. Without positive, undeniable proof, the only way Genevieve Stroud could be arrested was to catch her in the act. And Philip was prepared to allow for one, and only one, attempt.

He invited everyone—Woody, Chet, Mrs. Quigley, Polly Jane and even Betsy— to join Elizabeth at the jailhouse for a harvest picnic he'd ordered and had delivered at his expense from Ferris's Freddy-fried Chicken on the northern outskirts of the capital. After they had eaten, they all gathered in the cell to look at the beaming prisoner's latest painting—a bright, cheerful watercolor of pastel shirts bobbing and fluttering on a clothesline (all she could see of the outdoors from her high barred window). Elizabeth announced happily that at last she had achieved movement and life to her renewed hobby. Phil put his hand on her shoulder. Her shining face turned toward him as she thanked him for having the art materials sent out from the Fredericton art shop. Then Woody looked cautiously at his watch and the jovial air disappeared; anxiety crept in like the damp night air.

While they'd been eating, gathered with the pretense of gaiety throughout the jailhouse and with Beth's cell door flung wide and ignored, Philip had explained deductions they'd made, then painstakingly outlined the plan for the evening. Now, nerves were obviously attacking his godmother. Her hands were shaking and her glasses continually slipped to the end of her nose as she perspired.

"But how can you be sure Esther was Genevieve's birth mother?" she asked.

"I'm *not* sure. But that's the best motive we have for all the murders. Everything ties in, you have to admit. The first name change to a French version, the Stroudsville connection, the reason she moved to Victoria and tried so hard to get close to Elizabeth— not that that was her only incentive for making friends with you, Beth," he added sensitively with a glance in her direction. "I'm sure, in retrospect, that she pitied you as her younger cousin, being shut up in that huge house with a woman she'd grown to despise in her mind since she was a child. And she probably *did* genuinely like you. Who couldn't, after all?" Their eyes met warmly across Chet's shabby desk, still cluttered with plastic knives, forks and chicken bones atop a bright checked cloth.

"I believe she hadn't *intended* to frame you. The set-up just worked in her favor. Then she realized, perhaps, that with you out of the way in prison she might stand to inherit the Sanderson house herself. And because she *must* have been stealing the relevant paperwork from Bromley's offices, she also knew long before you did that Esther Grimball was actually a wealthy woman. Perhaps she would get blood tests and sue in court if she had to. She's a determined schemer, regardless. But I believe she wasn't just after the money and the property. She demanded a kind of recognition which had been missing from her life, and which Esther likely refused to give. Who knows? I'm sure we'll be able to piece more together after tonight."

"But I still don't understand," cried Elizabeth in confusion. "I thought—that is, remember when Genevieve came here and tried to lie about sending me the flowers, Phil? She could hardly keep a straight face, nor could she look me in the eye when I thanked her!"

"Yes. Double bluffing, I suppose." Philip smiled. "I recall you said she was no good at lying. She's had everyone fooled."

"So then, why not just introduce herself when we first met? Why not tell me everything? We could have shared—"

"Ulterior motives in a mind as warped as hers can lead to reasoning which is completely rational to them, totally irrational to the rest of the world." Philip shook his head slowly. "I've seen this kind of justification in so many cases."

"But why kill the others if she just wanted Esther dead?" Chet said through a toothpick propped in his molars.

"Well, we're still only guessing at this point, remember. I suspect, though, that Esther had caught Oliver trespassing: either stealing the gun or blowing up cartridges virtually in their backyard. It's possible she *did* know later that he was involved in the bank robbery. It might have been Esther after all that he'd intended to meet that night, to scare her or maybe even to kill her to keep her quiet. But my gut instinct is that no matter how it came about, Genevieve Stroud is at the root."

"Evil bitch," Woody said.

"Obviously she wanted anyone connected with the new codicil dead. Why? I have yet to figure out completely. But when that's sorted, we'll also find most of the answers, no doubt. It's my bet she didn't want anyone to know there'd been an addition, a second witnessing. So Wilf, Mary and Bromley himself all had to go. Luckily, Wilf's fairly tough to fight his way through at least two doses of poison. For I suspect he never had flu at all, that she'd tried poisoning him at least once before. Now, tonight, we're also relying on Genevieve believing that Mary didn't take her sworn secrecy very seriously. If she even *suspects* that P.J. also knows about the codicil..."

"Tssk! I don't know how she can just kill people off for no reason. I mean, she doesn't even *know* if I know," Polly Jane said. She bit her lip with worry.

"She can't take any chances at this point. Why do you think she's removed all the evidence from her home and gone elsewhere? She knew damn well we were on to something. That's why she came to see you. Now then, are we all set? Everyone knows his or her part? And Mrs. Quigley, you ride shot-gun on Elizabeth until you hear from us. Oh, and neither of you eat or drink anything unless you've prepared it yourself. Don't even use your tea bags if they've been around longer than yesterday. Sulphuric acid and M.C.P.A. can appear in the damnedest places. All right, troupes? Let's go!"

Elizabeth stood tentatively and took Philip's arm as she led him aside. "I'm scared, Phil. The risk... "

"Beth, you'll be fine as long as you keep your wits about you. Mrs. Quigley's a staunch old girl and—"

"Oh, good grief, I'm not scared for *me*! I'm worried sick about *you*!"

Phil sucked in his breath sharply and took her hands in his, clasping them tightly to his chest. As he bent to kiss her softly, Trudy, Betsy and Polly Jane stood quickly to wrap up the remains of the picnic while Woody winked amiably at Chet as they headed for the door.

• • •

The rich amber glow of the September moon shone radiantly down in sparkling shadows along the flagstone paths of Polly Jane's garden. Swathed in white cotton with a billowing veil of tulle trailing behind, a figure danced gracefully among the tall, feathery marsh plants near the bird fountain. Limbs were stretched taut as a silent waltz accompanied the solo ballet. The dancer swooped to one side, lightly tripping toward the crest of the knoll where the roses climbed the trellis near P.J.'s house. Then, back again toward the weeping willow. Both dancer and willow were now swaying in the golden light as stars flickered high above. This was the time to feel wholly alone, yet exultant in the whispering breezes and cricket trills of the autumn night. Though the white tulle which wound about the mouth, nose and eyes slightly impaired sight, the melodious mental rhythms kept the replica of an old-fashioned Harvest Hunt Ball alive with motion for close to an hour.

And of course the dancer was *not* alone. Lurking in the limbs of a pine tree at the far side of the garden, a pair of eyes never wavered from the swooping figure. As a cloud passed over the ochre moon, dimming the slightly overgrown trail, the dancing figure stumbled and then a heavy force created a slam against the wood-pile that caused immediate pain and a stifling shortness of breath. But an instant later, the high-pitched singing of a violin rang out. Chet hit the ground running, the old signal bringing on a flash of decades-old deja-vu. Woody, too, left his station at the corner of the house and joined the chase, pausing only to bend over the figure in white, doubled over a cord of stacked logs.

"You O.K., Phil?"

Still gasping for air from the effort of shrilling the summons after being knocked in the solar plexus by the garden hoe, Philip nodded, gritting his teeth. "Go *get* her!"

Rapidly disentangling himself from the reams of white cloth, Philip swore. If Chet were fast on his feet as he'd once been... But then he heard a shout. As he hastened to run after them, in the direction of the street, a glint of metal shone in the moonlight just ahead.

"She's got a knife!" Woody bellowed at Chet as both men advanced and leaped on her with one motion, wrestling Genevieve Stroud to the pavement.

Philip arrived just in time to snatch the blade from her hand as Chet pulled her to her feet. Woody then yanked her arms roughly behind her back and predictably misquoted Thomas Gray: "A Halt called now, you tower of *Evil*."

She spat over her shoulder at him like a hissing cat.

PART THREE

"And the loud chanting of unquiet leaves
Are shaken with earth's old and weary cry,
(When) arose, on the instant clamorous eves,
A climbing moon upon an empty sky,
*

…Ah, faeries dancing under the moon,
A Druid land! A Druid tune!"
–Yeats

CHAPTER SIXTEEN

Rose Brock drove on through the early morning, rubbing her weary eyes. They had left behind a clear sky in Moncton, but as they neared Crabbe Mountain, rain was gently falling. The windshield wipers were starting to lull her into a dangerous doze and she thought about turning on the radio. But when she glanced over at her passenger, she was amused to see that the hippie-journalist with whom she'd been up all night had finally fallen asleep herself, mouth slightly skewed to one side just like Oliver had once slept. Rose unrolled the window an inch instead, to allow some fresh air to keep her alert, then clasped the wheel between both gloved hands. She was determined to make it back to Victoria before Philip Steele did any more damage with his misleading media quotes.

While going over the many truths in the case of Esther Grimball, Rose had come to a dawning realization about herself, just as she had watched from Jenny Connelly's picture window in Shediac as the sun rose over the ocean. She was finally *free*! It felt wonderful to at last have knowledge which would enable her to break the bonds of her abusive relationship. Rather than despise the early-thirtyish woman beside her, she felt she owed her a great deal. Their frank honesty throughout the hours before daybreak had led them both down a path of personal awakening.

Victoria was only another few miles. Then they could set their confrontations in motion. No more sitting quietly in a corner and waiting for permission to speak! *Action* would set her free. Galvanize her spirit. It had been a sad, but most enlightening week.

•   •   •

Someone was pounding heavily on the door knocker of the cedar-shingled salt-box as rain drummed on its sagging roof. The mums in the window boxes shook as the frames were rattled by the persistent hammering. Polly Jane sat up in bed, glanced at her alarm clock which read "7:15", then threw back the covers, reaching for her fuzzy slippers with her toe as she tucked herself into her robe. Good heavens! She'd over-slept. They all had, she thought, as she noticed the door of the guest room still closed and presumed that poor Bethie could well snooze until noon. She scuttled downstairs. As she hurried to the front door, she passed the library and noticed Phil's angular body stretched out in exhaustion on the couch within, an ice-pack still on his abdomen and a pillow over his face.

Worried that her mail would not get sorted in time for Carol's imminent arrival, she flung open the door, prepared to get rid of whoever was creating such boorish noise. On the stoop stood a belligerent Mort Henry.

"Where the hell's your godson, P.J.? I gotta speak to him."

"He's fast asleep, Mort. What's the hurry?" Polly Jane put her fuzzy pink dressing gown between the door and her angry neighbor to bar his way.

"What the gol-dang does he mean, arresting my insurance broker and haulin' her off to Fredericton, eh? She ain't got no partners in the business, you know. It'll be mod'rate tied up for months in court!"

"Mort, what on earth are you talking about?"

"Whatcha think? My policy!" whined the man. "You know, 'cause of Mary's dyin' 'n' all. I got a right to that money and I need it *now*. I'm takin' a trip up north for some huntin' this year and I want to rent a cabin."

P.J. stared at the man before her as though she'd just heard a description of an albino tiger with purple polka-dots running loose in York County. Then she shook a twitching finger in his face hissing, "Mort Henry, you should be ashamed! Standing here practically at dawn with your knickers in a twist over a few measly dollars so you can go off and shoot some innocent deer on the money from your wife's murder! I've never heard the likes of it! Genevieve Stroud is a homicidal criminal. She should have been locked up years ago but now that she is, all you can do is complain you might have to wait a few weeks until you can go beer-guzzling with your buddies. Now get out of here! We were up all night and I've got two exhausted people inside whom you've no doubt managed to awaken!" With that, Polly Jane spun around on the heel of her slippers and marched through the door again, shutting it firmly behind her.

Appreciative applause stopped her as she headed back upstairs to change and get herself ready to work in the front. Philip had entered the hall, clapping his hands inaudibly, laughing gently.

"'Atta girl, Godmother! Don't ever lose that spunk!'"

"Oh, Phil, dear. He's such a useless man! Even Mary had more sense. How are your ribs? You're sure nothing's broken?"

"Well, it was quite a whack, but I can honestly say I've never felt better in my life. And just grateful she didn't fancy a bit of night-time sharp-shooting instead."

"Why do you suppose she didn't just stab you—'me'—right away?"

"She knew all that swaying and prancing would just cause the knife to glance off, I guess. Thought she'd knock the wind out of you first! I appreciate your leaving your gardening tools handy at the side, by the way!"

He smiled as he heard a light tread on the floor above him. He felt his heartbeat quicken. "Thank you so much for letting Beth come here last night, P.J.. It would have been dreadful for her to go home to that cold, dark house alone. And there was no way I wanted her behind bars a second longer. We'll go over to the Sanderson place today, do some more standard procedure stuff, then she can settle into her home. In as many rooms as she likes!" He then said, under his breath, "Bless her!"

His godmother touched his cheek merrily. "If blessings are all you say from now on when you mutter away to yourself, I can go to my grave a content woman." She slid past him to get dressed and on the stairs passed a refreshed-looking Elizabeth on her way down.

"Good morning, Mrs. Whistler. I'm just—"

"Now how many times do I have to tell you, Beth? You just call me plain old P.J. I refuse to answer to anything that makes me sound like some painter's ancient mama in a rocking chair."

Elizabeth laughed. "O.K., P.J. I just wanted to say I thought I'd found my freedom in that jailhouse, but this morning, despite the rain, I feel as though it's literally the first day of the rest of my life!"

Philip heard this as he stood at the bottom of the stairs, feeling suddenly shy and uncertain. It was a most unusual emotion for him. As Polly Jane continued her ascension, Elizabeth walked slowly down to meet him. She stood on the last step, from which height she could look directly into his eyes. They paused for a long tentative moment that way, just looking at each other, swallowing each other.

Philip cleared his throat, smiling weakly because his pulse was racing at a most alarming rate. "Beautiful morning, beautiful woman," he whispered.

"It's raining," she teased.

"You're free."

"All thanks to you."

"You'd never have been there in the first place if I hadn't arrested you."

" Mmm. A synonym for 'arrest' is 'attract', you know."

"It's the first time I've ever made an 'arrest' of this kind, then."

"For me, too."

They stood still, not touching, only looking more deeply into reflecting glimmers beyond their dark round pupils. Finally, self-conscious, it was Elizabeth's turn to clear her throat. "It *is* a beautiful morning—the most gorgeous I've ever seen."

Philip grinned and imitated her. "But it's raining!"

"Good thing the skies stayed clear as long as they did last night for your moon dance! Oh, I *wish* I could have seen you!"

"I wasn't nearly as graceful as P.J. is, I can assure you—and as Woody and Chet will take every opportunity to tell you, as well as the whole of the Fredericton detachment. But it fooled Genevieve for the split second we needed it to."

"You risked your life for me."

"No. *Because* of you. You know, I quite like you there on that step."

"Why?"

"You're at the perfect level for me. I don't have to dip." He leaned toward her, never taking his eyes from her alive, glowing face.

"You calling me names? What do you mean 'dip', mister?"

"Mmm. I mean *this*," Philip said, as he closed his eyes slowly, their lips meeting with a hunger they had not yet felt for each other. Prior to this moment, their kisses had been brief, feathery questions. Now, Philip pulled her toward him with both hands, a passionate craving overtook them and as the rain pelted harder on the cedar shakes above, the intensity of the kiss also increased into a most profound answer.

A slight cackle of delight trickled down from the top of the stairway. The couple came up for air. As Elizabeth unwound her arms from about Phil's neck, he looked up at his godmother, now fully clothed and preparing to descend again.

"It looks as if I don't need to worry about making you two any breakfast; your hunger seems to have acquired a taste for something other than my waffles, Philip."

And she peered over the tops of her glasses at them and giggled.

•   •   •

In a hospital bed in Fredericton, Wilf Graham rolled over and moaned. Marcia, sitting at his side, reached for his hand and clasped it tightly.

"Bethie. I–I shouldn't have told her. I didn't know…"

"Shh, dear. Everything's fine now. The real killer's in prison. Elizabeth's out free and happy. She and Philip called me this morning before I left to come here. Don't fret or you won't get well."

"Oh, God—I ache all over. Feel like someone took my insides and stretched them outside and up over my head. And this I.V.'s in wrong; the vein shouldn't be…"

"Yes, Wilf. But they saved your life." Marcia was used to his complaining, especially when he was ill. Maybe it was time he retired. He was just sixty, but perhaps it was time he went on to something new, found some hobbies. No one knew better than Marcia that doctors always made the worst patients.

Wilfred moaned again. "But I–I can't. My gut's all bruised and my throat feels scraped clean."

Primly, Marcia pursed her lips together and raised her eyebrow at him. "Perhaps now, dear, you'll be cured of your sweet tooth."

•   •   •

"There's some quote about not bequeathing a tumbled-down house. I can't remember it…" mused Woodbridge as he and Philip entered the Sanderson house later that morning.

"Small miracle!" Phil grinned. "But are you really so sure the old lady bequeathed the house at all? There's an awful lot unanswered about that latest will of hers."

"If Madame Accused doesn't decide to tell us what she did with it, how will we know what was in the codicil? Even if Wilf Graham gets better, he didn't get a good look at it, you said."

"No, that's true. But I have a feeling Esther kept a copy here, didn't give them all over to Bromley after the signatures. We'll have to check through every possible place, and Elizabeth is coming over here in a few hours to show us a few hiding spots her aunt kept."

They began the search on the ground floor in what had been Esther's own bedroom. It was full of cheap clutter. Her bureau was stacked with magazines and newspapers which Woody offered to sort through. Decidedly better than the bottom of a garbage dumpster, he thought. Philip picked his way through her clothes closet, checking in several shoe boxes which were piled in the back on a shelf. However, they revealed only loafers and slippers from various decades. Esther, it seemed, had thrown nothing away. Next, he searched under her bed. Here, he revealed a box of jewelry in which were either old and expensive heirlooms, or particularly good imitations. Phil couldn't tell.

Suddenly an exclamation from his sergeant caused him to stand abruptly. He hurried to join him at the heavy cherry dresser.

"Got something?"

"Maybe so. Take a look." Woody handed over a series of newspaper articles, yellowed and brittle with age, paper-clipped together at the top.

"VICTORIA JUVENILE ACCUSED OF DISORDERLY CONDUCT" read one headline from a Saint John newspaper almost forty years old. The article went on to describe the behavior of a teenage boy from the village who had 'teased and grabbed at several women who complained to the owner of *The Horse and Harbor* tavern on Hampton Street'. The boy remained unidentified as he was 'under an age' and the women had decided not to press charges, despite his repeated threats to 'get them yet'.

A second, less yellowed article was boldly titled: "RAPE VICTIM DEMANDS RESTITUTION". The story had appeared in 1943. It told of a woman, Emma Lyn Meyers of Church Road, Harriston, who had been walking home from a baby shower one summer evening when one T.J. Brock of Victoria had leaped from the bushes and 'attacked her in a sexual manner'. Ms. Meyers, it said, would see the twenty-six-year-old man prosecuted."

A sequel to this article was immediately behind it in the pile and Philip read the first paragraph with keen interest. 'Thomas Jacob Brock of the village of Victoria, north of Fredericton', it said, had been acquitted of rape and assault on a 'legal technicality'.

Woody was still riffling through more papers. "What do you think, sir?"

"I think our Miss Esther Grimball might have had it in for the Brocks as much as they were vindictive toward the Sandersons and Grimballs," Philip said, reading on. An entire roster of birth announcements from a hospital in Stroudsville, Vermont was next, dated 1937. One of the names appearing was 'Jennifer Brown', newborn daughter of an E. Grimball.

Woody glanced over his shoulder. "Well, that just confirms what we already knew about Genevieve Stroud."

"Yes. But why 'Brown', I wonder? Why not 'Smith', or 'Jones'? Why give the baby a name at all if she was immediately going up for adoption?"

"Maybe she really cared about it, but her family insisted she give it up—or she'd be written out of their wills? Maybe the adoption agencies needed more reference. Who knows?"

"Or maybe she wanted that name to be kept because it reminded her of the father."

"You mean Genevieve's biological father might have been a Brown? Old Maid Esther had been running around with Farmer Brown, eh? Sounds like a dirty nursery rhyme."

"Or *Brock*. Very similar surnames."

Woodbridge stared. "You think she was in love with Jake Brock? A.k.a. Thomas Jacob of Victoria?"

"Whatever made us believe she'd been in love with *any* man? That was a conclusion to which we never should have leaped. If she kept all these articles, it's my bet Jake Brock raped her as well. The Sanderson family would have never wanted that to be made public, so they sent her away when she discovered she was pregnant. But she wanted Brock held accountable in some way, so chose a surname which was close to the baby's father's. It makes sense, Woody. No wonder she was so disagreeable about men all her life, no wonder she didn't want Genevieve back in town, haunting her, making friends with her niece. If in fact, she even knew who she was."

"And no wonder Genevieve killed her own half-brother, if that's the case?"

"Hmm. Perhaps. I still think there's more to that death than just personal emotions like anger or jealousy. Let's keep searching. Elizabeth will be here in another hour."

Leaving the bedroom, they entered the large parlor which they had used last Saturday as their meeting room. Despite the musty aura and the dust sheets covering the antiques, it occurred to Philip that at one time it must have been a most beautiful chamber. Someone long before Esther Grimball had clearly once cared about keeping up the appearance of wealth. The Victorian architecture of Fredericton, renowned for its heritage buildings, had extended to many of the outlying towns and villages in the Upper River Valley; Victoria was no exception. The huge windows of this room were draped with a heavy gold brocade with tassels. The walls had been stenciled along the marbleized ceiling border with elaborate designs. Intricately carved tables and chairs lay beneath the dust covers. Lying atop the darkly stained hardwood floor, the carpet was of an ancient Oriental design, woven with pine greens and wheat golds.

"I hope Elizabeth will bring this room back to life—*make* it a living room," Philip said, thinking of Genevieve Stroud's odd metaphor for her own gathering rooms.

"It must have been something at one time," Woody agreed.

"I'll take the far side; you can go through this end." They began again, turning out drawers, checking underneath the furniture, behind paintings on the wall, but to no avail. "Why don't you finish off here then take the kitchen and the cellar?" Phil suggested, twenty minutes later. "I'm going up to the third floor and I'll work my way down to the second."

"Aye, aye, Captain."

The men separated and Philip climbed the two flights of stairs to what must have been built originally as servants' quarters. The rooms here under the eaves were compact, undecorated and most now even unfurnished. He checked under the single iron-clad bed in one tiny gabled room, almost choking from the layers of dust and mouse droppings which had settled on the pine-board floor. Brushing off his pants and sweater as he stood up, he crossed to the tiny closet door, yanked it open. As he turned on his flashlight and bent down, he noticed the dust in the closet had been disturbed. He could even detect a small footprint, completely intact. Yet the room's floor outside the closet had seemed untouched.

He studied the print for a moment and then, suddenly inspired, began tapping the walls of the four-foot square space. Hearing one paneled section decidedly hollow and feeling as though he'd just been transported to the pages of a Hardy Boys story, Philip pushed and pried on the panel until it swung open, revealing a narrow set of wooden stairs leading downward. Despite stepping lightly as he descended at least forty steps, his shoes echoed against the battered old unfinished wood. He remembered now that Elizabeth had several times mentioned hearing people 'going up and down the stairs' while she'd been lying in her drug-induced state of repose. She had even distinctly described hearing 'Chet' climb from the third floor before going back down and leaving the house to get his cigarettes. But when Phil had questioned Chet on this point, he'd insisted he had only gone up and down the first flight of *main* stairs; he'd never been on the third floor, he'd said.

Philip came to a landing where he noticed a paneled cut-out, behind which he clearly could hear Woody rummaging noisily in cupboards. This had obviously been the servants' entrance through to the kitchen, long ago blocked off. Grinning, he tapped on the wall.

"Detective Woo-woo-woodbridge!" he called in a haunting ghost-like voice.

"Hey! What the hell?" came the startled exclamation from the other side.

"I'm behind this wall. I know where Stroud's been hiding out and how she knew Chet had left the house and how she got at Mary so quickly! Meet me in the cellar. I'm going on down."

He turned to proceed down one last, narrow flight at the bottom of which, in the gloomy darkness, he tripped over something which forced him to sprawl against the wall. The wall flung open with the force of his weight and he tumbled out onto the cement floor of the basement, his flashlight knocked from his right hand.

"Geez! Are you all right?" asked Woody, helping him to his feet.

"Turn on your flashlight, will you? Shine it right in there."

In the strong beam, both men stared at the pile of junk inside the little cupboard-like opening behind the pantry wall. Lying there upon the floor sat a bag of pretzels, several juice bottles, a briefcase, a cushion, blanket, and a green metal tin labeled "Langley Landscaper's Lawn and Garden Spray—for the unwanted growth of weeds, burdock and sumac."

Woody shook his head and swore under his breath. For once, no classical poet sprang to mind as he simply said, "Well, holy crap."

CHAPTER SEVENTEEN

Half an hour later, they gathered in the parlor: Woodbridge, Philip, Chet Anderson, Elizabeth and Polly Jane. Elizabeth had, with a great flourish, flipped and snapped all the dust sheets off the furniture and extended her hand with a newfound hostess' pride, indicating that her guests should sit in the over-stuffed chaise longues or davenports. Philip had started a fire in the wood furnace in the basement and already the deathly chill of the house had diminished. Outside, the rain had let up. A hint of bluer sky could be seen above the tree-line of the gully.

"So, start at the beginning, Holmes." Chet said, then screeched his violin-string sentry call.

Woody covered his ears and said, "Not *again*!"

Polly Jane chuckled, patting Elizabeth's arm. "Those boys used to drive me crazy when they were teenagers with that silly whistle."

"Yes, but it served me well last night, P.J." Philip put in, patting his abdomen. "If Chet hadn't leaped out of that tree as fast as he did, I might be lying next to Wilf in the hospital."

"Or worse." Elizabeth shivered.

"And even though Betsy and I were at our separate windows with our phones close at hand, we neither of us saw a thing. So we were worse than useless," lamented Polly Jane.

"Not at all. I felt more secure having all those pairs of eyes, and the extra back-up."

Woody cleared his throat. "If you don't mind, sir, I'd like a shot at piecing everything together before you fill in the blanks for us."

Bowing his head in assent, Philip said "Fine. It'll be excellent preparation for your new promotion."

"Say again?"

Philip smiled tenderly at Elizabeth. "Well, it's not official yet, but this was my last case. I'm quitting the force. And I'm going to recommend that Detective Inspector Zareb Norbert Woodbridge replace me. So please proceed—with as few literary quotations as possible, if you don't mind."

Grinning broadly, Woody stood up and threw back his broad shoulders. "I guess it really began back with the death of your teacher friend, Miss Grimball. Percy Collins. From what I can gather, Oliver Brock had had an obsession with you for over a year because you'd been so kind to him. And when you started seeing Mr. Collins, the evil violent streak which apparently runs in the Brock family reared its ugly head once more. Oliver knew where Percy lived, on that farm just out of town, and he used to pull pranks with Paul Guthrie's herd of dairy cows. He'd likely seen the teacher driving home from school at the same time every day, on his way to do chores with his father and uncle. Guthrie said you could set your clock by him, almost. Anyway, before he accidentally shot that Holstein then had his gun taken away, he'd likely already been getting ideas. He practiced spooking the herd around the pasture and one day last May he skipped his classes, went out to the Guthrie place, cut a section of fence, and herded the cows out into the road. He timed it perfectly with Collins' return home. His car came around the bend, swerved to miss the animals, and crashed head first into the telephone pole."

Turning ghostly pale, Elizabeth gasped. Polly Jane gallantly moved over to allow space on the davenport sofa for Philip, who sat down and put his arm comfortingly around Beth. His godmother rested her hand on his shoulder for a moment, then patted his knee wordlessly as Woodbridge coughed and continued.

"It would be hard to say, I suppose, whether the boy had had fatal consequences in mind for poor Mr. Collins. Right, sir? Like as not, he just hated him because he was so jealous, and wanted to put him out of commission for a while. Or maybe to scare him off? But we've checked into some of Genevieve Stroud's records, discovered she had been showing a farmhouse out on that road at four o'clock that afternoon. We can only surmise, until such time as the evil witch admits it,—"

"If ever," Philip said, lips pursed.

"—that she saw young Brock leaving the pasture right after the accident had been cleared and later, knowing of his infatuation for Elizabeth, put two and two together and came up with her own charming form of blackmail."

"But I still don't understand how Genevieve Stroud is connected with all of this." Chet complained. "It makes no sense to me at all."

Woodbridge looked at Philip. "Perhaps you'd better take over. I get stuck on some details in that myself."

"It's another tragic story, I'm afraid. As we've just been able to piece together today, we now think that thirty-four years ago, Jake Brock, in his mid-twenties and still unmarried, continued the tradition of animosity which his father had harbored toward the Sanderson family for firing him. He raped Esther Grimball who was of course older than he and considerably less agile. We're fairly certain, having glanced at some of the notes Stroud kept in her briefcase, that she was the result of that unfortunate crime."

"Good Lord!" Chet said, shaking his head in disgust.

Polly Jane was startled. "But of course! That makes more sense than a single middle-aged spinster in that decade going out and getting herself pregnant. Ever since you told me about her pregnancy, Phil, I found it hard to believe Esther had had some love affair, or the like!"

Esther's niece bit her lip. "It also explains her uptight cynicism and bitterness toward the world—men especially."

"Right," Philip said. "But her family—her parents and grandparents—either didn't believe she was raped or refused to believe that she wasn't partly responsible for her own condition. With all the strings their wealth could yank, they arranged for Esther to be sent off to New England to have the baby. She named her Jennifer Brown. We think because "Brown" was close to "Brock" and perhaps Esther always thought to make the Brock family responsible in some way, likely after her parents were gone. Or perhaps it just began as a clerical error, and she had originally written "Brock" as the father. Who knows? Regardless, the baby was immediately put into a huge orphanage on the outskirts of Stroudsville, Vermont. Here's a copy of the birth record from the orphanage." Philip handed Elizabeth one of the plastic bags in which all of the evidence from Genevieve's briefcase had been placed.

"Oh, so she really was my cousin! What a shame we couldn't have been friends. Instead of—"

"Don't forget, Beth, that she could just as easily have killed you. For some reason, she didn't. Though she used you to get information on her background, she must have actually thought of you as a friend as well. Even a sister figure? Perhaps she didn't realize she had been conceived through rape. She knew Esther had given her up for adoption and probably resented, even hated her, for it. That was her motive for coming to Victoria in the first place."

"But how on earth did she know Esther was her birth mother? That's what I can't understand. The hospital wouldn't have released parental information without the consent of both parties." Chet shook his head, confused.

"No, they wouldn't have. But today Woody and I discovered, in this brown briefcase of our Mrs.'Stroud's', that she had been receiving information and money for many years through the family lawyer, Beaufort Bromley—from right here in Victoria, New Brunswick. Whether it was Esther herself who set up this secret arrangement after her parents were gone, or whether it was someone else in the family, we may never uncover. It was certainly enough for our resourceful Genevieve to go on, though."

"So she moved here, got herself set up in offices right next to Bromley's and what—broke in at night and stole files?" asked Beth.

"As near as we can figure. Or at least she read whatever she needed to know in situ. That is one reason his unfortunate secretary was fired; Bromley thought it was she, of course, who was carelessly misplacing things. Naturally, when she was let go, it made it that much easier for Genevieve to continue researching and to kill off the old man without anyone discovering it for nearly a week."

"Ooo, that Satan spawn! I used to play bridge with Beaufort, years ago now. He was a very upstanding human. And she killed him—why? Because of the codicil to Esther's will, which otherwise only Mary and Wilf knew about?" Polly Jane asked.

"Yes. Plus, of course, she was pretty sure you had heard about it too, P.J. That's why you were next on her list, why she attacked 'you' dancing in the garden. She couldn't risk word getting out that there had ever been anything other than the original will, but until today we didn't know why."

"Do you mean—you mean you finally found it?" Elizabeth spoke up querulously.

"Woody—?"

"Yes, she'd swiped all the copies from Bromley's office. They'd been in three different files and she found them all. But he must have suspected something was up. He just hadn't started putting it all together. I guess we shouldn't read the will right now. Officially, another solicitor will have to be appointed?" He looked questioningly at his superior, who nodded. "But suffice it to say the *original* will was to have looked after the needs of both

Esther's niece and the daughter she'd been forced to give up, with the necessary information attached to contact her."

"So, why did Esther change that recently, then?"

"Remember, Stroud said she'd tried to persuade Esther to buy life insurance but had had no luck?" Philip supplied. "I suspect had Esther fallen for the offer, her daughter would somehow have made herself the benefactress, unbeknown to Esther herself. Or perhaps she confronted her mother about her birthright. We may never know. If she's unwilling to give an honest account before her trial, as I suspect... It's even possible threats were made. By them both. Regardless, Esther obviously knew something about Genevieve and was not at all impressed, because less than a month ago she drew up the codicil which would leave her birth child out completely. When Genevieve discovered this latest addition in Bromley's filing cabinet, she must have become murderously angered. And that triggered the chain of events which led to all these killings, I'm afraid."

"The evil Brock streak seems a genetic predisposition through generations, then!" Polly Jane shook her head in wonder.

With a toothpick hanging from his open mouth, Chet asked in awe, "How the hell have you ever put all this together in just over a week? And where's the bank robbery fit into all of this?"

Woody said, "That had me confused too. But Inspector Steele here, he never lets a little thing like a twist in criminals' noggins interfere with problem-solving. Eh, sir? Phil? I've just figured this out—you see, last night when we took Genevieve Stroud or whatever her legal name is, in to be booked, we did get a few answers out of her. Flippant though they were."

"Indeed. She was certainly glib about the few things she was willing to share." Philip put his arm around Elizabeth's shoulders.

"She's signed an initial statement which admits she'd been psychologically blackmailing Oliver Brock, whom she'd also discovered through more of Bromley's documents, was her probable half-brother. At least, this revolting thing," Woody said, holding up a piece of onionskin in another plastic sleeve from the briefcase, "dated thirty-four years ago, says 'Esther Grimball, daughter of Patty Sanderson and John Grimball *alleges* that Thomas Jacob Brock is her attacker in a criminal rape, uncharged due to parental sanctions.'"

"Do you mean they wouldn't even believe her when she had the courage to *tell* them the truth?" Elizabeth asked, slipping away from Philip's grasp in her indignation. "That doesn't sound like my grandfather!"

"Didn't I tell you a few days ago that your aunt must have had her reasons, Bethie? That she probably deep down, really did want to take care of you in the only way she knew? She's been trying to protect you, from the world as she perceived it."

Chet Anderson didn't care about all these emotional issues. "Go on about the blackmailing."

"Genevieve Stroud either saw Oliver Brock's connection with the Collins' death or she may have caught him stealing the rifle out of the cellar here. Or perhaps both. We hope if we can't get it out of her, we'll get Hauche or another of the thieves to cough up something Oliver might have said. He and Daddy Jake were under Stroud's scrutiny, I expect. I'll say this for her: when she sets her mind to something, she doesn't take kindly to impediments of any sort. Hell, last night she was strong as a bull, wrestling off both me and Chet, ready to slash us into strips. If Phil hadn't grabbed her knife … Anyway, she saw a useful purpose for poor old Liverwurst. She found out he and his dumb-ass cohorts across the gully were planning on holding up the bank and she promised she wouldn't let on to the cops about Collins *or* Oliver's part in the robbery if he would take Elizabeth away. See—" here Woody paused, his voice softening politely as he looked in her direction, "she didn't want to kill you. She thought you'd been as much Esther's victim as she was herself. But she didn't want to share any of her inheritance, either. So, knowing how Oliver felt about you, she told him she'd help him get the two of you to a deserted hunting cabin in upstate Maine which she knew about from her real estate work. Providing he *stay* there with you. And drug you and keep you hostage, if that's what it took."

"*What?*"

Philip's lips stretched to a thin grimace at Elizabeth's exclamation. She moved back into his protective arm. "That's ridiculous. They were going to *kidnap* me?"

"Well, this is what she's telling us, be it nonsense or not. And what she likely told Oliver. So he was lulled into a sense of security, could daydream about his fantasies coming true with his beloved teacher. If you disappeared and no one knew about Esther's codicil, Stroud could prove who she was and live here in this house on her own. In time she'd declare you 'deceased' and collect your share of the Sanderson/Grimball estate as well. And then be able to sell up," Philip said, glancing at his godmother as she squeezed his arm. "She might have even made your disappearance look like a suicide-at-sea, body never to be discovered, but with a forged note which left no doubt as to your 'intention'."

Chet said, "*Hell.* Wouldn't put it past her, considering."

"That's it!" Woody was on a roll now. "That's why the kid stole all the extra jewelry and the watercolor paints from his parents' store when he took the rest of the things for the robbery. He figured, in his little dopey-brain, he'd offer them to you as lures or something, Miss Grimball! Ah, I see—"

"Elizabeth, please, Sergeant."

"And with his share of the stolen money, I'm sure he felt he'd be rich enough to live forever in some secret camp in the hills of Maine, in a whole other country. Philip still insists those fake brooches and things are in some hollow tree somewhere in the ravine. But we're damned if we can find them!"

Elizabeth was struggling to take in all of this. Quietly, in a near monotone, she mumbled, "I had dreamed Oliver tried to give me a locket. That night in the cell." She shivered, and shimmied closer to Phil's warmth.

Chet was still perplexed. "If Genevieve already knew about the robbery, what the devil was she doing depositing money in the bank that day?"

"Ah, that's where her cunning twist comes in. This much she did admit to last night. You see, according to her, the idiot thugs were ten minutes late getting there. Stroud had had an extra thousand dollars meant to be taken off her person by Oliver, in front of the bank tellers. Presumably, when the other two crooks were with Mr. Ouellette. It was meant to be taken by her half-brother and used to help get her cousin 'out of the way'. There's your familial loyalty. She told us that if we ever did get wind of her connection, she thought it would throw any suspicion completely off her, having had that much money stolen herself. Oliver had told her he was getting a thousand from the thieves, so she said she'd match it if he could wrangle it from her in front of a witness. But they were late, and she couldn't keep just hanging around the bank doing nothing, so she'd been forced to deposit it."

Philip took up the story again. "Yes, she's admitted this much, I suspect because it demonstrates how clever she is. But we've not got much else. We figure she'd planned to get Oliver and Elizabeth dispensed with Friday night, drive them over the border herself. Then she'd be free to kill Esther on Saturday. And she'd left a little reminder note to Oliver wrapped around the cash in her purse." He removed the crumpled note which read:

```
          To Liv -

     ̲L̶i̶z̶ ‖
               - Viv
```

Phil passed this to Elizabeth who glanced at it, shuddered, then handed it to Chet.

"But since she'd had to deposit it all instead, she took the note home and tossed it, which is how Woody came to find it. Two of the closest rural borders close at midnight, so that's an '11' there, those hand-written lines. The time she'd planned to meet Oliver with his hostage."

"O.K., yeah," Chet said, mulling it over. "She called him Liv, as did most of the younger folk hereabouts. And I bet when she explained to him they were half-siblings, she told him to call her 'Viv'. But in secret, like. Oliver would have loved having that secret code with someone—would-a made him feel important, part of something, you know?"

Woody snorted through his long nose. " Liv and Viv, for God's sakes!"

Chet mused on. "So, basically her time confirmation to him was: *Dear Liv, Getting rid of Liz at 11, Viv.* That what you mean?"

"Simple enough for the big lummox to understand, cryptic enough to mean nothing to anyone else if discovered," Woody said.

"I've been thinking," reflected Philip. "This may be a stretch, but remember we found that list Genevieve had made of potential high-value properties here in the village? This house was listed, but so was Brocks' store. Maybe she wanted Oliver conveniently out of the country too. Maybe she was planning her next attack on the rapist who'd fathered her!"

There was a subdued silence while everyone pursued this train. Then Chet nodded. "Seems like she did her killings to both get revenge *and* to gain financially."

"So, when Oliver wasn't able to 'rob' her of her purse as planned, she deposited the cash, then threw out the note when she got home. And when Oliver and the gang did show up at the bank,

Genevieve pretended to be just as frightened, just as surprised, as everyone else?" Polly Jane asked.

"Actually," Phil said, "she was double bluffing again. She *could* have acted that way. But instead she was fairly calm and pretended to be amused by it all. Which was more in keeping with the personality she was known for around here. Cool, level-headed, detached."

"And she must have intentionally given us the wrong license number of that stolen Plymouth! That car belonged to an elderly man all the way up near Campbellton. I spent hours on that red herring! What an actress," Chet said, not without some admiration.

"'After a well-graced actor leaves the stage,… murder, though it have no tongue, will speak,'" Woody misquoted.

Elizabeth laughed despite herself. "Never mind getting him promoted, Phil! He can come and teach my English classes."

"Except he mixes two Shakespearean tragedies into one, then thinks no one will notice." Philip said.

"Whatever! Anyway, Stroud had been laying the ground work for all of this since she moved here years ago. When she stole the codicil copies from Bromley's office, she must have decided to get rid of Doc Graham and Mary Henry almost immediately. We think she began poisoning the doc with treats she kept sending over for him starting at least two weeks ago. Mrs. Graham told us she never used to send baked goods to the house. Then out of the blue, she started."

"And as for killing Mary, now that I think about it—remember the day Mary came in with cinnamon buns, P.J.? She said someone had narrowly missed her with a baseball. Of course, she'd just blamed some reckless kids on their way to school. Normal enough, but now…I wonder."

Polly Jane was in television-detective mode again. "You know what, Phil? A few days before you arrived, she came in and said a car had almost hit her, too! Of course, I thought she was just exaggerating to get attention."

"I'll make a note to question Stroud on those," said Philip.

"By then she'll have made up all kinds of other stories and she'll have her lawyer wrapped around her little finger!" Chet said mournfully. "Good Lord, you'll never get the truth out of that hustler!"

"Don't need it now," crowed Woody. "We've got enough evidence here to put her away for four or five consecutive life sentences. We found the weed-killer which we know her prints will be on, we've got her belongings and documents from her hiding place, we know how and why each of the murders was committed…"

"Whoa! Back the cart up there, Woody. Go back to why she killed Oliver in the gully that night! You're starting to confuse even *me*!" said his boss.

"Well, correct me if I'm wrong, then. You usually do. But I think we suspect she'd arranged to meet him Friday night, was going to help him bundle Elizabeth into her car and whip them across the border to the hunting cabin, getting back just after midnight and ready for her homicidal Saturday planned here at the house. But something must have gone wrong. He showed up early to confront her? Maybe because Oliver hadn't got his extra cash 'payment' from her after all? Maybe because he simply couldn't coax Elizabeth out of the house without help? He was supposed to return the rifle to the cellar from the getaway car, bribe Elizabeth out. But maybe he was threatening Stroud with the gun instead, as he'd seen Elizabeth leave to go off to the Grahams' and the plan was unraveling. For whatever reasons, Stroud no longer felt she could trust him. What's the expression? He was a loose cannon. So she somehow big-sister-sweet-talked the rifle from him and then shot him in cold blood. Obviously, they were both wearing gloves while handling the thing. Then she just slipped back into the cellar herself and replaced it."

"That's why she wasn't home that night, when I walked over there after leaving Dr. Graham's," Elizabeth thought aloud.

"Yes, and if I hadn't already decided to quit the force, I should be fired for being so slow to pick up on that." Philip winked. "I was just too carried away with whisking you off to jail."

"My gosh," P.J. said. "That's probably how Genevieve got her chest cough. She'd quit smoking a few months ago, but had often told me when she was out in the damp, cool air at night she would start hacking again, worse than when she'd been on the nicotine."

"That and the fact she was spending a good deal of time living behind the walls of this damp house," Philip agreed.

"*What?*" Elizabeth, Chet and P.J. gasped in unison.

"Now who's getting ahead of himself?" Woody grumped, pouting.

Phil laughed. "Touche! Go back and continue."

"So she snuck back in some time later to replace the rifle, maybe thinking she could inadvertently get Elizabeth framed for the murder—conveniently get her out of the way that way, instead of held in a cabin in the wilderness of Maine. MacCarrey, one of our investigators, found the cellar door lock had been jimmied. It might have been Oliver, of course, but because of the hiding place, we suspect Stroud. And we think she'd been sneaking in for some time. But that night Esther must have heard her, caught her in the act, something. So somehow, Genevieve got her up to the kitchen then pushed her down the stairs, left the gun beside her on the floor. Her own birth mother."

"And I didn't hear any of it because of the sleeping pills! I'm never taking another one of those again!" vowed Beth.

Philip leaned close, whispering, "You'll never want to."

As Elizabeth blushed, Woody went on. "We discovered earlier, before you all got here, that Stroud had been virtually holed up in the servants' stairs—a sort of hidden passage behind the walls which goes from the cellar pantry right up to a little closet-room on the third floor."

"You're kidding!" Elizabeth's jaw dropped. "I've lived here almost all my life. I've never heard—"

"I'll show you later," Phil grinned.

"My goodness!" Polly Jane said in awe. "But how would Genevieve know about that?"

"Original blueprints of the house on file at the township offices? A realtor is always checking those."

"There's even an opening through one of the cupboards in the kitchen. They must have been added over when your family stopped using servants thirty or forty years ago, I guess. That's how Genevieve was able to hear and know everything which went on last Saturday. She heard Chet saying he needed more cigarettes. She was up the back stairs behind the wall of the guest room every time she heard him go to check on you, Beth."

"Good Lord!" muttered the local constable for at least the fifth time in an hour.

"When you thought you heard Chet going up and down to the third floor, it was really Genevieve. When you remember hearing Chet go out the front door on his way to the store, Genevieve heard the same thing and grabbed her chance. She crawled into the kitchen through the cupboard when Mary went down to stoke up the fire, took your quilt from your bed in the room next to the cellar door, went down, threw it over Mary's head and arms then strangled the life out of her."

The door bell rang and Woody raised his hand. "I'll get it. It's likely that nosy-parker, Mort Henry, wanting to know what we're doing over here. You go on, Phil."

"So then she threw your 'Threads' into the furnace and crawled through the cellar opening back into the servants' stairway. It's only about a foot and a half wide, so you'd never notice the missing space from outside. And that's where, this morning, Woody and I found the poison she'd used on Doc as well as this briefcase with all the stolen files from Bromley's office."

Elizabeth laid her head back on Philip's arm. "I can't believe all this. Genevieve was the only close girlfriend I've ever had, yet it was all based on lies. I wish I could have known her as a cousin. I've never had a relative near my own age. And none at all I could feel close to, since Grandpa died."

Woodbridge escorted Rose Brock and another woman into the room just as Elizabeth was speaking. The brightly dressed stranger with a red bandana tied across her forehead said with a beaming smile: "Well, I've read most of your diary, Cuz, so I already feel as if I know *you*! All that's left is for you to dig me!"

CHAPTER EIGHTEEN

"'Ah, would that this might be *the last*!' The last surprise, that is!" said Woody as he sat back in the chaise longue, hands clasped behind his head and looking about him with an air of satisfied completion.

Rose Brock had left again, with Chet Anderson. She was going home to sleep and Chet was on his way to arrest Jake Brock at the store on sexual assault charges filed by a young woman near Moncton two weeks previously. Jenny Connelly, sitting on the floor with her back against an ornate gold-leafed table, had been the reporter who had questioned the young woman and taken her description of the rapist. And, as Rose would testify that Jake was out late that night despite the alibi he'd forced her to contrive for him, yet another case seemed closed. Explanations and exclamations had gone on for over an hour after their surprising entrance. Yet still Elizabeth sat dazed. Philip had made tea for all of them and P.J. had even put a batch of oatmeal raisin cookies into Esther's huge old gas-burning oven.

"But I still don't understand, Jenny," Elizabeth said. "When did you first figure out Genevieve was the girl you'd known at the orphanage?"

"I *didn't* know for sure, of course, until Rose met me yesterday at the paper and started convincing me things were not at all as they seemed. I took her to my place for supper. We ended up talking all night. My husband went to bed and woke up this morning to find us in practically the same positions as when he'd left us!"

"But how the hell did Rose know?" Philip asked.

"She'd had enough of Jake. Who can blame her? Abusive, philandering husbands may be common, but it doesn't mean women have to put up with them. Losing her only son last week was something of an epiphany for her. You see, she'd always suspected since she married him that he was carrying on this whole secret life. She'd even gone to a lawyer six months ago—this Beaufort Bromley—to see about hiring a private investigator so she could charge Jake with adultery and get a divorce. Otherwise he refused to let her even consider it, thought of her as just a piece of his property, poor woman."

"You mean Bromley broke a thirty-four-year-old confidence? He told Rose about Gen—I mean *you*?"

"He did. Apparently told her he was ready to retire, and he was not bound to go on protecting a piece of shit like Brock anymore. He'd had his own investigator checking up on him years ago, too. He wasn't just involved with other women and one-night stands and sexual assaults. There're some files on him, Rose says, proving he's sold illegal pornography, black market bear organs, all kinds of things. You cops will have a good old time going through his files, I gather. But even though Bromley'd known about the birth of Jennifer Brown, and the circumstances of my conception—he'd had to forward money to me for several years at the orphanage, you see—I was adopted by a wonderful family named Russell when I was nine years old, and he lost track of me after that."

"And you're sure it was my Grandpa Grimball—I mean *our* Grandpa Grimball," Elizabeth corrected herself, smiling, "who sent you the money?"

"Yes. I know it wasn't my mother. Esther. Because Beaufort Bromley once added a typed note with his letterhead at the top, saying it was from my birth mother's father who wished to remain anonymous. I wasn't supposed to have that letter, of course, but a staff member at the orphanage left it on the seat of her car once when she took me shopping with my allowance. "

"My goodness! That explains why Esther used Grandpa as an excuse for 'losing' the family fortune. She and my grandmother were no doubt furious at him after he died, for secretly depleting the Sanderson wealth even remotely."

"Yes, just before I was adopted John Grimball himself sent me this card. I've kept it my whole life because it meant so much to know someone cared." She handed a faded rose-colored envelope to Elizabeth and, as she opened it, P.J. and Philip crowded over her shoulders to read the plain, hand-printed words, created for a child's eyes.

Dear Little Jennifer,

I am your grandfather and am writing to say that I am very sorry, but I won't be sending money to you anymore. But the good news is, you are finally going to live with some really nice people who will look after all your needs and hopefully your wishes. I hope you are well and healthy. I feel badly that you are going to be living so far away now. But my lawyer, who is sending this to your orphanage, says your new home will have several other children about your age living in it. I think this will make you glad and that you'll be much better off than you would have been growing up here, or at the orphanage too. Have a good life and please be happy.

Yours truly, John E. Grimball

Elizabeth sighed and handed the card back to Jenny. "I was only three when he wrote that; I wasn't living here yet. Oh, poor Grandpa. I don't believe he was ever very happy in this house. That's probably why he could relate to a child's unhappy home life. The Sandersons always ruled the roost here."

P.J. was enchanted. "So, to be clear—Genevieve-whoever-she-was grew up with you until the Russells adopted you?"

"Right. We were both in and out of a few foster homes as well, but mostly we were at the orphanage together and we were less than a year apart in age. Her legal name was Susan and she was always ridiculously jealous of me because my birth mother had named me in the hospital, and she was just named by the orphanage administrators. She thought my name "Jennifer" was so romantic, though really, I could have cared less myself. 'Jen' or 'Jenny' was fine with me. Sue always pretended her blood family would come back for her someday too, that they'd be richer than mine. She was jealous that I was sent money for clothing and toys from a 'rich relative', which was all I was ever told. And there was a volunteer at the orphanage who used to read Grimm fairy-tales to us. All us girls used to love 'The Worn Out Dancing Shoes' because it was about twelve princesses who all slept in the same room, which was like us at the orphanage. One of the li'l darlings was named 'Genevieve'. When Sue found out that was French for 'Jennifer', she wanted everyone to call her that instead."

"And then that just evolved into stealing your identity?" Woodbridge asked.

"She had *years* to think about it, to 'become' me, if that's what she did. She didn't leave the orphanage until she was sixteen, when she must have legally changed her name to 'Stroud' as well."

"And at sixteen or so, she must have become involved with her young social worker, this 'Pierre' from up in Montreal. Your orphanage was only about two hours south. So they got married, moved back to the big city. She got Canadian citizenship, which then made it easy for her to move and work here after they got divorced," summed Philip.

"God, what a schemer!" P.J. said.

"She always was. You see, that typed business letter from Mr. Bromley disappeared from the box under my bed not long after I swiped it from the car that day. I always wondered if it had been her. I guess that's how she could take on my identity, and to know about Victoria and the New Brunswick connections."

"And was it really *you* who got the real estate license in this province? As Jennifer Brown?" Philip asked.

"No. When the Russells adopted me, I became legally a 'Russell'. Until I married Jay. Jayson Connelly. We met at university, Dalhousie School of Journalism. He's a great guy. You'll have to meet him!" she bubbled to her newfound cousin. "No, Sue must have used both my original name—'Jennifer Brown'— and also 'Genevieve Stroud' as an alias. After all, she figured I'd never been interested in finding *my* roots. And as far as she knew I was living in Idaho with the Russells. She couldn't have known I'd want to go to one of the best journalism schools on the East Coast. So she figured, hey—if she couldn't find her own roots, she might as well take over mine!"

"So, you've been happy, then? Haven't needed to spend your life searching for something you couldn't even explain?" asked Beth, only a little wistfully.

"I've always been fairly optimistic. From what I saw in your diary—and I'm sorry now I repeated any of it in the Monocle, honestly, but the damn editor always takes my stories and rewrites them for sensationalism because we're such a new paper—but from what I read about your life, you've had more reasons to be unhappy than I've had, Cuz!"

"So reading my diary triggered something, some memory for you?"

"Well, the name 'Grimball' of course, really got me excited. It's not that common, and though I'd long ago forgotten the name of the town on Bromley's letterhead, I did remember it was in Canada, in a place called New Brunswick. And then when I kept seeing the name Genevieve Stroud—well, it really spooked me! Of course, I knew nothing about the Brock connection to me until Rose confronted me yesterday, angry I'd written another sensationalist article assuming you'd tried to escape from prison and that Jake's cousin had been the hero in the whole thing. Now, mind you, that wasn't how I'd drafted the piece at all, but again— my blasted editor. He's worked on tabloids his whole career; he can misquote and misrepresent with the best of them."

Philip tried to meet Woody's eyes, but his sergeant blatantly refused, looking instead at the colorfully-garbed hippie with her legs crossed like a yoga guru. While Jenny bubbled merrily on, a thought suddenly struck him and he interrupted. "Say, Jenny, did you send a letter to Genevieve, by any chance?"

"Right! How'd you guess? Just a few days ago, in fact. I did a few background checks after I read some of Beth's diary, then I tracked down the address of this Genevieve Stroud. On a hunch I wrote to her, confronting her, asking what the hell she thought she was up to. I suspect she'd already figured out who I was, that it was making me nervous. Someone had been calling the paper asking for Jennifer Brown Connelly. So I sent her a note and addressed it with her proper birth name."

"And P.J.—that was...?" Phil looked at his godmother with a glint of mischief.

She thought about it less than five seconds and then: "Oh, yes! Susan Margaret Smith!"

•　　•　　•

That night, after an early supper of superbly comforting oatmeal cookies, Woody left for Fredericton to finish paperwork on the case. Elizabeth asked Jenny, who kept falling in and out of sleep on the chaise longue, if she wanted to stay over.

"I've never in my life had a slumber party. I've never even stayed here all alone!" she pleaded with her cousin. She didn't add that with two violent deaths having just occurred in the sprawling house, and proof of a killer who'd been hiding behind the walls, she'd rather not be left by herself on her first night back. "I know you're exhausted from being up with Rose all of last night, but we still have so much to talk about and I can drive you home tomorrow. And then—"

"Easy, Cuz. I'd be delighted, actually! Just let me call my husband and grab an hour's shut-eye so I'll be good as new!"

"You can go up to the guest room and sleep," Beth offered. "But as for the telephone—we, um. We don't have one here." She looked embarrassed, so Philip gallantly stepped in.

"P.J. and I are on our way home. We all had very late nights last night, Jenny. Just give me your home number. I'll call your husband for you and explain the situation."

"Would you? That'd be great. You know, when I first met you last week, I thought you were just another old hulk of a pretentious copper. And when I realized it was my cousin you'd arrested—*Well*! Blood runs thicker than water, man, ya know? Just you remember that! Still, I guess you're not such a bad guy, after all." Unabashed, she reached out to pinch his cheek, then shook hands with P.J. saying, "I'll find the guest room myself, Elizabeth. Wake me up in two hours. Come up in your nightgown and we'll braid each other's hair, or something!" She disappeared in a cloud of perfumed air and Elizabeth threw back her head, laughing with joy.

"What a crazy, wonderful surprise ending to all of this!"

Polly Jane clasped the schoolteacher's hand in both of her own and looked sincerely into her eyes. "I'm so happy for you, Beth. I know the rest of your life is going to be a beautiful, exciting change compared to what you've been through so far." She glanced meaningfully in her godson's direction. "I'll see you in the morning, Phil. I have one last date with the harvest moon this year—thirtieth anniversary, you know—and then I have to get off to bed myself." She scampered down the street, leaving the couple standing side-by-side on the huge veranda.

Neither Phil nor Beth said a word for several minutes. They watched the orange moon, still rising over the dark forms of the rounded Appalachians, and listened to the light breeze in the crisp leaves clinging even yet to the maples which lined the street. Then Philip turned to her, perched on the railing of the porch and said, "What an unbelievable day!"

"What an unbelievable week!"

Phil laughed. "There's an understatement!"

"It's especially good to know that not only am *I* not a murderer, but I'm not related to one, either!"

"It's nice for me to know too, Miss Grimball. Because, all of that notwithstanding, I was going to ask you to marry me."

"Phil!"

"No, listen—I know we've only known each other for less than ten days and I know it's been under the most outlandish circumstances, but I also know that what I feel for you is—is *right*."

"But Philip, so much has changed. I–I need time."

"Oh, I'm completely aware of that, Bethie. I'm not pressuring you. I just wanted you to know what you should be expecting from me. No more surprises for a while! I haven't been fair to you, have inadvertently taken advantage of your situation. But now that you've regained your freedom and your health, you can do anything in this world which appeals to you. Have you even thought of all the possibilities? You're attractive, wealthy, still in your twenties. And, if you refuse to let me have my way, unattached! You don't even have to teach anymore if you don't want to."

She smiled. "Yes, but how do I know *you're* not just after me for my money?"

She was teasing, Phil knew, but he answered her seriously. "My parents are both gone now too, Beth. They left me our family's estate and a good deal of savings. I sold the estate to Toronto developers for a nice chunk of change, and my decision to quit the force is not a hasty one. I've been trying to get out for months, now. Oh, Elizabeth! We could have a wonderful life together—you have the same insights into people and situations that I do. We could travel, build a new home anywhere you want, or fix up this one. We can share our readings, hang your wonderful paintings, eat fabulous meals all over the world. And when we get too fat and stodgy, we can hike up Mount Everest or go rock-climbing or surfing. We could raise a family if you want, or just keep us as a cozy couple. I've never realized until I read your diary how lonely *I* was, too! I need you."

"Oh, Philip. This is so much. Too fast! But I–I feel the same way, I think… it's all been so confusing. I'm afraid to trust what anyone says, anymore."

"Well, before I leave you to your slumber party, I want you to come for a quick walk with me, O.K.?" He reached out his hand and took hers.

Slowly, in the moonlight, they strolled down the quiet street. When they reached the cedar-shingled post office, Philip held a finger to his lips and led her behind the salt-box house. There, along the garden path in the amber glow of the last full moon of the summer, Polly Jane Whistler waltzed to her far-off, long ago, silent music.

Elizabeth looked uncertain. "We shouldn't be intruding. She's so lovely, though!"

"I just wanted to make a point, Bethie," Philip said. "P.J. is a wonderful woman. But she never married and although she's led a full, active life, I know she misses the one man she truly loved. That's why she dances 'with him' like this every year. He died in the war, right after they got engaged at the Hunt Ball. It's such a tragic waste. And I don't want that ever to happen to us." He leaned way down to kiss her gently.

"It won't, Phil. I promise. I just need a little time."

"I fought for your freedom, and your innocence, Beth. Now, if time is the greatest gift I can give you, you have it. Because I love you and respect you."

She looked up to meet his eyes and knew that, with him, her life would never stand still again.

EPILOGUE

On a warm tepid morning the following June, Jenny Connelly hurried through the newly renovated "John Grimball Foster Home". The sound of children's voices came trickling through the kitchen's screen door; the kids were already up and decorating the seats which the caterers had set up in the back yard near the edge of the ravine. Good, that was getting done. Mentally, she went through her remaining check-list. That just meant: go to the florist's, get the flowers on the table and on the tiny altar in the gazebo, make sure the cake Polly Jane had made was out of the freezer and—oh, yes—put Grandpa Grimball's favorite old rocking chair which had been stored under dust covers on the main floor, out in a place of honor because Bethie said she could always imagine him in it. It would be her special addition to the ceremony. Thank God it didn't look like rain! The apple trees were still in radiant pink and white bloom. Jay had strung colored lights among their branches for the dance later on.

"Jenny! Jenny!" Little Clarissa came running up to her as she hurried out to supervise the seating arrangement. "Look what Ben just found under that rock!" On the palm of her tiny hand lay a few pieces of costume jewelry, well weathered but still glinting in the early sunshine.

"Yeah, Jen! Look what else! *Paints*!" Ben came up and held out a still plastic-packaged set of cheap watercolors. "May I keep them? Huh?"

"Me too! I can wear the earrings for the wedding!" Clarey chimed in.

Jenny smiled fondly down at them. "You'll have to ask Beth when she comes down. But I'm sure she won't mind."

Her husband Jayson crossed the lawn heading toward them, a slight frown creasing his dark, haggard face. He'd just returned two days ago from doing a story on Oriental girls in China who were unwanted and neglected, left for dead. All because baby boys were the preferred gender there. He was making arrangements for several of them to fly here to their small new orphanage where, at their young ages, Beth and Jenny were sure they would quickly be adopted. Then he would fly to Freetown, Sierra Leone, the country from which his great-grandparents had fled to come to Halifax. And from which, now that it had been made a republic a year ago, he wanted to rescue more orphans.

"You still look worn out, hon. What's wrong?" Jenny queried, concerned.

"Just jet-lag, I think. I'll be more energetic by the reception tonight. You'd better save me a polka!"

"A *polka*? What happened to that crazy-fast jive dancing you taught me at university eh, man?"

"I'm too old for that now. Anyway, you white gals don't have the right rhythm for it."

"How dare you!" Jenny laughed. "Well, then, it's that new Cowboy Boogie or nothing, mister! Besides, I promised some of the kids I would teach it to them before they had to go up to bed."

"Does that mean I can wear my cowboy boots with my tux?" he grinned.

"Don't even think about it!"

Beth's happy voice behind them broke in. "Jay, you can wear whatever the heck you want! This is my day and I want everyone to be comfortable and relaxed."

Jenny sighed. "If I relaxed, nothing around here would get done!"

Her cousin hugged her. "I know, Jen. You've worked so hard for the ribbon-cutting ceremony last month and then to get ready for today. It shouldn't be Phil and me who are flying off to Greece. *You're* the one who needs the holiday!"

Laughing, Jenny said, "Well someone needs to stay here to make sure these little scamps do their homework every night! Then when school lets out, you and Phil can come back and look after them all summer long, and Jayson and I will bug out!"

"Only if you take the money for your trip out of our joint savings account! You haven't touched a penny of it yet, Jen Connelly, at least not for personal use!"

"Let's not argue about *that* again—today of all days!"

"It's really your money more than it is mine," Elizabeth persisted stubbornly. "She was your mother; she was only my aunt!"

Jayson feigned aggravation, putting his hands tightly over his ears. "Enough already! Keep this up and I *will* wear my cowboy boots, girls—and nothing else! How would that look in your wedding album, huh? A great big naked black buck standing there? And do you really want the children traumatized?"

They giggled as Jenny hurried off to the florist and Beth went back upstairs with a mug of coffee, to have her bridal bath.

•　　•　　•

Several doors down and across the street, another flurry of activity was being launched. Carol Caribou was busily sorting the mail by herself while Polly Jane scurried about the kitchen in her fuzzy pink slippers. Phil entered, wiping his eyes sleepily and smiling at his godmother affectionately.

"Oh, Phil. This is the last chance I'll ever have to make you your favorite blueberry waffles for breakfast. But I've been so busy finishing off the quilt, I think I've burned the first batch. And honestly, I can't find my glasses anywhere and I have a few last stitches to do..."

"P.J...."

"Yes, dear?" Polly Jane said abstractedly as she poured cream over the waffles.

"Take a deep breath and relax. They're on top of your head."

"What are?"

"Your glasses, silly!" Phil was chuckling now.

"Oh, fiddlesticks! Really, I am the most ridiculous old fool. I don't know how you've put up with me all winter."

"There's nowhere else I would rather have been."

"Even when I asked you to dig out the eaves troughs? And replace shingles on the roof?"

"Especially then. And now we'll be living as neighbors—me, Beth, Jen and Jayson and all those wild kids! How will *you* manage to put up with *us*?"

"Oh, it's wonderful, truly, to hear all those children's voices laughing in a house which for years and years has been smothered in silence, so—so dormant and still. I just love them all so much, already, and most of them have only been here a few months!"

Philip kissed the top of her hair and placed her glasses back on her nose where they promptly slid down to the end, causing her to peer over their rims. "And they just adore their Aunt Polly!"

"Well, poor pumpkins need *some*one to love them, after all most of them have been through."

Woody appeared, his tall broad-shouldered body already handsomely ensconced in his best man's tuxedo of blue. "Ah, thou that listens to the sighs of orphans, and drinks the tears of children."

P.J. and Philip laughed and the bare-footed groom added, "That's just a tad in bad taste, isn't it, Woody *Word*pecker? Seeing as how it's from Confessions of an English Opium Eater?"

Woody grinned wickedly, "You mean that's not what we're having for breakfast? Why the hell aren't you dressed?"

"Give me a break! It's only 8:30!"

"How about you go get ready and I'll polish off the rest of these waffles for you?"

"You'll do no such thing, Inspector Woodbridge," said Polly Jane. "Here's your own batch and they're luckily not as burned as poor Philip's! Did you sleep well? That mattress in the guest room is frightfully lumpy."

"Never felt a single bump! I saw your quilt in the den. It's beautiful! It must have every color of the rainbow in it!"

"Yes, it's my special wedding present for Elizabeth. She lost her old quilt which her mother had made her when Genevieve burned it in the furnace. I wanted her to have something really bright because she's always loved color so much and never seems to get enough of it now. Jenny's influenced her a lot in that way, I think."

"Maybe you can show it to my wife Glenna when she gets here later on. She'd love to see it I'm sure."

"Did you see the painting Beth did for P.J.?" Philip asked. "It's hanging in the hall. Come see!"

The threesome left the table and went to examine the enormous two-by-three foot watercolor.

"Good Lord! It's magnificent! So much movement and energy! The only thing is, I can't tell if the subject is Polly Jane herself, or you, Phil," chortled Woodbridge wickedly. "You're both so graceful!"

Ornately framed, the canvas interpreted the multi-colored leaves of autumn, waving in the light of a full ochre moon. In the center, with billowing shrouds of transparent white all around, a dancer whose feet were not touching the ground, pirouetted in elegant, classic proportions.

• • •

Later that afternoon, an ecstatic bride looked up into the face of her smiling new husband as on all sides, well-wishers joined them in their ceremony of union. Next to Elizabeth and an empty rocking chair, stood Jenny, Polly Jane, Marcia Graham and Trudy Quigley, as well as Julia and Katherine, the first two girls to come and live with them at the old Sanderson house. Next to Philip stood Woody, Chet Anderson, Wilf Graham and Deputy Commissioner Cobalt, or 'Blue', the friend of Phil's father who had finally accepted, with great disappointment, the resignation of his favorite inspector. The men all had puro Cuban cigars in their mouths, compliments of Santana who had sent a box along with Woody.

The Reverend Baker who had presided over so many funerals in the village of Victoria only nine months before, was now very excited to be launching this first wedding of the summer. Nearly the whole town had turned out to sit in the back yard beside the new gazebo, with giggling children surrounding the couple as rice and rose petals were scattered in all directions. Soon, reflected the minister, this village would learn to become a lot less racist as orphans from Atlantic indigenous reservations, from east coast inner cities and from third-world countries afar would bring Victoria to an enriched level of shared joy.

Jayson Connelly, dressed impressively in an antique satin morning coat which had belonged to John Grimball himself, was the official photographer of the wedding party. But when Mort Henry offered to take a few shots with him in them as well, Jay couldn't resist the urge to hike up his trousers in order to exhibit his alligator-skin cowboy boots.

And for once in his life, the newly promoted Inspector Zareb Norbert Woodbridge croaked out a timely and entirely relevant quote: "Though some may venture far abroad/ Whilst others rest 'neath summer's bud/ Such warmth extends from hat to *boot*/ The love we share in friendship's blood."

E N D

ACKNOWLEDGEMENTS

I would like to express gratitude first and foremost, to my late grandmother Victoria Ivanel (Lipsit) Johnson (1906–1992) of Straffordville, Ontario, for her constant support and encouragement in all things literary and theatrical—especially in the cozy-mystery genre. Oh, those Ngaio Marsh and Agatha Christies we shared! (Rehearsing lines from <u>The Mousetrap</u> was an especial favorite pastime.) Oh, the Murder She Wrotes and Rockford Files we watched together! And the treasure hunts and word play! (Grandpa Ho shared the familial love of words by spouting his classical quotations —as Woody and Philip do—and his often-risque 'punnies'). Thank-you for my first typewriter, my first writing desk which was once yours, and indeed the very outline of this novel—originally drafted out in 1947 when my own father was still a child. More on this graceful woman who is much like Polly Jane, can be seen at the bottom of the webpage: https://mckencroftproducti.wixsite.com/jivanelauthor/still-life

My other grandmother, Dorothy Hawkins McKenzie (1913–1990) also deserves my gratitude as she and her daughter Joy were always in cahoots for gifting me diaries, blank notebooks, quality pens, low typewriter tables—and for framing and hanging various letters and poems from my earliest pre-teen works. And much thanks to the latter for sending a certain poem to Anne Millyard (Annick Press founder and Robert Munsch 'discoverer') when she was just starting Books By Kids. Thus, <u>Another Wordsandwich</u> and my 'Night of Flame' are now part of Canadian publishing history in The Osborne Collection at the Toronto Public Library. And, when I was eleven, it was Anne who first wrote:

"J. organizes her material well and knows how to set up suspense."

Other great supporters and/or Beta-readers (of either this manuscript or others like it) have been Jane Wright, Ian Moir, Richard Reich, Marianne Bell, Peter Wright, Curtis Sullivan, Scott Giroux, line-editor extraordinaire Joy Cehovin and Canadian authors Tim Wynne-Jones, Chris Scott and A.J. McCarthy. Huge cheers to the latter, as well as cozy mystery authors Mairi Chong and Jinny Alexander, for reading ARCS and reviewing prior to publication. I want to give a shout-out to two generous enthusiasts of my writing in general—Phillip Mellor and Annette Maeckelbergh-Mcgill. Thanks to Alycia Bartlett, Sandi Tattersall, Norma Jean Saulis and Dr. Mary Ann Bramstrup for their help in some true- life detail-sorting. Gratitude to Richard Reich for his artistic advice and the author photo.

Jennifer Johnson, who happily used to swap her Nancy Drews for my Trixie Beldens, critiqued a very early version of <u>Just A STILL LIFE</u> in the mid-1990s and noted several times in the margins: "Sorry—this bit defies imagination." (Well, she obviously hadn't read <u>Nancy Drew and the Flying Saucer Mystery</u>; thankfully, we were both too old by the time that one came out!) I hope those 'stretches' have since been successfully relaxed in revisions and not instead snapped to breaking point, like the elastic buckle ends of Trixie's saddle girth... or did someone intentionally fray those? I can't remember.—J.I.J.

Credits of quotations where authors or sources are not mentioned directly in the text:

"...murder cannot be hid long" speech by Gobbo in The Merchant of Venice, Act 2 Sc. 2, by William Shakespeare

"the tongue no man can tame is an unruly evil", paraphrased, from James 3:8, KJV, Bible

"flash upon that inward eye", from I Wandered Lonely As A Cloud, by William Wordsworth

"Ah, would that this might be the last!", from My Mary by William Cowper

* others 'quoted' by the character Woody with no citation, are of my own creation. – J.I.J.

ABOUT THE AUTHOR

J. Ivanel Johnson is the pen name for a disabled author/playwright who now resides on a remote farm in the Appalachians of New Brunswick. She strives always to write about marginalized and culturally-diverse characters, many based on people from the First Nations, inner city or mountain communities where she has previously lived and taught across the UK, USA and Canada.

Her most recently-published fiction includes 2019's *Iron Bone*, a short story about coping with disability in the groundbreaking *Nothing Without Us* anthology by Renaissance Press, as well as works in other literary journals and anthologies.

Just A STILL LIFE is her debut novel, first outlined 75 years ago by her Ontario author-grandmother.

NOTE FROM THE AUTHOR

Word-of-mouth is crucial for any author to succeed. If you enjoyed *Just A STILL LIFE*, please leave a review online—anywhere you are able. Even if it's just a sentence or two. It would make all the difference and would be very much appreciated.

Thanks!
J. Ivanel Johnson

We hope you enjoyed reading this title from:

www.blackrosewriting.com

Subscribe to our mailing list – *The Rosevine* – and receive **FREE** books, daily deals, and stay current with news about upcoming releases and our hottest authors.
Scan the QR code below to sign up.

Already a subscriber? Please accept a sincere thank you for being a fan of Black Rose Writing authors.

View other Black Rose Writing titles at
www.blackrosewriting.com/books and use promo code
PRINT to receive a **20% discount** when purchasing.

Manufactured by Amazon.ca
Bolton, ON